THE HERO CHRONICLES
TRUST

THE HERO CHRONICLES
TRUST

BY TIM METTEY

KENWOOD PUBLISHING GROUP
www.kenwoodpublishinggroup.com
Cincinnati, Ohio

ISBN-10: 0-9885425-2-8
ISBN-13: 978-0-9885425-2-5

To the children who lost their lives in
the Moore, Oklahoma tornado.

ACKNOWLEDGEMENTS

I would like to thank my family, friends and fans that have given me so much support while writing *Trust*. I also need to thank some important people: Karen, Katie, Joodi, Lauren, Ben, Lori, Rick, Carolyn and Mickey for editing, tweaking, and pretty much doing everything to get it to this point. Without all of you, my book would still be just a dream, sitting on my shelf. I look forward to working with all of you for years to come.

OBSESSION

CHAPTER ONE

It had been nearly three months since I was told that I was part of an ancient group called the Thusians, the secret guardians of mankind destined to sacrifice our lives at any given time. I would have thought that after finding this out everything would have become really complicated for me, but it hadn't. It was nice and quiet.

Everything I went through to get to this point was worth it, because now I had Elle. I still couldn't believe how such a wonderful, amazing girl ended up with me. We were inseparable during the summer. Unfortunately now I was keeping more secrets from her. It was for her protection, but I still hated it.

Elle and I were lying in my front yard under the shade of the towering oak trees, enjoying each other's company like we had done most of the summer.

"Nicholas, what's wrong?" Elle asked for the hundredth time.

"Sorry, I'm just preoccupied today."

"It's okay. I just wanted to make sure it wasn't me."

How could it be her? She was nothing but wonderful, my reason for living.

"Elle, it's not you. You know that. I'm just thinking about the last interview I did. It wasn't very good."

Last year when I confronted the mob of reporters at the school's entrance, I told them if they would leave me alone I would do interviews. To my dismay, Cora, my aunt and guardian, made sure I did every interview they requested. It had now become the thing I dreaded most. I had to relive the worst day of my life, the 10-10 Earthquake, like it was some recurring nightmare from which I couldn't wake up.

"Sorry, Nicholas, I know how much you hate doing interviews, but at least that was your last one until next summer."

In addition to me only doing interviews in the summer, Cora had told the media that I would only answer questions over the phone. She also required that they never say where I live or where I go to school, even though they were camped outside of my school last year telling the world all of that information. Cora thought, better safe than sorry.

Cora had even talked to Ester Theasing, the head of the Thusian Council and a friend of ours, about doing the interviews to make sure it was safe for me because of Xavier and the Seekers who were trying to eliminate me and any other Thusians. Ester didn't have a problem with it.

Chase Letterby started visiting us more midway through the summer. After the attack last year he left as soon as his doctor talents were no longer needed. No one had heard from him for a while. Even his regular TV appearances had stopped. But as more time passed during the summer, he started to frequent our house again. Cora didn't seem to mind his company, despite his countless attempts to get her to go out with him. He was fixed on the one woman he couldn't have, Cora.

Elle and I continued to lie beneath the trees. She went back to reading her book while rubbing my head. Her hand moved slowly through my hair, making me forget all of my worries. With every pass, a wave of relief went through me. I had positioned myself on her lap facing our driveway, so I could watch my new obsession. A large house was being built next door. It was hard to believe that the lot had been completely wooded just a month ago, and now the house looked close to being completed. Cora was not happy about the new house and the new neighbors that came with it. She still wanted our privacy, and the trees surrounding us had given us ample protection, but now they were gone. She even tried to buy the lot, but it had been sold exactly a week after we moved in last year.

The workers swarmed over the site like ants working hard on their hill. It was amazing to see such a large home being built so quickly. For some strange reason it was fascinating to me. I had no interest in design or architecture, but it still captivated my attention.

Cora and I had been in five different houses in six years, but never a brand new house—one freshly built just for us. Our new neighbors were about to get the fresh start I had wanted after the earthquake, but never got. Maybe that was the reason for my obsession.

NEIGHBORS
CHAPTER TWO

"Nicholas, Coach Miller is here to see you," Cora yelled up to me. I was in my bedroom lying on my bed, daydreaming about Elle, who had gone home. He had told me that he was going to visit during the summer, but I wasn't really expecting him to show up the first week of football tryouts.

"Coach Miller, would you like something to eat or drink?" Cora offered as I walked down the stairs.

"No ma'am, I'm fine. Please call me Aaron."

Cora smiled and walked into the kitchen, leaving both of us standing in the hall. I felt awkward around him. I still felt so guilty for faking my injury last year. It was like I let him down, even though the team won the state championship.

"Son, can we talk?"

I walked him into the family room. I sat on the couch and he took a seat across from me.

"So, how has your summer been?"

I eked out a "Fine."

He nodded his head as if to say he understood and that

we didn't need to continue. "I hope you've considered my offer. The team and I really need you."

How could this legend need anything from me? I'm just a quitter.

"You would be one of my varsity assistants, if you agree to it."

I didn't say anything.

"You know, this is the first time I have ever asked a student to help with the team." He paused and took a deep breath. "After everything with Oliver, they need a real leader, one they can look up to." Coach Miller's voice was quieter when speaking of Oliver. Did he feel sympathy for him? He was staring at me, waiting for an answer.

"Okay, Coach, I will think about it and let you know in the next couple of days."

He smiled as though I had said yes. "Great, Nicholas. And remember—if you ever need to talk about anything, I will always be here for you. We have more in common than you know."

What did that mean? I smiled and he stood. I walked him to the door and he left.

Later that evening, I joined Cora on the front porch. She was doing a crossword puzzle, and I was daydreaming again about Elle, which was always my favorite pastime. I tried to picture what it would be like to have no secrets at all, just to live a normal life with her. We would go off to college, get married and maybe even start a family. It felt so good to just sit there with these thoughts comforting me, allowing me to forget about everything that had to do with Thusians, Seekers or Xavier. The sun had already started to set, sending in a cool, calming breeze that welcomed in the night. It was refreshing after the long, hot day. I closed my eyes and listened to the wind moving through the trees, rustling the leaves on its journey by.

A loud, wrenching sound shattered my peace. It was like a lawn mower going over a piece of concrete. I sat up to see where it had come from. Then the sound happened two more times. Our porch lights flickered and then were extinguished, along with all the lights in the house. The loud noise had come from somewhere out by the street. Cora and I both walked down off the front porch to see what was going on. We saw the problem immediately. One of the large work trucks from next door had backed into an electric pole, knocking it over and sending it into the street. The workers were all scrambling around. One of the workers saw us and hurried over.

His tool belt bounced along with his belly. He was very out of breath by the time he reached us.

"Ma-ma'am," he stuttered, taking off his white hard hat. "I am so sorry for this inconvenience. We have already called the power company and they are on their way to resolve this situation."

Cora didn't say anything; she just politely smiled. He put his hat back on, tipped it and hurried back to the mess.

"Well, I guess we'll be without power for a while," Cora said.

I went upstairs to relax in bed. The Illinois Power & Electric trucks' lights were flashing through my window, illuminating everything in my room with a yellow glow every couple of seconds. It was soothing. The pulsing light put me into a hypnotic state.

I could hear Cora busy preparing something in the kitchen. My stomach was growling relentlessly. When I went down to the kitchen, I was shocked to see that Cora had not actually fixed anything. She had gotten take-out from a restaurant. She must have slipped out while I was in my room.

"Cora, what are you doing?" I asked, dumbfounded. She always made everything we ate. She prided herself on her delicious, gourmet meals.

"Oh, Nicholas, I didn't feel like cooking tonight. Besides, the power being out made it too difficult, so I just went out and got food." She never made eye contact with me; she just continued to set out dinner.

The power outage was just an excuse. She could cook a gourmet meal with a couple of matches and paper plates. About a month ago, she mentioned that I was getting to the point where I didn't need her anymore. She thought she was becoming useless. I tried to convince her that she wasn't, but I knew what she meant. She had spent so much time over the years keeping me hidden and protecting me, but now there was no real need for that. Ester Theasing had told us we would be safe from any more attacks, which reinforced Cora's thoughts of not being needed. This had to be the reason for the slow decay of Cora's vibrant personality.

The flickering candlelight couldn't hide her depression at the dinner table. Her eyes looked sunken and hollowed, and her always perfectly-styled hair was falling down in several places. There was a knock at the door, snapping Cora out of her trance. When someone unexpectedly came to our house in the past, she would have normally become focused, but it didn't seem to be a big deal to her anymore. I knew Ester said we were safe, but I still kept up my guard.

"Nicholas, are you expecting anyone?" Cora asked.

I wasn't. Elle was at church and my friend Eric was over at his girlfriend's house. "No," I said.

Cora slowly walked toward the door.

"Nicholas, could you start cleaning up the dishes for me?" she asked when she was almost to the door.

I had gotten up and began to clear the plates when Cora rushed back into the kitchen, scaring me.

"Nicholas, run!" Cora said, in between yelling and whispering. I didn't know what to do. I was stunned.

"What are you talking about?"

"There's no time to explain—you're in danger. I will keep whoever they are busy at the front door. Go out the back and run straight to the Theasings' house. Tell Ester what's going on and then call Chase."

"Who's out there? What's going on?" I whispered urgently.

"There are Seekers here for you." She shoved me toward the back door. "Move, and when I open the door, you run for it," she yelled louder because I was still standing there stuck to the floor.

I dropped the plates onto the table. Both of them fell off the side, shattering on the floor. She crept to the front door and I ran to the back. I looked at Cora, and from where I was standing, I could see a woman peering into our window next to the front door with both hands up framing her face. It was too dark to see who it was. Cora was at the door, getting ready to open it. Then two loud thuds rattled our front door. Cora pulled away, startled, and then moved back into position.

What was I doing? I couldn't leave her. Cora was scared for me but I didn't feel anything. There was no fire in me warning of danger. But I still couldn't trust that feeling and leave Cora to face whatever was on the other side of that door alone, just in case I was wrong. Even though the fire was absent, I couldn't leave her defenseless.

Cora looked back at me and mouthed the words, "Go now." Before she had time to fully open the door, I was next to her. My fear of something happening to her made me get there faster than normal. She had the door a quarter of the way open. Realizing I was now standing next to her, she grabbed my arm and tried to pull me back. She started to slam the door with her free hand, but I stopped her.

"Cora, it's okay, I know them," I said, recognizing the two people in front of us. "Riley and Genevieve are the ones who saved me in the park."

Cora still had a tight grip on my arm and on the door knob. I opened the door all the way so we could see both of them on the porch.

"Wow, you guys have a funny way of answering the door. How about a little gratitude?" Genevieve said sarcastically.

"I'm sorry for scaring you, Cora," Riley said. His Irish accent was less obvious than last spring. I had never really gotten a good look at Riley before. He was tall and slender. He reminded me of a greyhound with his narrow face and wiry frame. Genevieve looked like a movie star, dripping with sex appeal. Her radiant skin was still lightly tanned. She was tiny but not like a little girl. Her brown hair was pulled back in complex braids. The nurturing way she had spoken to me in the park last year had been replaced by sarcasm, which sickened me.

"My name is Riley and this is Genevieve. We are fellow Thusians like the two of you. We have been searching for you both for many years, Cora. We caught up with you a year ago in Tatesville, and we followed you here so we could watch after you both. Luckily we did, because we were able to save Nicholas."

I looked over at Cora. The light had returned to her eyes. She was the Cora of old, vibrant and in control. She was in her protecting mode; she had a purpose again—to keep me safe.

The four of us just stood there in silence, waiting for the next person to make a move. Cora wasn't impressed by what Riley was saying or willing to let them get any closer to me. She had somehow managed to get her foot in front of me just in case.

"Maybe we could come in so we can talk," Genevieve urged.

Cora didn't budge. She wasn't going to let them into the house under any circumstances.

"Cora, can we invite them in?" I asked, but it was like I wasn't even there. Riley tried this time.

"Cora, you are right not to trust us, but please just give us a chance. We would like for you and Nicholas to come to dinner tonight at our house. We still have power. I thought it would be the neighborly thing to do since our workers knocked out your power."

Neighborly? The house I had watched being built all this time was theirs. The fresh start I dreamed of having belonged to these two.

"We have had dinner already," Cora said, showing her contempt. They weren't winning her over tonight, that was for sure.

Riley smiled. "Of course you have, but please come next door in a half hour, even if it's just to talk."

Cora's gaze was cold and hard.

I glanced at Genevieve, who was staring at me just as intensely. A sparkle appeared in her radiant green eyes that restored her beauty for a split second, but then it vanished. Riley grabbed her arm and pulled her away.

Cora turned to me. "We have to go now," she said, shutting the door and locking it, still watching them as they vanished next door. *Not this again*, I thought. I wasn't going to run from the very two people who had rescued me. If I was going to eventually die anyway, I wanted to at least spend as much remaining time as possible with Elle.

"Cora, I'm not going anywhere. You know this. What's gotten into you? They saved my life—that has to count for something. They're not the bad guys."

She turned to me. "I'm grateful they saved your life, but that's where it ends. I have a bad feeling that being around them will lead you into more danger or maybe something worse."

"Worse than my Thusian Final Sacrifice? You know, the one where I'll most likely die for a complete stranger? Cora, I am *not* moving and I *am* going over to their house to hear what they have to say, with or without you."

"Nicholas, if that's your decision," she paused, collecting herself, "I will go with you, but I want you to know that I don't support this at all."

LEFTOVERS

CHAPTER THREE

Cora and I drove over to their house. She insisted that we drive even though they were right next door, just a two minute walk. Cora was definitely back in control.

Cora grabbed my arm before we got out. "Nicholas, even though you think you know them, we still can't trust them," she said. "You let them do all of the talking."

"Cora, they did save my life," I reminded her again.

"We're here, aren't we? But still, we can't assume anything. Please listen to me. I've been doing this a lot longer than you. I know what I'm talking about. You have to trust me."

I nodded. She was right, she had a lot more experience and I should listen to her. But deep down inside I felt like they were fine, like I was supposed to be with them.

We got out of the truck. The house was even more incredible up close. It was at least two times the size of our modest house. The house looked like it was a luxury log cabin or a ski lodge. There were windows and lights everywhere, making large, dramatic shadows. We walked up an ornate brick path lined with freshly planted trees, bushes and flowers.

Cora was about to knock on the oversized wooden door that should have been on the front of a castle rather than a home, when the door opened.

"I'm so glad you both decided to come over," Riley said, smiling. He had on a bright teal polo and a pair of khaki shorts. He looked like he was ready to go out on his yacht or something.

"Why, thank you, Riley," Cora said, walking through the door and handing him a bottle of wine that she had gotten from our pantry. Cora never drank alcohol—she thought it made people look and act unsophisticated—but she always had a bottle on hand for cooking purposes.

We followed Riley into the house. It was almost completely empty. The floor plan was open, with tall, vaulted ceilings, which made the large, empty house look even barer. We walked over to the only piece of furniture that I could see in the house. It was a large, round metal dining table set for four. Riley motioned for us to sit down. Cora walked over and sat facing the door. I sat right next to her.

"Genevieve will be out in a little bit and then we can start to eat, only if you'd like more dinner, of course. I got the food from a little restaurant in town, Marcello's. It's supposed to have the best Italian food around." He picked the same restaurant that Cora had gotten our food from earlier. We should have just brought over our leftovers to save them the trip. I laughed. I must have laughed too loudly, because Cora kicked me under the table and shot me a dirty look.

"I would also like to apologize for the lack of furniture; the workers just finished. Our furniture will be here tomorrow," Riley said, changing the subject.

"I don't mean to be rude, but let's skip the small talk. Why have you been searching for us?"

Cora had just told me to let them do all of the talking and then she went and asked him the million dollar question right away. Riley's face showed that he was shocked, too. I was sure he was thinking, like I was, that it was going to be a long evening of trying to figure each other out, like a courtship or a game of chess.

"Cora, if you don't mind, I would like to wait for Genevieve. Then we can discuss—" Before he finished, his eyes looked past both of us. I turned to see Genevieve gliding down the hallway, coming toward the room. She looked like a Greek goddess straight from Olympus. Her hair was pulled back in another elaborate style, different from the one just thirty minutes ago. She was wearing some simple silver jewelry that was a perfect accent to her dark skin. Her white dress was cut well above her knees. The fabric looked like it was made of a loosely woven silk. She was incredibly beautiful, but she didn't stir any emotion in me. Elle was the only one who stirred those types of feelings.

Genevieve sat down. "Okay, so what did I miss, kids?" Again, the way she spoke didn't match her elegant appearance. She was rougher and more sarcastic, not polite or nurturing at all.

"Well, Genevieve, Cora just asked why we have been trying to find them all this time," said Riley.

"Wow, you don't mess around, do you?"

Cora didn't look at her. "We are only here because you saved Nicholas, but if we don't get some answers right now, we are leaving," Cora said, starting to stand.

Riley motioned for her to stop and she slowly sat back down.

"Cora, we haven't really been searching for the both of you," Riley said. "We have only been searching for Nicholas."

Cora grabbed my arm under the table. By her grasp, I could tell she was preparing me to run.

"But before you go racing out of here, let me explain why only Nicholas. As I told you at your house, we are Thusians too. My family can be traced back to some of the original Thusians and my great-great-great-great-grandfather was even a Keeper. The Keepers were the ones who knew all of the bloodlines and history and made sure they were respected."

"Riley, we already know what Keepers are," Cora said.

He smiled and continued, "Of course you do. The reason why we were looking for just Nicholas is because he discovered his Thusian talents, going through his Realization, on the same day both Genevieve and I did, October 10th."

"I'm sure there were other Thusians who discovered their talents the same day as the three of you," Cora said. Riley was trying to link me to them and she was clearly trying to derail any effort for a connection.

"Cora, you're right, but we are the only three that discovered significant talents and are still alive today."

Cora looked partially satisfied with his answer. I looked

over at Genevieve, who was not paying attention. She was playing with the paper napkin on her plate, making it into some sort of flower, not interested in the conversation at all.

"Beyond the fact that we are all alive, I was also drawn to Genevieve and we were both drawn to Nicholas."

"You were drawn to me?" I had to say something because that sounded weird.

Everyone at the table was now looking at me. I even got Genevieve's attention.

"Yes, we were drawn to you, Nicholas," Riley said. He looked at Genevieve and she spoke up as if on cue.

"Yeah, we were," she said, like she had been coached on what to say.

"You see, we are all being drawn together. Nicholas, don't you feel it?" Riley asked.

Everyone was looking at me. My stomach started to feel sick with nerves. I grabbed a couple of Tic Tacs and popped them in my mouth.

"I do feel something, but I'm not sure what it is."

Inside of me, I could feel something drawing me toward both of them. I wasn't sure if it was gratitude for them saving me or curiosity, but something was there deep inside.

Riley smiled in triumph and Genevieve went back to her paper flower. I avoided looking at Cora. I was sure she wasn't happy with my answer.

"Of course he feels drawn to you. You two saved his life. That's the only reason why we came over here in the first place," Cora said. Then she looked at Genevieve. "And if I were a teenage boy, I would definitely be drawn to you the way you're dressed. It's nothing more than a cheap, physical attraction with you."

I couldn't believe she just said that. It was kind of funny, though Genevieve didn't think so at all.

"I don't have to take this crap, especially from a nobody like you." Genevieve stood up ready for a fight, her napkin flower falling to the ground. Cora remained in her seat. She didn't look threatened in the least.

"Genevieve, sit down now," Riley said firmly.

It took a minute or so, but she eventually sat down in her chair, picking up her flower from the floor and playing with it, but with less enthusiasm.

Riley continued to talk as if nothing had happened between the women. "After I discovered that the three of us had our Realization of Talents on the same day—and in such dramatic ways—I had to find Genevieve and now you, Nicholas, so we can find the 4th Thusian, which will help form The 7."

I glanced over at Cora. She looked puzzled by what he said.

"What is The 7?" I asked.

"The 7 is a group that was formed when the Council created the Seekers. The Seekers, you know, were used by the Council to eliminate the Keeper. That Keeper's name was Finn Wren. He was one of the oldest and wisest Keepers the Thusians ever had; he was in his 90s when he was finally killed. The Council used the Seekers to kill him in order to gain power, but not before he foretold about The 7."

"Wait a minute. I thought the Keeper wasn't able to keep track of the growing population of Thusians, because they were able to marry non-Thusians. And because of this population explosion, the Seekers were formed and used by the Council to eliminate the Thusians who didn't know about our traditions, right?" I asked, remembering what Ester had explained to me in the vault last year.

"Of course that is what you were told; that is what they told all of the Thusians. But the Council wanted the power for themselves, and they used the Seekers to take it from the Keeper. Anyone who stood in their way was killed by the Seekers." Riley looked at me to make sure he had answered my question. I wasn't sure if I believed him entirely, but it was an answer.

"But why would they need a group of people to kill one Thusian Keeper?" I asked.

"Keeper Wren had hundreds of loyal Thusians protecting him. It was a bloody period in our history," Riley answered.

I had no idea if he was lying or not, but I could tell that he believed what he was saying.

"Okay, now let me explain The 7 to you in more detail." He paused and looked at Cora and me, then continued. "The 7 consists of three Seekers and four special Thusians. The three Seekers represent evil, everything that is wrong with the world. The four Thusians represent the goodness in people, the part that is self-sacrificing with no thought of one's own well-being—everything the Thusians stand for. Together they make up The 7, representing the balance between good and evil."

I already saw a flaw in this; I was surprised Cora didn't speak up first.

"Riley, three Seekers and four Thusians aren't balanced. It favors good by one whole person." I didn't have a problem with that, but his explanation was still flawed, which drew into question his credibility. He seemed prepared for this question.

"Excellent point, Nicholas. I asked my dad the same question when he explained it to me when I was young. He told me that a group of three Seekers and three Thusians isn't balanced at all—it's uneven. Evil will always win when it's a fair fight, three on three. The expression that good always conquers evil isn't exactly true. Evil will do anything to gain an advantage, so that's why good needs extra help. Good values life and evil doesn't. So that's why there has to be a fourth Thusian to make it fair and balanced between both sides. Then once The 7 is formed, we will fight, representing both the Thusians and Seekers. The winning side will determine everyone's fate, giving us the opportunity to finally end the Seekers' terrible reign of terror over us."

I wasn't sure if that made sense, but I believed him. However, if it were up to me, I would want hundreds of Thusians fighting the Seekers, not just four of us.

"So that's why we have been searching for you, Nicholas. You are one of the 4. Now that the three of us are together, we can find the 4th. He or she will have more talents than we do, and once we're all together, we will all develop more talents as time goes on."

"This 4th, whoever it is, just started to get his or her talents now?" I asked.

"Well, actually no. He or she would have started developing them last year. Even though we didn't actually meet up with each other before you moved here, I believe that's when this person would have started gaining talents, because we were so close to each other. But I'm not 100-percent sure."

"Riley, I'm not saying I believe you, but how are we supposed to find this 4th? It sounds impossible."

"It will be difficult. We'll have to be careful while we're looking and hope whoever it is won't draw too much attention to themselves with their newfound talents. We have to get to them first, before Xavier and the Seekers do."

Then I thought of Elle. Could she be the one we are looking for? Could she be the 4th? As soon as I got to Winsor, I had been drawn helplessly to her. The love I felt for her was something deeper and more mystical than just a high school romance.

"Nicholas, I'm going to rely heavily on you in finding this person, because you have been here in the community and you have most likely met them or seen them already. You might even be friends with them. I've taken a job at Winsor High as a history teacher and Genevieve is going to pretend to be my wife. She will be scouting out any leads that we come across while we're in school. Nicholas, is there anyone Genevieve should start checking out?" he asked, eagerly waiting for my answer.

I wanted to say the 4th had to be Elle, but I restrained

myself. I still didn't know if I believed their story or if they could be trusted.

"I can't think of anybody right now, Riley."

Genevieve cleared her throat and said under her breath, but loud enough for everyone to hear, "Yeah right."

I looked at her. "What's that supposed to mean?"

Her beauty was once again tarnished by her tone. "I know you think we should check out your little girlfriend, Elle. I have been following you back and forth from her house for too long. Cora's got at least one thing right tonight. Boys always think their physical attractions mean so much more than—"

I stood and my chair fell backward, interrupting her. Everyone at the table jumped to their feet except Genevieve, who was not even paying attention to me, twirling her paper flower between her fingers.

"Elle is not just a physical attraction. She is someone I care about deeply, more than you will ever know or understand. I did consider her, but I wanted to think things over before telling you to start looking at her. I'm not sure I can even trust the two of you."

Genevieve stood and smiled at me like a little kid who was just teasing her brother until she got what she wanted.

"Thank you, Nicholas. That's all I wanted you to admit. You think she is a possible candidate. I will start checking her out." She turned and walked back toward the hall and added over her shoulder, "But I doubt she's the 4th."

I felt like chasing her down to give her a piece of my

mind, but all I wanted to do was get out of this place. The walls felt like they were closing in on me fast.

"Cora, we're leaving." I turned my back to Riley and walked to the door. "Don't contact us again. When I'm ready, I will contact you," I said loudly enough so that Genevieve could hear me wherever she was in the house.

SUBPOENA
CHAPTER FOUR

By the time I got home, the anger I was feeling toward Genevieve and Riley had grown unbearable. My stomach twisted into knots. I couldn't believe that she had tricked me. Normally, so much intense rage would trigger the fire in my stomach, sending bitter acid into my throat. But to my surprise, it wasn't there. I just felt plain anger, nothing else. It had been so long since I had a normal emotion without some sort of weird Thusian reaction. As unwanted and unbearable as this anger was, at least it was a nice, normal feeling. Cora didn't seem bothered at all by what had happened. I knew she didn't trust them, but now she was relevant to my well-being, giving her purpose once again. I called Elle right when I got home, knowing that she was still at church. I did it just so I could hear her voice on the message.

"Please leave me a message, not too long, not too short, one that is just right. *Beeeeeep*."

"It's Nicholas. Give me a call when you get done. I want to see you tonight."

Genevieve's comments started to ring in my ears. *Thank you, Nicholas. That's all I wanted you to admit. You think she is a possible candidate. I will start checking her out.*

I didn't want Genevieve anywhere near Elle, examining her like she was some sort of lab rat. Deep down inside I knew that they weren't going to hurt her, or even let her know what they were doing, but it still angered me.

The phone rang.

I picked it up and said quickly, "Hello?"

"Is everything okay? Your message sounded so sad," Elle said.

Of course I couldn't tell her what was wrong, so I was going to be vague, hoping I wouldn't have to lie to her again for the millionth time.

"I'm fine. I just miss you terribly. So how was church tonight?" I asked quickly, hoping to get her talking about what she did and not about what I did.

"It was church, but it would have been better if you were there with me," she said with a sigh. "You should come sometime."

"I would love to," I responded. The last time I was at church was the Sunday before the earthquake with my parents at Mt. Vernon Baptist Church. Cora always made sure we avoided public places. Churches are always filled with people wanting to get to know you. It was definitely a place we had avoided. "That would be great, Elle. You know I want to be anywhere you are."

Elle giggled.

"So are we going to see each other tonight?" I asked, hopeful. Being with her would help ease my troubled mind.

"Nicholas, I really want to, but it's too late. We can see each other tomorrow." It wasn't like her to turn me down.

"Are your parents in the room with you?" I asked.

"Yes, have a good night, Nicholas," she said, "and make sure you get a good night's sleep. Bye."

I was filled with excitement when I heard those words. We had worked out a code earlier in the summer after I told her that I only get a good night of sleep after spending time with her. So now, when she wanted me to come over later, she would say, "Make sure you get a good night's sleep." Once she said that, I had a green light.

This was exactly what I needed. Spending time with her would make everything better. It was only 10:00 p.m. I still had two hours until I was in her arms with the stress of the day melting away.

I ate two packs of Tic Tacs while I waited to leave. I got to her house a little earlier than planned, and then slipped down through her window into her bedroom in the basement. Everything was better when I was with her. My nerves and anger subsided. We spent our time holding each other and watching old re-runs of *Friends* on her small TV on her dresser. The warmth of her touch and the smell of her perfume took my cares away. She was intoxicating. No words needed to be said. With her, nothing could ever be wrong.

When I got home later, the effect she had on me started to wear off a lot faster than normal. All of my anger crept back. It seemed to be even more intense this time around. When I closed my eyes to try to sleep, I was once again fighting the darkness that plagued most of my dreams.

When I awoke, it was 8:30 a.m. I reached for the phone immediately to call Elle. The phone rang twice and then her groggy voice answered.

"Hello?"

"Hey, Elle."

"Nicholas, it's 8:30 in the morning. Are you okay?" Her voice was filled with panic.

"Yes, I just wanted to see if we could spend the day together."

"Of course we can. Haven't we spent every day together this whole summer? Are you sure you're okay?" she asked again, sensing something was wrong. "What's going on?"

"Everything's fine, I just miss you," I said in the most normal, nothing-is-wrong voice that I could muster.

That did the trick, or at least she didn't push me any further.

"Oh, Nicholas, I miss you too. Let me get dressed and I will be over in an hour. But you owe me a back massage for waking me up this early, and it better be a good one."

"It's a deal. See you in an hour."

A massage was a small price to pay.

Now with Elle coming over, I was able to relax and think about Riley and Genevieve. The two of them had gone from being my rescuers to becoming another big question mark in my life, another secret. Could Elle be this 4th Thusian Riley talked about? Half of me wished it was her so that I could share everything with her, no more secrets. Then maybe we could have a future together, but it was selfish of me to want such a thing. It would be a death sentence for her if she was a Thusian, and a world without Elle Canan was one I didn't want to know. As those thoughts went around in my head like angry hornets, a vision of Genevieve flickered in. Where did that come from? Why was I thinking of her? I didn't know, so I did my best to block it out.

I waited for Elle on the front porch. The smell of Cora's coffee was unbearable today, making my constant nausea swirl throughout my body. A gentle breeze helped calm my upset stomach.

I didn't notice Elle's car pull into the driveway until the sound of her closing the door broke my trance. She looked amazing. Every time I saw her, it felt like the first time all over again. She was my beautiful angel. The butterflies in my stomach came alive; a lump in my throat made it difficult for me to breathe. She was wearing plain-old ripped jean shorts and a red tank top. She had her hair up in a black Cincinnati Reds baseball hat. She was simply awesome.

I met her at the bottom of the porch with a kiss. Instantly everything was good in the world.

"So you missed me, huh?" she said in a very innocent, but patronizing tone.

"Terribly," I said, taking her hand. "Sorry for calling so early." I looked down, feeling embarrassed, like I was a little kid apologizing for eating a cookie before dinner. Elle put her hand under my chin and raised my head so I would make eye contact with her.

"Never apologize for missing me."

Smiling, I picked her up in a big hug and spun her around to her delight.

We spent the rest of the morning inside with Cora. They talked about some book they had both read. Cora loved to read and so did Elle. They had grown very close to each other over the summer. Elle had become like a little sister to Cora and Cora loved everything about it. Cora had never asked my opinion on clothing, food or anything else like that, but now she asked Elle's opinion on everything. Cora was a strong, independent woman who never needed or looked for any advice or help, so I found it odd. I guess she missed having friends and Elle was a perfect fit.

"So guys, what do you want for lunch? I was thinking about making portabella mushroom paninis with balsamic vinaigrette, sliced tomatoes, avocados and provolone cheese. What do you think?"

"Everything you make is incredible, Cora. You know that," Elle responded.

Cora smiled and went to the kitchen.

"I love your aunt. She knows we would love anything she makes. I still remember that time I saw the gourmet lunch she made for you when we ate under the stairs for the first time last year. It was incredible."

I had come a very long way. Just last year I was hiding from people during lunch, but now I had a girlfriend and friends, with no reason to fly under the radar or just blend in anymore.

"So, Elle, that reminds me, are we going to eat under the stairs this year?" I was joking, but she paused to think about it. She put her finger up to her head, pretending to really think hard.

"Well I guess it's up to you. As I recall, you were the reason why we sat there in the first place."

"Hang on. You're right that I was originally the one who sat there, but even when I wasn't trying to hide anymore, you still insisted we sit under there, remember?" I grabbed her and started to tickle her.

She flashed her crooked little smile and broke free from my grip. She stood up and straightened her clothes like she was a mess and said, "Well then, Mr. Keller, we will have to see if I eat with you at all this year."

She was so cute when she was trying to be funny. I couldn't be any luckier.

Cora brought out our lunches. We took them out to the porch. We were about ten minutes into our lunch when Elle asked something I was hoping she wouldn't.

"So what did you do last night while I was at church?" An innocent question, but how was I going to answer it? I was tired of lying. I was going to try the truth, or at least some form of it.

"Cora and I went over to our neighbors' house for dinner."

Elle looked like she had just seen a ghost.

"You went to someone's house for dinner—complete strangers?" She was joking with me, but she was right. Elle knew we avoided everyone, even now when we didn't have to. Some habits were hard to break.

"No, they aren't strangers. Cora knows him from college. He is the new history teacher at the high school."

"Oh, Mr. Riley Moore?" She said his name like he had been teaching at Winsor for years.

"Yes, how do you know him?"

"My parents are on the welcoming committee for new teachers to the school district. I met him and his wife about two weeks ago at the Winsor faculty dinner."

"His wife was with him?" I asked.

"Of course his wife was with him. She's the most beautiful woman I have ever seen, so elegant and nice." Genevieve, elegant . . . yeah, right. That was funny. She was far from that. From my brief encounter with her at their house, she seemed more rude and crass than elegant.

Then I heard the sound of a moving truck coming from the direction of their house. The sound made me sick. That sound normally meant *I* was moving again. Several moving trucks followed by their sea green truck backed down the long driveway. Elle seemed mesmerized with all of them. She stood to get a better view.

"Mr. Moore lives *there*?"

Her face showed her shock and I knew why. She had to be wondering how a teacher could afford a place like that.

"Nicholas, how can they—"

"Not sure," I said. I still wondered how they could build such an expensive house.

Elle sat back down, but now she had positioned herself

so she could watch the team of movers unload the fleet of trucks. Just days ago, I was fascinated by watching the house being built, but now that I knew who lived there, my interest had vanished. I didn't care anymore, not one bit. But Elle had picked up where I left off. I wished she knew that as the movers unpacked those trucks, she was that much closer to being examined by the very two people who were moving in next door.

Elle waved. I turned, hoping to see Riley. It was Genevieve. She was wearing a large sun hat and another summer dress similar to the one she had on last night, but this one had an elaborate floral pattern on it.

"Well goodness gracious, it's so good to see you again, Ms. Canan," Genevieve shouted. What was she doing? I had clearly told them I would contact them when I was ready.

Elle shouted back, "It's nice to see you again, too, Mrs. Moore."

Before I could stop Elle, she got up and walked toward her. Genevieve was already in our yard walking toward us. Cora must have heard Elle because she was now out on the porch, ready to swoop in if needed. I hurried to catch up with Elle.

"Your house is so beautiful," Elle said.

"Why thank you, dear. Riley and I have been saving to build our dream home ever since we met, and with a lot of help from my parents, we finally were able to. It's a little on the big side, but with some little ones running around in the future, it will shrink fast."

Elle laughed. I couldn't believe that she was falling

for this garbage. Genevieve quickly smiled at me and then focused back on Elle. Was she taunting me?

"Nicholas was telling me that Mr. Moore and Cora went to school together."

Without skipping a beat Genevieve responded. "Oh yes, they were close friends at Vanderbilt, maybe a little too good of friends." Genevieve gave us a wink, smiled then laughed. "But that was a long time ago and now Nicholas and Cora are like family." Elle looked at me and I forced a smile. Genevieve gave me a look again like she was having fun making me suffer this way.

"Nicholas, I forgot to tell you, dear," the way she said it made my blood boil, "Riley was offered the assistant varsity coach position for football."

I had to compose myself to keep from showing anger. They were invading all of my safe places quickly.

"Wow, that's great," I choked out.

"I know you can't play anymore, but Riley would love for you to be part of the team. In fact, Coach Miller mentioned you may assist with the team this year."

I didn't say anything. Why did they fail to mention that they had already met Elle and her parents and that Riley was the assistant varsity coach? I started to clench my teeth, trying to hold back my anger.

"Nicholas was already asked by Coach Miller to help with the team," Elle said.

"Oh, then it's settled. I'll let Riley know you will help," Genevieve said with a big smile.

I wasn't sure if I was going to help. I still felt guilty about faking my injury last year. But what was I going to say now? Both of them were staring at me, burning a hole into me. I nodded in defeat.

"You two have fun. I have to go now," Genevieve said. She gave me one last look of triumph then headed back to orchestrate the movers.

"Elle, you know I haven't made up my mind about the whole football thing yet," I said, walking with her back to the porch.

"I know, don't be mad. You were forced to quit and I know how much you loved to play. So this is the next best thing. If you don't do it for yourself, do it for the team. They look up to you."

"They look up to me for the wrong reason. I am a quitter."

"Nicholas, don't give me that. You had no choice. They look up to you, not because you got hurt but because of who you are." She put both of her hands around my waist, staring deep into my eyes. I couldn't argue with her even if I wanted to. She had complete control of me.

"Okay then, that's settled. Now I have a random question about Mrs. Moore. She seems really young; do you know how old she is?" she asked.

"Twenty-eight or twenty-nine, I think." I didn't really have a clue how old she was but it sounded good. She then said something I wasn't expecting.

"Please don't think badly of me, because I know they're like family, but I didn't like how she was looking at you."

Where did that come from? Did she notice those looks Genevieve was giving me?

"What do you mean?" I asked.

"It might just be me being jealous, but I could swear she looked at you . . . Oh, never mind."

"Elle, what are you talking about?"

"She looked like she was admiring you," she said.

"Admiring me how?"

"You know, like she was interested in you."

"Elle, the whole time she was over here, she had her eyes fixed on you." I laughed. Genevieve likes me? That was a ridiculous thought. If she liked anything, it was how she was toying with me—that's it. "She's married to Cora's good friend. She's like another aunt to me."

Elle smiled, looking embarrassed. "I know, Nicholas. She is just so impressive, beautiful and—"

"Elle," I said, interrupting her, "you are stunning, intelligent, and perfect. Nobody could ever compare to you in my eyes." I sat her down next to me on our porch swing and put my arm around her and pulled her in close. "Elle Canan, don't forget that I love you so much it hurts, and I can't imagine life without you." I leaned over and kissed her.

After Elle went home, I sat down in the family room, looking at a magazine that had Dr. Chase Letterby on the cover with a caption that read, "Doctor to the Stars." As much as Chase was in the news, I was surprised the Seekers didn't go after him. Maybe because he was too big of a target with people everywhere knowing him. Xavier was more calculating. Dr. Chase Letterby was too easy, not a challenge. The doorbell rang. Cora was at the door and opening it before I even had a chance to move.

"Can I help you?" I heard her ask, but there was no reply. She shut the door and walked into the family room. She was holding a large, plain, tan envelope. She opened it and pulled out several pieces of paper.

"What is that?"

Cora was very focused on whatever was written on the pages. She flipped through them and said, "It's a subpoena for you to testify for the prosecution at Oliver Rail's kidnapping trial. It's signed by a Judge Barnhart and the district attorney, James Caldwell."

"Are you kidding? I gave my statement to the police a couple of times already. What do they need to know now?"

I called Elle's cell phone immediately, but she didn't answer, so I called her home and her mom answered.

"Mrs. Canan, it's Nicholas. Is Elle there? I need to talk to her."

"Nicholas, she can't talk right now. She is speaking with her father and our family attorney."

"Does she have to appear in court too?" I feared the answer.

"Yes, she does. I'll give her the message you called, dear."

I couldn't believe we would both have to relive that horrible night in front of an undoubtedly crowded courtroom.

After dinner, Cora and I ended up in the family room watching some old episodes of *The Lucille Ball Show*.

"Nicholas." I was lying on the couch and had to sit up to look back at Cora. She was sitting on the edge of our leather recliner with the TV remote in her hand. She turned off the TV, obviously wanting to talk.

"Cora, is everything okay?"

"I was going to ask you the same question. With our new neighbors and Oliver's trial, I wanted to see if you were okay."

"I'm great," I lied. She gave me a look that said, "Yeah right."

"Nicholas, I know you're not. After you got home from Elle's, you tossed and turned all night. I could hear you from all the way down the hall. The sounds of rattling Tic Tacs kept me up."

The Tic Tacs were always a dead giveaway of something being wrong.

"Cora, it's just a lot to take in."

"I know the answer to this will be no, but it's not too late to leave, to start over somewhere else," she said, hoping I would agree.

I shook my head emphatically no, so she would understand that no matter how bad it was I would never go back on the run, leaving Elle.

"I'm just letting you know it's still an option. So do you want to talk about having to testify?"

I held up my hand and said, "I don't want to think about any of that, Cora."

"Okay then, so what do you think about what Riley and Genevieve told us?" She sure was talkative this evening.

"Not sure what to believe. Did Ester or Chase ever talk to you about that stuff before?" I asked.

Cora sat there very quietly, like she was thinking carefully about how she should answer. It made me feel like she was hiding something.

"Cora, if you know something, you better tell me."

"I don't, but something about what Riley said sounded very familiar to me. I can't put my finger on it, but there was something, like a distant memory or connection."

I didn't know what she meant. Familiar, how? What did that mean? I definitely didn't think anything about that night was familiar in any way.

"Cora, I'm not sure I understand what you mean."

She shrugged her shoulders and said, "Nicholas, to be honest, I don't understand it myself. Did you understand everything they talked about last night?"

"I think I got most of it. But I don't understand why the group of seven has to be formed at all."

"Nicholas, I believe that the Keeper knew the Seekers would grow out of control, and The 7 was a way to set things right."

"But wouldn't it make sense for there to be a bigger group of Thusians with special talents to combat the large group of Seekers?" I asked. "How can four people fight all of the Seekers? I doubt they will limit themselves to only using three because some Keeper said so."

"If Riley is right about the Keeper setting up The 7, and if Ester is right about the Council using only the best Thusians to make up the original one hundred Seekers, then I think the Seekers would feel they need to abide by any order that the Keeper stated. They are still Thusians, so they'd still be compelled to follow the rules."

"I don't know, Cora," I said. "It doesn't make any sense."

We both just sat there. I had been able to block out most

of what had happened because of my time with Elle, but now my mind was fixed on Genevieve, Riley and the trial.

My head began to hurt. I didn't feel like talking about this anymore. I lay back on the couch and Cora turned the TV back on.

If Cora was right about how it worked and the Seekers would follow what the Keeper said, then I knew that Xavier had to be the leader of the three and that he would do everything in his power to stop us from forming The 7.

TRIAL
CHAPTER FIVE

I didn't see Riley or Genevieve the whole next week, which was a relief because I didn't want to feel like a prisoner anymore, trapped inside my house, avoiding them at all costs. I spent most of the week with Elle, because August 17, the date of Oliver's trial, was rapidly approaching. Elle's parents had refused to file charges against him after he took her from their house. Her parents knew he didn't intend to harm her, but the new district attorney, James Caldwell, was trying him for kidnapping anyway, despite the protests from Elle's parents and most of the town. James Caldwell was on the news every night leading up to the trial, talking about how Oliver was going to be tried as an adult, not as a juvenile.

No matter what TV station I turned on, he was there, talking about the trial. "Oliver Rails needs to understand that there are consequences for his actions. Even though he did not make the dock collapse during the party—the *illegal* little party that was on *privately-owned* property—he knew what he was doing when he took Ms. Canan from her house and put her in that perilous position."

"D.A. Caldwell, one more question?" asked the reporter, with his microphone right out in front to get every word he said.

"Just one more."

"Is it true that you are seeking the maximum sentence for Oliver Rails?"

He looked right into the camera and said, "I will be seeking the maximum sentence allowed by Illinois law for committing such a heinous act. This type of recklessness toward innocent individuals will not be tolerated while I am around." I turned off the TV. I couldn't believe he was trying to get the maximum sentence. As much as I despised Oliver for what he did to Elle, he shouldn't be charged with this. He had already paid heavily. His extensive injuries and being expelled from school were bad, but the worst thing for him must have been getting kicked off the football team. All of that was punishment enough in my mind. Being tried as an adult for kidnapping was way too harsh. Elle and I were going to be James Caldwell's star witnesses, and she was beginning to crack. She tried hard to act like everything was fine, but I could tell it wasn't.

Xavier, not Oliver, was the real reason the car went into the quarry lake, sending Elle and Oliver plummeting into the depths. I still remembered Xavier saying he didn't care how Elle and I died, just as long as we did.

Oliver's recovery from last spring's injuries had been a slow one. He remained in a coma for a month after the accident. Without Chase, Oliver probably would never have awoken. On one side of Oliver's face was a scar from his neck to his forehead, right along his eye. The scar was the result of hitting the windshield when the car went into the icy water. His good looks were now marred. He was a bully and a jerk, but Oliver didn't deserve what Xavier did to him and what James Caldwell was about to do next. Xavier and the Seekers almost killed him and James Caldwell was about to ruin what was left of his life.

The day before the trial, Elle cried most of the night. All I could do was hold her once I got to her house.

"I don't want to go. It was bad enough that I had to live through it. They can't make me go," she sobbed. She didn't want to relive those horrible memories. I couldn't blame her. I wanted to march down to the D.A.'s office and set him straight.

I, too, had strong emotions about testifying, but mine were different. I was upset at Oliver for taking Elle, but most of my anger was toward Xavier for almost killing her. I was afraid that the anger I felt would somehow come out in the courtroom and hurt Oliver's chances.

The August heat reared its ugly head the day of the trial with the sun beating down on Winsor. The grey suit Cora got for me was made out of a lighter material so that I wouldn't get overheated during the trial. I had gone through a pack of Tic Tacs that morning just in anticipation of what was about to happen. I hadn't been able to talk to Elle yet, which made me even tenser.

The old stone courthouse in downtown Winsor was not air-conditioned, so an already stressful situation was magnified by the heat. Inside the courtroom was a large fan that oscillated back and forth, pushing around the hot stagnant air with little relief. The courtroom's balcony was full of people who wanted to watch the drama unfold. The first floor was equally as crowded. The wooden benches were very uncomfortable, making it difficult to sit still. The courtroom hadn't seen much maintenance or attention over the years. Parts of the ceiling looked like they had been patched hundreds of times; cracks and water spots covered it. The bluish paint on the walls was chipping off in long columns.

Cora and I got there early, but not early enough to get a seat in the front. We settled for a seat in the back of the courtroom on the first floor, close enough to hear what was going on, but that was it. I could only see about four rows in front of where we were. I didn't really care to know what was happening up on the stand. I just wanted to get this over with.

"Nicholas, don't worry about anything. Just answer truthfully and this will all be over soon," Cora whispered to me, squeezing my hand.

I loosened my tie, hoping it would help cool me down and relieve some of my nerves, but it didn't help. Elle walked by me with her family and sat down next to their lawyer up front. I think I was more nervous for her than for myself.

The trial began. I blocked out everything that was being said. I didn't want to hear any of it. I closed my eyes and focused on my date with Elle on the golf course last year. The memory of such a perfect night blocked out what was happening in the courtroom.

Cora nudged me and whispered, "Elle."

I didn't realize that she was up on the stand. I sat straight up in my seat to get a better view. The fan was drowning out most of the dialogue between Elle and D.A. Caldwell, but I heard some of what they were saying.

"Ms. Canan, did you know that Oliver was going to drive off?" The D.A.'s voice boomed over the fans.

"No, but he wasn't going—" Her fragile voice halted, interrupted by D.A. Caldwell.

"Thank you, Ms. Canan. I don't need you to elaborate," his smug voice rang.

The fire that had been dormant inside me ignited for the first time in a very long time. The acid welled up into my throat. I didn't want to fight it. It felt good to feel hatred and anger toward James Caldwell.

"Ms. Canan, why did Oliver Rails come to your house in the first place? Was he looking for something?"

"Objection." Oliver's defense attorney stood.

But before he could say another word, James Caldwell said, "I will rephrase the question, Your Honor. Why did Oliver Rails come to your house, Ms. Canan?"

Oliver's attorney sat down.

"He was looking for Nicholas," Elle said quietly.

"I'm sorry. Can you repeat what you said a little bit louder for the courtroom?" James Caldwell said arrogantly, like he was having so much fun toying with her.

She took a big gulp, "Nicholas. He was looking for Nicholas."

"Nicholas who?"

"Nicholas Keller," Elle said, on the verge of tears.

"So why did he take you, then?" he asked.

44

I knew the D.A. was trying to trap her into admitting that Oliver took her against her will. My disgust for him for putting Elle through this was fueling the rage building in me.

"I guess he was trying to get back at Nicholas and that's why he took me," she answered in a very soft voice.

"Thank you. No further questions for this one, Your Honor," he said like she didn't matter, like she was nothing more to him than a means to an end.

The defense attorney then asked Elle a series of questions about how she knew Oliver and if they were friends. I couldn't focus on what was being said. I was consumed by the way that the D.A. had treated Elle. I had to control myself from jumping up and knocking him out.

Cora nudged me again. "They just called your name," she said.

I stood up. I could now see the entire courtroom. There wasn't an empty seat in the place. I walked up and stood next to the judge, not looking into the crowd. After being sworn in, I sat down. James Caldwell stood up with a couple of papers in his hand. He reminded me more of a used car salesman than a district attorney. His tight tan suit and thin blue leather tie looked like they were trying to escape off his body. It was not appropriate attire for an attorney at all; they were way too small for him. His comb-over didn't make him look any younger. I could feel another wave of acid pushing up into my throat as my contempt for him grew. I had to control it. I looked out into the courtroom for Elle, hoping to gain some composure. It seemed like everyone from the school was there along with half the town. Coach Miller was near the front of the courtroom, flanked by Coach Hoff and Mrs. Kitchen, our sophomore principal. I saw Eric, Livi and also Matt farther back. Then I saw Elle and her parents. She was not looking up. She had her head buried in her dad's chest. Seeing her that way intensified my disgust for the D.A., which didn't help me control anything. It made it worse.

"Please state your name," James Caldwell said.

"Nicholas Keller," I spat out.

"Could you please state your real name?"

"That is my real name," I answered shortly.

"No, I think your real name is Alexander Nicholas Taylor."

He was trying to make me look like I was a liar so he could gain an advantage over me, but it wouldn't work.

"That used to be my name, but it was legally changed to Nicholas Keller six years ago, so you may call me Nicholas or Mr. Keller if you'd like."

He didn't like that. By the look of some people in the courtroom, they were also stunned that I answered him so defiantly. Why shouldn't I answer him that way? The fact that he thought he was a big shot didn't mean anything to me.

"Mr. Keller, please stick to the questions that are asked of you," Judge Barnhart said. "I will not have that type of behavior in my courtroom."

"Yes, Your Honor," I said.

"Thank you, Your Honor. So, Mr. Keller, was Oliver a friend?" James Caldwell asked.

As soon as he asked the question I knew where he was going with this. He was going to try to make Oliver out to be some sort of monster who was trying to seek revenge against me by kidnapping Elle.

"No, not a friend of mine," I answered.

He followed quickly with the next question.

"He picked on you a lot?"

"No more than the other guys on the varsity team did." That wasn't exactly true, but he always had someone with him when he harassed me, so the answer wasn't actually a lie either. The D.A.'s face twisted with frustration, obviously not expecting that answer.

"But wasn't Oliver always picking on you in school and at football?"

"No," I said. He wasn't always picking on me because he wasn't always around me. The D.A. really should have phrased his question better. A glint of anger appeared in his eye.

"Did you see Oliver punch you the night of Homecoming?"

"I'm sorry, but I didn't see what he did." I knew he punched me, but I never actually saw him hit me. Again, James Caldwell should have phrased his question better.

The look on his face was priceless. He was fuming. Beads of sweat appeared on his forehead. I was enjoying putting him through this, embarrassing him for what he did to Elle. The courtroom was no longer silent. There was a lot of commotion. He walked up to the microphone and put his hand on it and whispered to me.

"I know what you're doing, you little punk. But it's not wise to mess with me. I know what happened that night and how you were able to save your little girlfriend. So you better start answering my questions, or I'll start to question you about how you were able to save them both. Or maybe I will call your little girlfriend back on the stand to put her through some more. You don't want that, do you?"

He leaned away. The judge didn't hear anything. She was preoccupied with the crowd. I grabbed hold of the seat, fighting back the urge to jump off the witness stand.

D.A. Caldwell resumed his questioning. "Okay, Nicholas, who did Elle Canan go with to the Homecoming Dance last year?"

"Oliver."

I didn't want to answer him, but I had to now. How could he know about my talents? He had to be bluffing. He was looking for an advantage of some sort and was trying anything. I couldn't see Elle's face because she was still buried in her father's chest. I was on the verge of losing it when I caught sight of Genevieve and Riley. Riley looked very calm and Genevieve looked so motherly, which caught me off-guard. Her eyes were full of compassion. I stared into them for a brief second. Just when I thought I couldn't control myself any longer, the anger was gone, extinguished. Somehow Genevieve was able to tame the anger, just like Elle. I became focused once again.

"Mr. Keller, why did you go to the rock quarry that night?"

"I went because I knew that Oliver had taken Elle with him and I wanted to make sure she was okay."

The D.A. smiled. "Why is that?"

He was leading me down a path and I knew what the outcome would be, but I had no choice. I had to say it.

"I was making sure she was okay because she would have never gone with him by choice."

"No further questions, Your Honor." He got what he wanted.

Oliver's attorney asked me if I thought Oliver would hurt Elle. I answered no. He asked a bunch of other questions, hoping to portray Oliver as a bully, but not as a kidnapper. Finally, I was dismissed.

What did James Caldwell mean when he said that he knew about how I saved her? Maybe he was part of Xavier's plan to get to me, or worse, was he one of the three Seekers? Regardless, I was more interested in getting to Elle so I could make sure she was all right and reassure her that everything was going to be okay.

The day's proceedings ended hours later. Cora and I were walking to our truck when the image of Genevieve sitting in the courtroom appeared in my head. How was that self-absorbed person able to calm me like Elle could? She was nothing like Elle.

I had to face the fact that I needed to talk with Riley and Genevieve to figure out what the next step was in finding the 4th. The world was not going to stop so I could try to have a normal life, which fell out of reach for me a long time ago. Time would move on with or without me. Hopefully, working with them would eventually give Elle and me some sort of future together.

**

"Cora, I think I should go talk to Riley and Genevieve."

Cora didn't say anything.

"I can't just sit around and do nothing."

"Nicholas, why the sudden change of heart? Was it seeing the two of them in the courtroom today?" she asked.

"No, it was because of what James Caldwell said to me when I was up on the stand."

"The D.A.?"

"Yes, when I was up there he whispered to me that he knew what happened the night I pulled Elle and Oliver out of the water. I'm not sure what he meant, but I'm afraid of who he might be."

"Nicholas, there is no way he is working with Xavier. He is just an overzealous D.A. trying to make a name for himself. That's it. How could he really know what you did?"

"Cora, do you know that for sure? Are you 100-percent positive? Because I'm not. I thought I could just put Riley and Genevieve off, but it seems like it's going to catch up with me whether I like it or not. No matter how hard I try, I can't avoid this any longer."

"If that's how you feel, then you should go and talk to them. Nicholas, I support whatever decision you make, but remember: once you go down this path, there is no turning back," Cora warned.

I couldn't help but think about how she said "no turning back." It had to be a reminder of her sacrifice and how she gave up the love of her life to protect me after the earthquake.

After the trial, I didn't get to see Elle. Her dad didn't want her to come over or for me to go over there. He just wanted her to be with family. More or less, he didn't want us to be together. He still blamed me for all of this. After the accident, he shook my hand as if to say thanks for saving her, but that gratitude was long gone. I could tell that Elle wanted to be with me, but she couldn't say it on the phone. She didn't give the code to come over, but it didn't matter. I was going to go over there anyway. I had to see her before I talked to Riley and Genevieve.

I waited until 11:30 to leave for her house. When I got there, the window was open, which was a welcome sight. I slid down into her room. She was not there. I sat on her bed waiting for her to come back. I didn't want to go out into her basement just in case her parents were still up. I longed to see her, to hold her in my arms and become lost in her deep greyish-blue eyes. I felt like I needed to wipe out the images of Genevieve from earlier because she was not the same as Elle.

I heard Elle and her dad coming down the stairs. The voices were getting closer and closer quickly. I was already at the window to make my escape when I heard the door open. I dove to the side of her bed.

"Elle, if he's not coming over, then why is your window open? Are you trying to sneak him in or something?" Her dad walked over to the window and slammed it shut. His back was to me. If he turned around he would see me for sure.

I couldn't believe that I hadn't gotten out when I had the chance. I squeezed under the bed right as he turned around.

"Dad, I wanted some fresh air in here."

"It's 90 degrees out there; we have the air conditioner on. What are you trying to do, cool the entire neighborhood?"

"Dad, I can open the window if I want to. Leave me alone." Elle walked over and opened the window back up. She turned and saw me sticking my arm out just far enough to get her attention. She walked out of her room like she hadn't seen me. He followed, slamming the door behind him. They continued to argue as they walked back up the stairs.

That was a close call. I think he would have killed me right there on the spot if he had found me. What was I supposed to do? Should I wait or leave? Either one had its faults. If I left, I wouldn't get to see Elle, but staying might mean I would get caught by her dad, and that would mean not seeing her for a lot longer. There was no question about what to do. I climbed up through the window and walked back to my truck.

Down the road from me a person darted from one car to another. My heart began to pound. Whoever it was, was lying down next to a car several houses away. I slowly crept toward the motionless figure, and then the front light of Elle's house came on. I scrambled to the side of the truck. As I slowly got in and backed away from her house, the figure went sprinting in the opposite direction. There was no doubt about it—it was Genevieve. Her long hair danced in the night air like it was mocking me for not being able to go after her. Nobody came out of Elle's, but I still couldn't take the chance of going after her just in case her dad was looking out the window for me. I would get my chance to set her straight soon enough.

NEW STUDENT
CHAPTER SIX

The darkness that haunted my dreams was absent when I got home, allowing me a full night of rest, which was a luxury that I welcomed after the long day. The extra rest made me feel full of energy. I was out the door before Cora made it down the stairs to start making coffee. I got into the truck and headed to Winsor High School. I wanted to get there early so I could go see Coach Miller about helping with football. This would also give me a chance to talk to Riley by himself without Genevieve. The clock in the truck read 6:15 a.m.

Pulling into the parking lot was different. I used to feel uncomfortable, almost scared of what was waiting for me inside. But now the school felt like home, a safe place. That's the feeling I used to get being with Cora, but now that feeling was gone because of our new neighbors. I was glad to have a place that brought me some comfort again.

There were some cars in the parking lot, but not many. The team still had about an hour before they had to arrive. I walked in the main entrance of the school. The ornate landscaping was not as incredible to me now. I guess I, too, had grown used to all of the roses and statues. It was sad not to appreciate such beauty anymore.

I almost fell over in shock when I went in. The once normal, plain brick and metal interior had been transformed into something that matched the outside. I couldn't believe it. The sterile interior now looked like a luxury four-star hotel. There were marble floors everywhere, which replaced the old orange carpet. The walls were covered in tapestries and plaques of all our school's achievements. Different colors were mixed on the walls, as if Michelangelo or Leonardo da Vinci had painted them. I didn't even recognize the office area where the secretary sat last year. It now resembled an upscale coffee bar or a posh trendy spa. Everything was modern, new and sleek. I walked down the hall in complete shock. What had happened to my safe place?

"Well, if it isn't the man of the hour." That whiny, high-pitched tone made me want to run and hide; it was my counselor, Joy Lemmins. She was standing in the doorway of the guidance office. The exterior wall was now etched glass with a large world map and big letters that spelled out "Guidance Office." It was quite impressive.

"So what do you think of the school's new look? Because I *loooove* it," she said. I didn't know how to respond.

"I think I liked it the way it was before. Wait a minute, what do you mean the man of the hour?"

"You are the reason we got this new look." She pointed to a metal plaque that was on the far wall opposite the guidance office. It was the size of a large movie poster. I walked over to read it and she followed.

The plaque simply read "In Honor of Nicholas Keller, Who Continues to Sacrifice Everything for Others."

I turned around. "Who did this?" I demanded, with the fire in my stomach coming to life.

"Don't get angry. You need to chill," she said.

"What did you just say to me?" I regretted my harsh tone before I finished asking. Joy Lemmins was odd and bizarre at times, but she was still my counselor. "Ms. Lemmins, I'm sorry. I didn't mean to say that to you. I'm just so angry about all of this," I said, looking around.

"Nicholas, I don't know why you are so angry. This was done to honor you, not to make you upset."

"But I didn't ask for it, did I?" I shot back, still on edge.

She pulled her large red-rimmed glasses down to the tip of her nose, peered over them and said, "Nicholas, there are a lot of things in life that we don't ask for. We just have to be grateful for the good ones, because there are far more bad ones."

I couldn't believe that Joy Lemmins actually just made a good point. As much as I hated this being done in my honor, it wasn't the worst thing in the world. I began to relax.

"I'm glad to see that you now understand that this was done out of kindness, sweetie."

"Who did this?" I asked in a calmer voice.

"That is a mystery, isn't it? The money came in right after the unfortunate incident last spring." She whispered, "You know, when the car accidentally fell into the water at the quarry party?"

I don't think I would say it was an "unfortunate incident" when Elle and Oliver almost died. She was so odd, and to think that just a second ago I was giving her credit for making a good point.

"Well anyway, I think it was Mr. David Rails. He is loaded. I'm sure he was grateful to you for saving his son. And also for having your family friend, Doctor Hotness himself, take care of Oliver until he got better."

"What did you call Chase?" I wasn't sure if I had heard her correctly.

Joy Lemmins' pale, white face turned a light shade of pink. She turned and walked back to the guidance office, her big, round, red earrings bouncing with each step as she retreated. She wasn't watching where she was going and walked into one of the desks. It sent her stumbling into the wall. After a whole year of being around her, I would have thought I'd be used to her antics by now.

I had to get to the locker room. I couldn't focus on the school's changes. I was here for a purpose. I walked into the varsity locker room, bypassing the lockers, and knocked on Coach Miller's door.

"Come in."

I opened the door. Coach Miller was sitting at his desk, holding a clipboard and studying it. He was probably looking over plays for this upcoming season. His face lit up with a big smile when he saw me standing in front of him.

"Nicholas, it's good to see you. How are you doing?"

"Fine," I said.

"So what brings you down here to see me?"

"I've thought it over. I will help out this year, if you would still like me to."

"Of course I do." He stood up, extending his hand for me to shake. I took it. "You are now my assistant. We knew this would be a good fit for you." He let go of my hand.

"We?" I asked, not knowing who else could make this decision besides him.

"My new assistant varsity coach, Riley Moore, also agreed you would be a perfect fit. You'll be on the sidelines with us during the games, and you'll talk to Coach Moore about anything you think we need to do on varsity. You were seeing things that no one else saw last year, so it's important to have those eyes. We need to have our most valuable player still part of the action."

Coach Miller's comment made me swell with a little pride. My dad would have been proud to hear that his son was the most valuable player.

"Go on out there with the guys. We will start the team meeting in a half hour."

I walked out of the office and the first person I saw was Eric. In a loud voice, he shouted like an announcer at a boxing match, "Ladies and gentlemen, may I have your attention? The first sophomore to ever play on varsity is now the youngest varsity assistant coach in Winsor history! Give it up for my best friend, Mr., I mean, Coach Nicholas Keller!"

The guys who were already there erupted into a loud roar. It was immediately silenced like a switch was turned off. Coach Miller had walked out.

"If this is how you're going to act, maybe you guys should go back down to JV. Their locker room is down the hall."

Nobody said a word.

"Couldn't let him get away with that, could I?" Coach Miller whispered to me. "And whatever you do, don't smile. You're a coach now."

It took everything in me not to laugh. Coach Miller walked back into the office and shut the door. Eric walked over to his locker. I followed him.

"Way to go, Eric. I don't think that stuff will fly up here on varsity." I hit him. A couple of the guys around me laughed.

"Did you guys see that? A coach just hit me. I am going to sue this place for everything it's got."

"Very funny," I said.

"But seriously, Nicholas, could you please tell whoever gave the money to fix up this dump to throw some of that dough to your best buddy? I need a baby-blue paint job on my car, to match my eyes." He blinked repeatedly.

I ignored him.

I hadn't really noticed before, but Eric had grown a lot since last year. He was now an inch or two taller than me. His long brown hair had been cut down to almost a shaved look. But his tan was still there. I had no idea how he kept it all year. It wouldn't surprise me if he had a tanning bed in his room.

"So how's football been?" I asked.

"It's hot out there," Matt said, sitting a couple of lockers down. He looked like he had grown a foot and put on a hundred pounds. I couldn't get over how much he had grown—he was massive before. He could go play for any college right now. "Luckily, Coach Miller has some of the practices in the gym when it gets over 100 degrees," Matt finished.

"Matt, you're so right. It has been brutal, but it's been well worth it," Eric said.

"Eric, what has gotten into you? I thought this was all for your dad?" I said to him, and Matt answered for him.

"I think it has to do with a certain new cheerleader, and also he's the varsity starting quarterback."

For the first time Eric didn't have anything to say. He just grinned.

"I thought you were going out with Livi?" I asked.

"I am. She's the new cheerleader," Eric answered.

"Keller, what are you doing on that side of the locker room? The defense is over here."

I knew that voice. I turned around and Chad was standing in the middle of the locker room, like there was an invisible wall preventing him from crossing over.

"Come over here, I want to show you something. But I'm warning you—don't get mad. I know you don't like this kind of stuff, but we decided it was fitting." I followed him, not sure what I was about to see.

He stopped and pointed toward my old locker. It had

Plexiglas over it. When I got closer to it, I could see that it was exactly how I had left it last year, with my framed jersey and all of my equipment untouched inside, frozen in time.

"What's this all about?" I asked. A couple of the defensive players who were on varsity last year huddled around us.

"Well, we wanted to honor your commitment to the team, so we left your locker as is, sealed." He tapped it with his hand, making a hollow thud.

"I'm honored, but it looks like I died or something." They all laughed.

"I guess it does." He laughed again. "We have decided to start a new tradition here at Winsor. The defense will vote at the end of the year on a graduating senior defensive player's locker to cover and seal for one year as a reminder of the commitment he made to the team. So we decided it should start with you. Even though you weren't a senior, it just seemed fitting. We all voted and it was unanimous."

I felt a little bit guilty because I didn't deserve it. But like Joy Lemmins said, I should focus on the good not the bad, so I did.

"Thanks, guys, it's awesome."

I saw Riley for a brief moment later during practice. I mouthed the words, "We need to talk."

He held up eight fingers and mouthed back, "My house."

After practice, I stayed with the coaches in the coach's office while they went over the next couple of days of practice. The meetings were exactly how I thought they would be. Coach Miller talked and everyone listened, just like when he met with the team. Coach Miller got out tapes of the next opponent. Before it started, he excused me to leave, and he told me that I didn't have to come to every practice until school started, which was a relief. I was happy to get out of there. I liked the idea of helping, but watching film of the next opponent sounded painful.

Most of the parking lot was now empty except for a truck with a flat tire jacked up just down from mine. It was the exact make and model of our truck, but a couple of years newer. There was someone sitting next to it. I backed out of my spot and pulled up to see if everything was okay. I recognized the player from football practice.

"Are you all right?" I asked through the rolled down passenger-side window. He got to his feet quickly.

"I'm okay. My dad must have used the spare, because it's not in the back, so I'm waiting for the tow truck."

"Well you are in luck," I said. "I have a spare that will fit your truck."

He looked at my truck and laughed, realizing that we had identical vehicles.

I got the spare out and rolled it over to his truck.

"Can I help?" he offered.

I turned to find him right behind me. He was a good head taller than me. He looked like he could hang with any of the bigger guys on the team.

"No, I got it."

He smiled. "My name is Bryce, Bryce Adams." He stuttered a bit and offered his hand. I leaned the tire against my knee and took his hand.

"I'm Nicholas Keller."

"It's nice to meet you, Nicholas." He brushed his jet black hair out of his eyes. In doing so he left a large streak of grease across his forehead. He looked ridiculous.

"Bryce, you've got some grease on your face." I motioned to my head, showing him about where it was.

"Great, what else can happen?"

He walked over to his truck. Using the reflection in his back window, he started to rub the grease off with very little luck.

"Wow, new kid at school and already making a fool out of myself," he mumbled, still trying to get the grease off his face.

A new student that wasn't me; I liked the way that sounded.

"Don't worry about it. I was new last year. I'll keep this between you and me."

He looked relieved. I wished that when I got here, or to any of the other schools I had attended, I could have had someone make me feel at ease about being new.

"So, Bryce, where are you from?" I asked while I was putting on the spare.

He paused for a second. I couldn't believe I had asked him that question. I dreaded being asked that when I moved. How quickly I forgot.

"I was born in Arcanum, Ohio, but my dad's in the military so we move from town to town about every two or three years. Hopefully this is my last stop, because starting over alone is tough."

"Alone?"

"Yeah, my dad is never home. He's traveling to the base in St. Louis. He moves me close to whatever base he gets reassigned to, which sucks. I wish he had left me back in Ohio. I hate moving." I had to agree with him on that. I hated moving more than anything.

"So where's your mom?" I asked.

Bryce's eyes never met mine when he answered. "She died giving birth to me."

I couldn't believe I had asked another question. What was wrong with me? Less than a year ago, all of these types of questions were asked of me and I hated it. And to ask about his mom, who was dead—I should have known better.

"Bryce, I'm sorry." I shook my head in disgust with myself.

"Don't worry," he said, smiling.

"So what grade are you in?" I thought that was a safer question.

"Senior, and I just made the varsity football team. I was pretty shocked I made it, because during the first week of tryouts I wasn't part of any of the drills. And they made us wear these disgusting white jerseys that looked older than my dad. Coach Stenger had us run along the sideline for a solid week, never practicing once. I thought for sure I was going to get cut."

"Did you have to wear equipment that was too big for you?"

He laughed. "No, the stuff they gave me was too small. Imagine me wearing that. I could barely move and the helmet felt like it was cutting off the blood to my brain. I couldn't tell if it was the heat or the helmet that made me dizzy. How did you know about the equipment?" he asked, still laughing.

"I was in your spot last year."

"Wait a minute, you're *the* Nicholas Keller?" He stood there with his mouth open. "The whole team talks about you—about how you were the main reason they won state last year, and how you saved all of those people during the 10-10 Earthquake, which was awesome, and then you saved Elle Canan and Oliver Rails from drowning. You're a hero."

I didn't know what to say. Now I was the one who felt uncomfortable.

"Nicholas, I'm terribly sorry. I didn't mean to upset you by talking about that stuff."

I was being silly. I just got done asking him about his dead mother and now I was upset over things that everyone knew about me.

"Don't worry about it, Bryce. I just don't think I'm a hero. No different than anyone else."

I figured I should change the subject, and I knew the perfect subject. "So, what do you think of Eric?"

"He's pretty full of himself, but hilarious."

At least Eric was still making the same impression on others as he did on me.

"So what position do you play?" I asked.

"Wide receiver." He looked at his watch. "Nicholas, it's good to meet you and thanks for the tire, but I have to go. I'm late. I have to meet the movers. They are bringing the rest of my stuff. I'll make sure to get the spare back to you. Also, one more thing, could you forget about all the bad stuff I said about tryouts? You're a coach now and I don't want anything to hurt my chances to start."

"Don't worry about it. It will be our secret." I smiled.

"Thanks, Nicholas. See you in school."

**

Cora was waiting for me on the porch, drinking a tall glass of lemonade. As hot as it was, I would have been inside with the air conditioning drinking the lemonade, not out on the porch.

"So how was practice?" she asked. I wasn't sure how she knew where I went—she was good. I sat down next to her and explained how the school was transformed with all of the new renovations and what Joy Lemmins had said. She just listened, not saying anything, just taking it all in. Every once in a while she would take a sip of her lemonade and then she would turn her focus back to me. I also explained about how I accepted Coach Miller's invitation to become an assistant coach, which brought a smile to her face but still no words.

"Aren't you going to say anything?" I asked.

"What would you like me to say, Nicholas?"

"Don't you think it's odd that someone would donate all of that money to remodel the school in my honor?"

"Nicholas, I think you should get used to odd things happening to you. And I'm going to hate myself for saying this, but I agree with Joy Lemmins. You and I need to not focus on the bad anymore, but the good. The school remodeling is a nice thing and it's a wonderful honor for such an incredible young man." She took my hand and put her arm around me. Cora was not very good at showing emotion, but when she did, it was nice. She made me feel good, just like my mom would have.

"So what time do we go over to Riley and Genevieve's tonight?" she asked.

"He told me to come at 8:00. Hopefully Genevieve won't be there. I caught her spying on me the other night at Elle's. Wait, how did you know I talked to Riley?"

Smiling, she said, "Because I know you."

WIRED
CHAPTER SEVEN

Elle came over after practice, which helped me stay relaxed while I waited to go over to Riley and Genevieve's. She apologized for not being able to get rid of her dad last night after the trial. She said he must have known something was up, because he wouldn't leave her alone and took her cell phone away. But she reassured me that we would spend the next couple of days together before school started. I thought she would have needed to recover after the trial, but she didn't. She was relieved it was all over and she could finally move on. It was the closure she needed.

After Elle left, Cora and I went over to Riley's. This time Genevieve opened the door, to my disgust. She was dressed in a form-fitting, short, purple dress, of course, leaving nothing to the imagination. Cora just shook her head. Genevieve's hair was pulled back into some small braids that formed a type of halo. Horns would have been more fitting for her.

"Come on in and sit down," Genevieve said.

The once empty room now had furniture in it, but not what I expected. With how big and expensive the house looked, I expected that the inside would be the same when the movers were finished. But it wasn't. It was simple, nothing flashy at all. The furniture looked like it was taken right off a department store's showroom floor. Large, black leather couches and matching end tables with lamps made up their family room with a big, off-white, shag carpet under the coffee table; nothing gaudy, just nice.

Cora and I sat down. I caught a glimpse of Cora looking around too. She would love to have a chance to decorate this incredible space. Her mind had to be busy thinking of all the wonderful things she could do in here.

"So, would either one of you like something to drink?" Genevieve asked.

I looked at Cora, shocked. We must have been at the wrong house.

Cora spoke, "Yes, that would be nice, thank you."

Genevieve didn't wait for my answer; she walked toward the kitchen. The whole house had an open floor plan so I could see her in the kitchen from the great room. She brought back a tray with a glass pitcher filled with some sort of brownish-orange drink and several glasses with ice in them. I was half expecting cans of pop at room temperature from her.

"I hope you would both like a Palmer?" Genevieve started filling a glass.

"What's a Palmer?" I asked.

"It's half lemonade and half sweet tea, named after the golfer Arnold Palmer."

I still couldn't get over how Genevieve was acting. Was

she putting on a show, or was she under strict orders from Riley not to screw up? What was going on?

"Sorry I kept you waiting. I just got back from football practice. Coach Miller kept us there late," Riley said as he walked into the room. His hair was still wet from the shower. He had on Winsor Cougars shorts and shirt and a pair of sandals. Riley settled in across from us.

"I guess I should start this off," I said. "Riley, I've decided that I would like to help you two find the 4th, because it seems like I'm not going to have a choice. This will also give me a chance to help protect the ones I love."

"Nicholas, it's good that you feel that way. There are still a lot of things that we haven't told you yet. I'm sure that you've heard some of this stuff from Ester and Chase, but we would like to go over it again. Did they talk to you about the Thusian Realization and your Final Sacrifice?"

"Yes, they did," I answered.

"Okay, but we will explain everything to you in more detail. I'm going to have Genevieve start, because she knows all of the inner workings of the Thusian's body better than I do."

Genevieve took a deep breath and started. "You know that Thusians are put on this earth to protect people. When they get this opportunity, it is commonly referred to as their Final Sacrifice, because most of the time this sacrifice leads to their death. Thusian talents are broken into two different groups to help you accomplish this sacrifice."

"Chase did tell me this part. One is physical and the other

is mental. And he also said we can't draw upon these talents at will."

"Nicholas, that's kind of right." She smiled at me. "Yes, the talents are both mental and physical in nature, but the part that Thusians can't draw upon their talents at will isn't exactly true. You have been drawing upon yours for some time. Your full talents will only be used when your Final Sacrifice occurs, but you are also able to use a portion of your talents for self-preservation and to protect others. For example, you walk out in front of a bus. A normal person probably would not hear the bus or have the reflexes or speed to get out of the way, but a Thusian would. We might think it's a close call, but our talents got us to safety. So you see, our talents will show up during these times.

"A quick side note about the Seekers and Xavier and why they are so dangerous. They create situations that we would normally get out of easily, if we were by ourselves. But what happens if there are other people around us during these situations? We are then compelled to save their lives and sacrifice ourselves, even if it's not the time for our Final Sacrifice. That's how the Seekers are eliminating Thusians. They create situations where we will have no choice but to save others.

"Now back to how the talents are divided. Thusian talents are both physical and mental, like Chase explained, but with us," she motioned to herself, Riley and me, "we don't just have one or two talents like most Thusians. We have multiple talents that are both mental and physical, which help us defend and fight against the Seekers. When normal Thusians react to a situation, they may be able to do some pretty miraculous things, like a mother lifting a car off her trapped child or a father stopping a gunman from hurting his family. But when you saved Elle and Oliver—that was an example of how you were able to use multiple talents, both physical and mental, to accomplish the rescue in the water. Most Thusians would have died while trying to save them. That's why Seekers can kill normal Thusians at will, like cats toying with a mouse. Cora was able to keep you hidden from the Seekers and pretty much everyone else, using a single mental ability—just one talent."

She took a deep breath. I looked away, realizing I had been staring at her without blinking. I was trapped by her words.

She continued, "Thusian talents come from how we are internally wired. We don't have super powers or possess some sort of magic. We process information faster and more efficiently than other people. Electric signals will direct blood and other chemicals to different parts of our bodies to activate our talents. When we use our talents, our bodies' physiology changes to aid or protect us. You could say that we are like chameleons, able to adapt to almost any situation. We are able to slow things down around us to help us make split-second decisions. Things aren't really moving any slower around us, but we are processing things faster, taking in more information. This allows us to slow time down in our minds, making our surroundings seem like they are slowing to an almost-stopped state. Here's another way to look at our mental talents: we are like super computers," she motioned to the three of us again, "able to process and analyze large amounts of information all at the same time. Regular Thusians are like home computers, only able to do some complex processes, and non-Thusians are more like typewriters. When we use our physical gifts, adrenaline plays a bigger part of our transformation. We get one hundred times more adrenaline pumped throughout our bodies than the average Thusian. It makes it seem like we have super-human speed and strength. There are hundreds of different variations of these talents, but this should give you a good basic understanding."

"Why didn't Chase or Ester tell us this stuff?" Cora asked her.

Riley answered, "Because the Council doesn't want Thusians to know, and I doubt Chase has a clue. Cora, you can't tell them any of this. I know that you think Chase and Ester are friends, but you have to understand that what we are telling you is a matter of life and death for so many people. We don't know who we can trust."

"Don't worry, Riley. We won't." I spoke up to reassure him and Genevieve, but mostly to let Cora know we weren't going to say a word.

I wanted to get back to what Genevieve was talking about to make sure I understood it correctly.

"So the three of us have multiple talents, unlike other Thusians who possess one or two?" I asked.

She nodded.

"And we have both mental and physical talents?"

She nodded yes again.

"Okay, that should cover the mechanics of our talents. Thanks, Genevieve. Now I need to tell you more about the search for the 4th," Riley said. Excitement filled his voice. "The person we are looking for will be drawn to us and we will be drawn to them. They will demonstrate all the talents that we have. This person will have more of our talents and will be able to use them better than we can because they were the last of the group, so they get the most. But more importantly, they will not understand what's going on. The Self-Realization of their talents will seem like one long nightmare, making what we went through look like a walk in the park."

I couldn't imagine how theirs could be worse than mine, being sick all of the time and not being able to sleep. I already felt sorry for whoever it was.

"One other thing that's important to know. The Seekers have the advantage over us right now because it's three on three. And I believe that they will still have a slight advantage when it's the four of us against the three Seekers at first."

"Wait a minute. You said that we needed the 4th Thusian to make it an even fight. Why look for the 4th when Xavier and the two other Seekers are still going to have the upper hand?"

"The reason why they have the upper hand is because if one of the three Seekers dies, they can and will just replace him with the next one in line. Xavier has replaced at least three Seekers since we have been looking for you. But that advantage will become their disadvantage over time, because we value life and each other, where they do not. This will bond the four of us together, making us stronger than all of the Seekers put together."

"Did you kill them? Those three Seekers?" Cora asked, sounding horrified.

"No, we didn't, but we would have, because it's us or them, and I prefer not to die just yet," Genevieve said. Her attitude had returned, but I had to agree with her on that.

"Besides the three, how many Seekers are there?" I asked.

Riley answered, "We don't know for sure, but we think that they are maintaining the original one hundred, which includes the three, that were set up by the first Council many years ago. They are very particular in keeping with the old traditions."

"Riley, why don't the Seekers just kill the Thusians off using the full one hundred Seekers? Why replace Seekers into this three?"

"Because, again, they like tradition. This is what Keeper Wren said should happen, and they follow everything that any of the Keepers said." I felt better about what he was saying because that's what Cora thought.

"I guess I'll have to have faith that you two are right about that," I said.

Riley and Genevieve looked at each other with relief. Then I looked at Cora. Her face still looked stiff with concern.

I couldn't help but think about Cora and what I was about to put her through. Cora and I were both relieved last year to not have to hide anymore, but now we were being asked to isolate ourselves once again. Chase and Ester were the closest Cora had to friends, and now she would have to keep everything from them. This would be harder on Cora than me. I still got to talk to my friends at school. Riley only wanted me, but he was asking Cora to be part of something that she couldn't help with. I felt horrible; I should have come alone to save her from this.

"Okay, now what?" Cora spoke up.

"Nothing for you, Cora. We just need Nicholas. No offense," Genevieve said.

"If you want Nicholas' help, you must have me, too. We are a package deal. There is no way I am going to let him get hurt. He hasn't yet, and I am not going to back off for anyone. Do I make myself clear? No offense." Cora said it with the same tone and attitude Genevieve had used. Genevieve smiled big, nodding her head.

"I think I'm going to like you," Genevieve said, looking at her and curling up on the couch.

"The next thing that we have to do," Riley motioned to the group, including Cora, "is make sure that we are careful while we are looking for the 4th. We should stay in pairs at all times if possible, because we are vulnerable alone."

I didn't like the sound of that. Someone would have to be with me while I was with Elle. No more being alone with her. Well, I guess I really never had any alone time with her before, but at least I didn't know they were there watching me.

"This will make it difficult for Xavier and the others to attack us," Riley added.

"Ester said he wouldn't attack again," Cora said.

"Of course he hasn't attacked again. Genevieve and I have been around the both of you 24/7. He is just waiting for his chance."

I felt like he was out there, but I wasn't sure Cora believed that. He hadn't tried anything since the quarry party in the spring, so why would he try something now? She nodded reluctantly anyway, but I knew her real hesitation was in trusting the two of them. We stayed a little longer, talking like we were long lost friends. Even Genevieve was nice. But in the back of my mind, I remembered what Cora had always taught me: never trust anyone, because this could still be a trap.

SCHOOL
CHAPTER EIGHT

Elle and I did spend the rest of the week together like she promised, but our conversations were centered on what colleges she was going to apply to. Elle's parents were trying to get her to focus on where she was going to college, which had become a very touchy subject with her. She wanted to stay close to home to be near me, but her parents, well, mostly her dad, wanted her to go away to school. I figured that I shouldn't talk about it because I didn't know what the future held for me. I didn't want to make any promises that I couldn't keep. So I just listened to her talk about how her parents didn't understand her anymore.

Elle didn't want to be at her house, so she spent every hour she could at ours during that week. Even when she was going on about her parents, it was still wonderful to be around her. Even her darkest days were bright and cheerful for me. I would find myself staring at her, still in disbelief that she was mine. How could such an incredible girl be with me? It didn't seem possible. I was nothing compared to her. Everything she did sparked my longing to be with her forever, free of all these secrets. But I would have to be content with what I had.

I increased my Tic Tac intake on the first morning back to school. My nerves were making me feel a little sick. It wasn't as bad as it had been at the last five new schools, but the habit of popping Tic Tacs continued. Cora was up before me, drinking her coffee in the kitchen as usual.

"Nicholas, are you ready?" Cora yelled to me. I was brushing my teeth.

"Almost," I said with a mouthful of toothpaste.

"Hurry, I have something to show you."

I finished, grabbed my empty backpack from my room and walked down the stairs. Cora was standing by the front door. Without any words, she opened the door and walked outside. I followed. I couldn't believe what I saw. Tears rolled down my cheeks instantly. I was looking at a ghost from my past.

"Nicholas, I've been waiting a long time to give this to you," Cora said.

Behind our truck sat my dad's orange 1973 Ford Bronco. It looked the same way it did on the day of the earthquake when I left for school.

"Cora, where did you get it?" My voice was broken and I was doing everything I could to fight back more tears.

"After the earthquake, I had all of your parents' possessions stored away in a safe place. And this is something your dad would have passed on to you for sure. So I thought this was a perfect time for you to get it."

I ran down to the truck to rub my hands on the hood to

make sure it was real. The orange paint was still faded in all the right spots. The top still showed some small spots of rust. I opened the door and found my dad's old black flashlight and maps in the driver's side door just as he had left it. In the back seat was the old Nerf football that we used to toss back and forth. The inside smelled of oil and leather; it was incredible. Cora gave me a couple of minutes before she walked over to the truck. I wiped away my tears.

"Cora, I don't know what to say." I gave her a big hug.

She held on to me tightly and said, "Your dad would have been so proud of the man you are becoming." She handed me the keys. "Now, this is not a license for you to come and go as you please. We still have rules."

"I know, Cora." I smiled.

She smiled back and laughed. "Have a good day at school."

I got in and sat on the worn, black leather seat, still in shock. I loosened my grip on the keys so I could start the truck. The engine choked, then roared to life. I checked all of the mirrors and they were perfect, no need for any adjustments. I put on my seat belt and backed out of the driveway. Cora had said that I could use the truck for driving to school this year. I had no idea she meant this truck. The drive to Elle's house was filled with incredible memories of my mom, dad and I taking different trips in the Bronco. I always knew when we were going to go somewhere because Dad would be washing and polishing it.

I pulled into Elle's driveway. I didn't need to go get her; she was waiting outside. She walked down the driveway slowly, making sure it was me. When she saw me she hurried to the truck. She opened the door and got in. I totally forgot to get out and open the door for her.

"Elle, I'm sorry for not getting the door for you."

"Don't be silly. My hand works just fine. Where did you get this truck?" She looked over at me and asked, "Is something wrong?"

"No, nothing's wrong. Everything is perfect." I'm sure I looked like I had been crying. "Cora got the truck for me. I mean, she got it from where she had stored my parents' stuff. This surprise was waiting for me earlier. This was my dad's Bronco. He got it from my grandpa when he was old enough to drive."

"Nicholas, I love it."

Elle didn't say anything on the ride to school. She just held my hand tight.

I felt invincible driving my dad's truck and having the girl of my dreams right by my side. At school, there were no cameras or reporters, no one trying to take a picture of me, no reason to hide. I was relieved. I guess the radio interviews I had done worked, keeping the media away.

My dad's truck was by far the oldest vehicle in the lot, surrounded by every kind of nice car imaginable, but mine was the best. I got out before Elle and opened her door. We walked into school together, hand in hand.

"Nicholas, I have to hurry to the guidance office for new student orientation, okay? I'll see you at lunch." She kissed me on the cheek and hurried toward the office.

Elle never ceased to amaze me. She started a new-student

program this year to help all the new students find their way around the school to their classes. She was just too good to believe. I wished they'd had that program last year. I would have gotten to know Elle a lot quicker.

I was greeted by Eric and Livi. They were linked together, arm in arm. I had to laugh because they looked like the Odd Couple. She was so proper, dressed in clothes she had probably picked out weeks ago just for the first day of school. Eric's clothes looked like he had picked up whatever was closest to him on the floor when he woke up. I guess opposites do attract.

"Hey, Nicky, my boy, I love what you've done with the place."

I shook my head and walked over to them. "Eric, you know I have no idea who did this to the school. So, how does your schedule look? Are we in any of the same classes?"

Livi answered, "I doubt it because somehow, Eric has volleyball, water polo and outdoor recreation all in a row. How you were able to get three gym classes in the same semester, I will never know."

"We have a pool?" I asked, not sure where it was.

"I got three gym classes because of my good looks, my dear, and of course we have a pool, Nicholas. Where have you been?" he said. At least school would be about the same as last year with Eric around.

"So what are you guys waiting around for?" I asked.

Livi answered again. "Mr. Moore to walk by on his way to class."

"Coach Riley Moore?"

"Yes, all of the women at the school have been talking about him. I overheard Joy Lemmins saying how gorgeous he is, in a rugged, real-man way."

"But Eric, why are you waiting with Livi? Shouldn't she be here with her girlfriends, not her boyfriend?" I asked.

"Her friends are all more interested in Bryce Adams, the new kid, you know, the wide receiver from the team. They think he looks like a young Johnny Depp. So I am standing in for them. Anyway, Coach Moore has a smokin' hot wife for me to check out later, and Livi will stand with me when I want to catch a glimpse of her."

Livi dropped his arm immediately, gave him a dirty look and stormed off.

He shrugged his shoulders. "What did I say?" He chased her down the hall.

School was as good as I had hoped it would be. It was normal, nothing out of the ordinary. The only thing that I was bracing myself for was the earthquake drill like the beginning of school last year, but after the first four classes, it still hadn't happened. I hoped that Cora or Ester had somehow made it so there wouldn't be one at all this year.

When Elle and I got to lunch, I had to bite my tongue. The revamped and newly-remodeled interior of the school had not bothered me much after the initial shock, but when I saw the new lunch options, I nearly lost it. I almost grabbed Elle's hand and led her back under the stairs, away from all this.

The lunchroom had most of the same types of food as last year, but it had been transformed into five actual restaurants, each having its own unique sitting area. Instead of lunch ladies, each had its own staff dressed in the theme of their restaurant. I couldn't believe it. It was like we had five different restaurants that had set up right where the food court used to be. Off to the side were different food carts selling everything from hot pretzels to ice cream. Right in the center of the lunchroom, hanging on its own stand-alone pillar, was a plaque saying that the lunchroom was dedicated to me. I knew that this was a nice thing, but it was making my day a little less normal than I had wanted it to be.

Elle got her food from the Greek restaurant. Everywhere we went, people were staring at us. I couldn't tell if it was because I was officially with Elle or because of the new décor in my honor.

"Nicholas, don't worry about the people staring. They are just envious of you," she said with compassion, because she knew it was making me uncomfortable.

Out of the corner of my eye I saw Bryce. He was sitting in a corner eating his food, reading a book by himself. A couple groups of girls were eyeing him from different tables, but he was completely unaware of the attention he was getting. I remembered how I was feeling the first couple of days of school, not really knowing where to sit or what to do.

"Elle, I'll be right back."

I walked over to Bryce, who looked stunned to see me, knocking over his milk in front of him.

"Hey, Bryce, do you want to sit with Elle and me?" I asked.

"Nicholas, that would be great," he said, trying to clean up his milk while gathering his things.

To the dismay of the girls staring at him, he followed me over to where Elle was sitting away from their view. We sat down.

"Elle, this is Bryce. He's a—"

"Nicholas, I know Bryce. I took him and a couple of other new students around the school today for a tour."

"I knew that. I was going to tell you that Bryce is a Scorpio and loves long walks on a beach," I said with a grin. She hit me.

Elle then started to ask Bryce a bunch of questions. Before she asked too many, I kicked her under the table. She smiled and realized what she was doing and stopped.

We were eventually joined by Amber, Chad, Livi and Eric. Livi must have forgiven Eric for his comment earlier, because they were joined at the hip again. Amber walked around the table and gave everyone hugs except for Bryce; she just shook his hand before she sat down.

The guys talked about the upcoming football season. Elle and the girls were already busy talking about Homecoming. Every so often Elle would reach over and squeeze my hand just to let me know she was still thinking of me, which sent much-welcomed electricity charging through me.

Sitting there, I realized that I had part of the normal life that I longed for—friends and a girlfriend.

With about five minutes left of lunch, Riley walked over behind me. At first I didn't know he was there, until all of the girls at the table got quiet and began staring right behind me.

"Hey, Coach, how's your first day of school? Do you need help finding your class?" Eric asked, laughing at his joke.

"Actually, I'm here for Nicholas. We are having a short coaches' meeting now. And next time, Eric, respect your coaches more or you will be the one who needs help finding your playing time," he emphasized.

Eric went silent. That was twice in one day he had gotten in trouble for something he said. I had to hand it to Eric. He was definitely entertaining, even when he was not trying to be.

I followed Riley out of the lunchroom and down to the locker room. There was no one in there, not even Coach Miller.

"So, how's your first day?" Riley asked.

"Okay," I responded. "How's yours?"

"Fine, but I forgot how much I hate waking up early. Football is one thing, but teaching is another. I nearly fell asleep in my first two classes. I should have been a P.E. teacher, not a history teacher. The running around would have done me some good.

"The reason I called you down here is that I need to get an idea of who could be the one we're looking for. Do you have any other possible leads yet?"

"Riley, it's only the first day back," I pointed out.

"I know, but start looking at your friends. What about Bryce or Chad?"

"Not sure. This is only the second time I've talked to Bryce. I haven't really had much time to get to know him yet, and for some reason I don't think it's Chad."

"Remember, Nicholas, the Seekers are also looking for the 4th. And if they get the opportunity, they will kill whoever it is. And if Xavier can get one of us to sacrifice ourselves as well, he will, so we need to work together and be extremely careful."

I started to feel like I had another Cora here at school.

"If you ever need me, come to my classroom, 211. If I'm not there or down here, find Coach Miller. Even though he doesn't know about the Thusians, he is still someone we can trust."

"You think Xavier is here looking for the 4th?" I asked, already knowing that he was.

"Absolutely. Xavier doesn't come out to play unless it's for something big. That's why he tried to kill you in person. I think he knew you were part of The 7. Also, one more thing, do you remember what Xavier looked like?"

"No. One minute I was walking in the park, then I felt a sharp pain and then I awoke lying on my back with my head in Genevieve's lap. Why?"

"I was hoping you saw what Xavier or the others looked like, because when they saw us coming they took off. Neither Genevieve nor I got a good look at them."

"No, I didn't see a thing. You know I would have told you if I saw him."

"I wasn't sure if you would. I didn't want to push it in front of Cora just in case you were keeping it a secret, because I know you do that from time to time to keep the people you love safe."

"I do occasionally keep secrets, but not this time, Riley."
He nodded.

"Riley, is Genevieve with Cora right now? You know how

we are supposed to try to stay in pairs." With all of this talk of Xavier, I was beginning to worry about Cora being home alone.

"No, Cora thinks she doesn't need a babysitter, and Genevieve thinks she shouldn't waste her time with someone who isn't even part of the 4."

I started to object but he put his hand up to stop me.

"Nicholas, Cora is part of the group. It will just take the two of them some time. Even with Genevieve acting nicer, she still is hardheaded."

Riley pushed a pink piece of paper into my hand.

"Here's a note to get you back to class. See you at practice."

COACH'S WIFE
CHAPTER NINE

Coach Miller had me run most of the drills he used to do at practice. He spent more time watching and breaking down technique for the players, more one-on-one stuff. It seemed really weird that I was giving orders to the players that were my grade or older. But the weirdest part was that they actually listened, never questioning me once, always saying, "Yes, Coach. No, Coach." Chad was a big reason for the respect I got. The first time I was running a drill with the linebackers, I told Chad to drive through the ball carrier when he hit him. It was something Coach Miller had yelled at practice a thousand times. Everyone around quieted to listen to his response. Without hesitation, he said, "Yes, Coach Keller," and got back in line. From then on, I had everyone's respect.

After practice I was hanging out in the locker room with Eric. He was going on about one of his you-will-never-believe-what-happened-to-me stories, most of them about Livi or one of her girlfriends. I didn't care much for the gossip, but he was a true showman—funny and entertaining—regardless of what he was talking about.

"So, Nicholas, are you going this Saturday?" he asked, changing the subject.

"To what?"

"Are you kidding? You've been here for a year. Do I really have to tell you again?" Eric rolled his eyes.

There was no way he could be talking about the quarry party. The last one ended with Elle and Oliver almost dying. Plus, I doubt the school would allow one to happen.

"You aren't talking about the quarry party, are you?"

Eric pulled a piece of paper out of his locker, like he was pulling out the golden ticket. "Why yes, yes I am, and here's the map. *OHH! AHH!*" He fanned himself with it.

"Are you crazy? Don't you remember what happened at the last one?" I scolded.

"Easy, Coach Keller," he said with thick sarcasm. "They aren't doing anything stupid this year and they even got permission from the school board, the city council, and the owners of the quarry. The place that they picked has no water and it's a big, open area. Some parents and staff helped to plan it. Relax. The real thing that caused all of the problems was the rite of passage, and that will never happen again. Chad took over the captain duties from Oliver and made sure it would be safe with no crazy challenge. There's going to be a band there, the Rusty Griswolds. They rock. It's going to be epic." Then he echoed *epic* several more times like he was using a microphone.

It did sound a lot better than some crazy stunt between the football captain and another unlucky player. But why hadn't Elle mentioned anything about this? She knew everything that happened at the school, well, most things. Was she still too shaken up about the last one and that's why she didn't say anything? I was still scarred from it and I was not the one trapped in the car.

I called Elle immediately when I got home.

"Did you know about the quarry party this Saturday?" I asked.

"Yes."

There was a long pause on the phone.

"So are we going?" I asked. I had to be careful not to upset her if, indeed, she was trying to avoid talking about it or going to it.

"Not sure, do you want to go?" she asked apprehensively.

That was a loaded question. If I answered yes, she could be upset because I was being insensitive to her feelings, but if I answered no, she may think that I didn't think she was strong enough.

"I just found out about the party from Eric today. How long have you known about it?" I said, avoiding her question.

"I knew something about it before school started, but not much. Chad had asked me earlier in the summer if I minded if he put it together. He circulated the map at lunch today after you and Coach Moore left to talk. I thought Chad would have told you. So do you want to go?" she asked again.

"Elle, to be honest, I'm not sure. It's really up to you."

"You're so sweet, Nicholas. I wanted you to decide because I didn't want to upset you."

"I was doing the same thing," I said.

"I just thought it would bring up bad memories for you, Nicholas. That's why I didn't mention it to you earlier."

"Bad memories for me? I wasn't the one who almost drowned in the sinking car."

"I don't remember much of that night," Elle said. "You are the one who had to watch us go into the water and then pull us to safety, not knowing if I was going to be okay. You sat all of those days in the hospital, waiting for me to wake up. I just woke up and there you were." She actually seemed okay with it.

"If you really don't care, I say we go. Amber and Livi want us to go, and I heard there's going to be a band," she said.

"Okay, let's go, Elle. It'll be fun."

**

Our first football game of the season was here. I was as nervous and excited as if I were playing. The stadium was packed like normal. The roar of the crowd was just as deafening as last year and the lights were just as bright. Off in the distance, thick mountainous clouds were illuminated with heat lightning, as if God was excited for the game too. Henry Theasing, Ester's husband, was leaning up against the fence, talking to Coach Hoff just outside the tunnel. He waved me over to congratulate me on another accomplishment, becoming the youngest coach in Winsor's history. It was difficult to blow him off because he was with Coach Hoff, so I thanked him several times and then went out onto the field to stand next to Riley while the team stretched. I hated talking about myself.

The game went by so fast; we won by 24 points. Our defense was just as strong as last year, but now we had an extremely potent offense that made it look like we were in a position to repeat as state champs. Our offense was led by Eric and surprisingly, Bryce. Eric had thrown him a total of three passes that all resulted in touchdowns. No matter where Eric threw the ball, Bryce was there to make the spectacular catch.

When I got home, Riley, Genevieve, and Cora were sitting in our family room. I wasn't sure how Riley beat me home, because he was still talking with some of the coaches when I was getting ready to leave.

"So what are you guys doing here?" I asked, hoping they were just talking about the game. I wanted to go get cleaned up so I could go over to Elle's. I didn't feel like talking about any Thusian stuff. I stood between the hall and the family room, trying to make whatever it was faster by not sitting.

"Nicholas, you made plans without letting us know," Cora said.

"What are you talking about? You saw me at the football game, and I just made plans to go to Elle's after the game. How was I supposed to tell you?"

Riley spoke, "No, we mean going to the rock quarry for that party."

It hadn't even dawned on me to tell them about it. "Sorry, I totally forgot."

"It's okay this time, but we have a problem now. One of us has to go with you," Riley said, reminding me.

"Anyone can come. I will give you the location and you can all hang out around the party, but don't be seen."

"That's the problem," Cora said. "Someone has to actually be with you. If someone tries something at the party, we may not get there in time. From the outside it will be tough to get through all of those people. Xavier made one attempt to kill at the last quarry party. We can't give him another chance. Remember, he needs others to be around so you will sacrifice yourself for one of them. A party like this gives him plenty of opportunities to kill you off."

"Nicholas, you have to be focused on finding the 4th. Being blinded by love isn't helping anything," Genevieve said.

I ignored her. "Well then, who should I take? I can't take my aunt or a teacher—" I paused, realizing who was left.

"You will take Genevieve," Riley said.

"You want me to take the coach's wife to a high school party? That is going to be awkward."

"Listen, Nicholas," Cora said. "I know it might be strange, but I agree with Riley on this. Genevieve would blend in the most. This is for your safety."

"Don't worry. I'll give you plenty of space if you want to get personal with Elle."

"Okay, that's enough, Genevieve," Riley said in a threatening tone. He turned back to me. "Nicholas, there is only one other solution: don't go to the party."

"That won't work. They are looking to kill other Thusians too, remember? Not just us. I'm sure there will be dozens of Thusians there, and also maybe the 4th. I have to go," I said, fishing the pack of Tic Tacs out of my pocket. "Fine. Genevieve can go, but only if she parks the attitude at the house."

"She will," Riley assured me. I avoided looking at her and went upstairs.

Later that evening at Elle's, I had to break the bad news that Genevieve was coming to the quarry party with us. Cora decided I should tell people that she and Riley were going out of town for some college reunion stuff, and we felt bad leaving Genevieve at home alone in a new city.

It didn't seem to bother Elle at all. She simply said, "That's great. She will have so much fun with us." I was glad she thought it was great, because I was dreading it.

RITE OF PASSAGE

CHAPTER TEN

I drove over to pick up Genevieve before I went to get Elle. I wanted to lay down some ground rules before I took her anywhere. Following me to Elle's when I didn't know she was there was one thing, but being around us in person was another. She came walking out in another form-fitting outfit. She was wearing a ribbed white tank top with another black one underneath and a pair of ripped jean shorts. She had a long silver rope necklace that had a loose knot in it and matching silver bracelets. Her hair was pulled back in a black baseball cap with a large "NYPD" on it. She was not dressed to blend in. Instead, the complete opposite: to stand out. Every guy at the party would be staring at us—well, just her.

She got into the truck.

"What are you wearing?"

"What do you mean? I look nice," she said, running her hands down her sides onto her jean shorts like she was pressing out imaginary wrinkles.

"Nice, are you kidding? Everyone is going to be staring at you."

"Does everyone include you?" she asked with a mischievous grin.

"Very funny, Genevieve. You aren't going to make this easy, are you?"

"I will be on my best behavior, I promise, cross my heart. I bet no one will even notice little old me."

I was too flustered to lay down any ground rules. I just wanted to hurry up and get this night over with. I rolled down my window to get some fresh air. This was going to be a long night.

When we got to Elle's, I told Genevieve to get in the back so Elle could sit up front. I rang the doorbell and Elle answered. I don't even remember walking to the truck with her. I was too concerned about what she would think when she saw how Genevieve was dressed. But when I opened the truck door expecting to find an empty passenger seat, Genevieve was still in the front putting on bright red lipstick in the truck's visor mirror.

"Give me one sec." She finished by blowing a kiss to the mirror and then she turned and said to Elle, "Don't you look cute? Let me climb in the back so you can sit next to Nicholas."

"Don't be ridiculous, Mrs. Moore, you can sit in the front." I was burning holes into Genevieve with my eyes, but it didn't seem to bother her. She got out and waited for Elle to get into the back. I slammed the door out of frustration. She knew that Elle was too polite to make her get in the back seat. I took a deep breath and got back in.

"Elle, you've lived in Winsor for a long time, right?"

"Yes," Elle said cheerfully.

"So what's this quarry party all about?"

Elle explained the history of the quarry party and some other school traditions. I wasn't really listening to them. I was concentrating on finding the party. We were getting close to the quarry entrance because we had just passed Maple Dale, one of the Winsor elementary schools, when Genevieve said something that snapped me back into focus.

"Did you hear the Oliver Rails verdict was handed down from the judge today?"

Elle didn't say anything. She had been leaning forward when she was talking, but now she was back against her seat, disappearing into the darkness.

"Genevieve, Elle and I don't care about any of that." I gave her a dirty look.

"Oh, I'm so sorry. It must be difficult for you two, especially after all he put you through." What was she doing? She was supposed to be on her best behavior.

"No, it's okay, Mrs. Moore. I'm fine," Elle said from the back, still lost in the shadows.

"Okay then, Oliver got 120 hours of community service and is on house arrest for three months. You know, when they make you wear that ankle tracker thingy. D.A. Caldwell's kidnapping charge was thrown out and he got some lesser charge. Not sure what it was, though."

We sat in silence the rest of the way there. I was now navigating the quarry roads from the map. Luckily, I caught up with two cars and followed them. With Genevieve talking about Oliver, I was concerned about Elle's well-being and not how to get to some party.

When we pulled into the area where the party was, it looked completely level, like a bulldozer had smoothed it out just for this. There were several large gravel and sand mounds around the outside, but that was it. Right in the middle was a huge stage. The stage had everything: lights, large speakers and it even had two jumbo video screens that flanked the stage high up over the speakers. I was shocked. I guess I shouldn't have been stunned. Winsor did everything bigger and better than anyone else. Why should this be any different?

I parked and we walked over to the stage. Elle took my hand as soon as she got out. Her hands were cold and clammy. She was clearly shaken up about what Genevieve had said in the truck. It had brought to the surface some feelings and memories that we had tried to get past.

"Do you want to go?" I asked quietly.

"No, I'll be fine." She laid her head on my shoulder. Genevieve followed behind us. I didn't look back. I was glad I didn't have to see her face, because I would probably have said something that I shouldn't have. Off to the side of the main crowd of people were Eric, Livi, Chad, and Amber.

"Hey, guys," Amber said. She gave each of us a hug. When she saw Genevieve she paused, confused. Her mouth fell open, looking her up and down.

"This is Genevieve, I mean, Mrs. Moore, you know, Coach Moore's wife. Riley and Cora went out of town for some college alumni thing, so I invited her to come along," I said. The group just stared at her.

"It's nice to meet you," Livi said, breaking the awkward silence. "I'm Livi." Then she introduced everyone else in the group.

"Does anyone else want to go look around?" Amber asked. Like they had just received some girl code, they all headed off, including Genevieve.

When the girls were far enough away, Eric started in on me. "You have to be kidding me. She is ridiculously hot. You dog." He hit me on the arm.

"What do you mean?"

Chad, normally the silent one, spoke up. "What he means is that you have two of the hottest girls we've ever seen with you, besides *our* girlfriends, of course," he added, and Eric nodded half-heartedly.

"She's a friend of the family."

"Dude, it wouldn't matter if she were your sister. She's still hot," Eric said.

"That's sick," I responded.

"You know what I mean. You are what legends are made of." He slapped me on the back.

When the girls got back, the band had already started playing. Genevieve had disappeared, which was a relief. The group of us sat in the back of the large crowd on a blanket that Livi had brought. I had never heard of the band, but it seemed that a majority of the crowd had. Elle was pretending that everything was fine.

"Are you okay?" I whispered.

She shrugged her shoulders. "I guess." Her fake smile faded. "The whole trial thing just makes me upset. I thought I was over it, but Mrs. Moore talking about Oliver being sentenced brought back some memories. Also, I kind of feel bad for Oliver." What? She had to be kidding. With everything he put her through? He was the reason she was on that dock in the first place.

"You shouldn't feel bad for him. He brought it on himself."

She looked away, apparently upset with what I said. How couldn't I be upset with Oliver? He put my angel, the love of my life, in danger. Then Xavier's voice from that night flooded my thoughts. *Oliver and Elle are on their way to the rock quarry, and there is no way you will be able to get to them in time before they die.*

If Oliver hadn't taken Elle, she would have died for sure, because Riley and Genevieve wouldn't have been watching over her. She would have been left defenseless against Xavier and the Seekers at her house. I guess I should have been thanking Oliver, not hating him.

"Elle, you're right to feel bad for Oliver. I do too. He didn't know the dock would collapse."

She turned back to me. "Thank you, Nicholas, for understanding. I love you."

Our moment didn't last long. Genevieve was back.

"Nicholas, may I speak with you for just a moment?" she asked, looking very serious. I looked at Elle, hoping she would be okay with it.

"Go ahead, I'll be here." She smiled and kissed me on the cheek. The smile and kiss made me feel like I could go.

"Nicholas," Genevieve grabbed my arm and pulled me away, "could you hurry? I don't want to keep you too long. It might raise suspicion."

Genevieve guided me away. I looked back and the only one who was still staring at me from the group was Eric. He was holding his thumb up in the air and mouthing the words, "That-a-boy, you stud."

"Genevieve, what do you want? Did you find something, or are you just trying to cause more problems for me?"

"Listen, I know you would rather spend time playing kissy face with your little girlfriend, but we have a job to do."

"So did you find something, or not?"

"Yes, Xavier and his Seekers are here or were here." Genevieve pointed to the two large screens up over the stage, which were broadcasting a close-up of the lead singer to the crowd. "The brackets have been loosened. You can see them swaying back and forth."

I squinted up at them, but I couldn't tell anything was wrong.

"Are you sure?"

"Nicholas, use your talent to slow things down to take a closer look. Think about all of those kids getting crushed, or worse, your friends or Elle getting killed by the screens. That will trigger your talents."

My heart started to pound when she said that; the fire inside me started to burn. I concentrated on the screen closest to where we were standing. Everything around me slowed down and the bottom corner of the screen became magnified. I could see the screen bouncing to the beat of the music slowly, not attached to the support, each time distancing itself a little more from the back.

"Do you see how it keeps moving away? If the concert continues, it will fall in the next fifteen minutes or so, killing and hurting a lot of people."

"Let's just unplug the electric. That should stop the vibrations from the speaker," I said.

"I thought of that, too, but if we cut the electric, the crowd closest to the stage will push up against it to see what happened, causing the screens to fall for sure, killing even more." Genevieve's voice was filled with panic. The stress was showing on her face. I didn't feel panicked at all. Then an idea came to me. I knew what we had to do.

"I'll create some sort of distraction behind them, to draw them away from the stage. Then you can cut the power, Genevieve."

"We can't divide up, just in case that's what Xavier wants us to do."

"We have to protect them, right? Just be careful. You will know when it's time to cut it. Then I will meet you at the truck. Stay with the crowd to hide. The Seekers will be distracted by me and won't give you a thought."

She didn't question me further and disappeared into the crowd. Now what was I going to do? I had to come up with something fast that would get everyone away from the stage.

I saw the band's large box truck. I ran over to it, still not sure what I was looking for. I saw several metal lids with metal handles on the side; they looked like big sleds. Then I had an idea. I grabbed two of them from the back and ran over to where I had been sitting.

Amber was the first one to see me.

"What are those for, Nicholas?"

Everyone looked at me, including Bryce who had joined the group now.

"I'm here to challenge Chad to the rite of passage."

Elle jumped up and said, "No you're not. Are you out of your mind?"

I ignored her and looked right at Chad.

"Oliver chose me to challenge at the last quarry party, so that makes me responsible to challenge the next captain, and that's you. So I challenge you to sand boarding. I saw it online being done in Nicaragua on some active volcano. The one who makes it to the bottom of that hill still standing or in one piece wins." I was pointing to the large pile of sand and gravel behind them.

All three of the girls were telling us to stop, to not be stupid. I wished they knew that I was trying to save people's lives.

"So, Chad, what do you think?" I asked. Amber was trying to pull him away, pleading with him not to listen.

Chad smiled. "Keller, you're on."

Eric was pumping his fist in the air like he just won something. Chad grabbed one of the metal tops and followed me to the pile. As we got closer, it got taller, a lot taller. It had to be over five stories high and 100 yards long. From where we were sitting it didn't look so big. What was I thinking? I didn't turn back to see if Elle was following me. I couldn't bear to see her face right now. We started up the hill. The pile had become solid from sitting over the years. Only a thin sheet of loose sand and gravel covered it. I heard the buzz behind us getting louder and louder as we climbed higher. Eric was in his element, promoting the challenge. He must have run around to everyone telling them about the challenge, which is what I was counting on. By the time we got to the top, the entire party was around the pile, cheering loudly. There were just a couple of people next to the stage now. Then the stage went dark. Genevieve had done it. We had done it! But now I had to go through with this crazy, stupid stunt.

"Keller, I knew you were brave, but this is insane."

I smiled. Just last year, I was upset that Oliver was doing something so dangerous and here I was about to do something as dangerous, if not more so.

"So what are the rules to your rite of passage?"

"The first person who makes it to the bottom on two feet either standing or crouching wins."

I looked down the large sloping hill. I stepped into the metal box top. Chad did the same thing. We were so high up that I couldn't make out anyone's face. But it didn't matter; I knew Elle was down there, ready to kill me. I might save her the trouble by killing myself right now.

"Ready, set, go!" I yelled.

The fire inside me filled my body. My muscles pulled and

strained. I could feel the blood pumping through them. We were only ten feet into our descent when everything slowed down. The rough ride now felt like I was on a smooth sheet of ice. Chad, on the other hand, was jerking back and forth violently, trying to maintain his balance. He was a blur. We were only about a third of the way down when he slowly started to lean my way. His blurred body indicated how he was trying not to fall, but it was no use—he was about to. I hit his shoulder like I was falling toward him. It did the trick. He slowly centered himself on the metal lid and grabbed both sides of it, crouching down and stabilizing himself. I was lucky that he fell toward me. If he started to fall away from me or forward, I might have had to do something drastic that would draw a lot of attention. But I would have had to chance it since I put Chad into this dangerous situation.

The farther he went down the hill, his motion became more erratic. He became blurrier because of all of the back and forth movement. Still in slow motion, he was moving fast enough to create large blurs of movement around him. I could barely make out the shape of his body. He was getting tired from the jarring, but we were close. He just had to make it to the end.

We only had about 20 yards left before it would slope gradually to the end. Just then I saw Chad start to move quickly forward. He was getting ready to wipe out hard, face first. In my mind, I could see all the different possibilities of what was about to happen, and there was only one scenario where Chad wouldn't get hurt.

I leaned hard on my box and swerved in right behind him. I kicked my lid toward him. It hit his and sent his sled back underneath his feet, making him regain his balance. I hit the surface of the hill hard. The initial impact didn't hurt at all, but then time went back to normal. The other hits after the first hurt. Chad stood up to the roar of the crowd. I slowly stood up at the bottom of the hill. I could feel the stings and burns on my back from hitting the gravel pile. I held my hand up to show everyone I was okay. The crowd cheered.

AFTERMATH
CHAPTER ELEVEN

Eric was the first one to run up to me. "Nicholas, you are the greatest; that was incredible. You make me want to date you myself. I love you, man." He gave me a big kiss on the cheek. He grabbed my hand and held it up in the air. He yelled to the crowd, "He did this for you, even with a bad vertebra. He could've died." Everyone cheered, loving it.

I was mobbed by the football team. Chad came up to me. "Nicholas, I don't know why, but somehow I think I owe you a big thanks."

Amber grabbed him and pulled him away from the crowd. Elle was nowhere to be found. Livi came up to Eric and me.

"Bryce is taking Elle and me home. When you boys grow up, you know where to find us." Then Livi disappeared into the crowd.

I rushed to the truck after escaping everyone, so I could go to Elle's immediately to apologize. As I got closer, I didn't see Genevieve waiting for me. I scanned the lot frantically looking for her. What if Xavier got her? To my relief, she was sitting on the back bumper.

I got into the truck slowly, still aching from the rough landing. Genevieve hopped in.

"You sure know how to make a distraction," she said, in her normal sarcastic tone.

"You should talk. The way you dress is a distraction." I started the truck and pulled out.

"Does it distract you?"

I was a little taken aback by the question, but not surprised. "What I am distracted by is that Elle isn't with me now."

"Nicholas, you had to do something. It's not your fault she's acting like a typical high schooler."

"No, she should be mad. I was doing the very thing I refused to take part in last year because of the danger, and now I go and do something even more dangerous. She cares for me and doesn't want me to get hurt. She could've died during one of these damn rite-of-passage stunts. And what gives you the right to bring up Oliver to her? You had to have known it would make her upset. You can't always do what you want." I was seething with anger.

"Are you done lecturing me?" Genevieve asked. "Because actually, I do have the right. I was testing her to see if she had characteristics of the 4th Thusian."

"What, by torturing her?"

"No, by testing her mental and emotional states. The 4th would be upset, but also would be able to put that behind them. So far, I'm not convinced she could be the one. She looked pretty shaken when I talked about Oliver."

I gripped the steering wheel tightly.

"Nicholas, I think you were amazing tonight. You saved all of those people from dying, and from what I could see, you saved Chad at least twice from getting hurt. You sacrificed your body to do so, and I bet you have the scrapes and bruises to prove it. That makes you a hero."

The word *hero* sent white hot anger pulsing through my body. "I'm no hero. Don't call me that ever again, do you understand?" I yelled.

The rest of the way home I pretended she wasn't in the truck with me. It was the only way I wouldn't kick her out and have her walk home. When I got Genevieve back to her house, she jumped out of the truck and went inside without another word.

Cora was already home when I pulled into the driveway. I told her what happened in as much detail as I could. She listened closely, making sure not to miss anything I said.

"Have you told Riley? He needs to know all of this, because we didn't see anything on the outside of the party."

"Genevieve can tell him."

"No, that's not good enough, Nicholas. You should really go over there and talk with him."

"The only thing I'm going to do is go over to Elle's."

Cora started to question me again so I just walked out the front door, slamming it behind me. Why was Cora all of a sudden so interested in talking to Riley about things? It didn't matter now. My main concern was Elle. How could I have done this to her? I had to try to make her understand why I did the rite of passage. I really had no idea how I was going to do that because I had thought it was a dumb idea the first time I heard about it.

I was happy to see her bedroom window was open. It gave me hope. I slid down through it, but her room was completely dark. I could see her silhouette standing in front of me. I started to talk but she grabbed my hand and led me to her door. She opened it slowly and I saw both of her parents on the couch watching TV. She whispered, "You need to go. This isn't the best time, Nicholas."

I couldn't tell if she was upset or not from her whisper.

"No, I have to explain," I pleaded quietly.

"I don't want to hear it right now."

"I don't care if your parents catch me. I have to tell you why I did what I did," I said, hoping she would give me a chance.

In my mind there was still no good reason for me to have done what I did. I led her to her large round chair and sat her down. My eyes had somewhat adjusted to the darkness. Elle looked upset. Maybe the light being off was a way to keep me from seeing how truly upset and angry she was. I sat her down and knelt in front of her.

"Did Genevieve make you do this?" she asked bitterly. Elle didn't call her Mrs. Moore as usual. Right then, I realized that Genevieve was part of the reason she was mad.

"No, I didn't do it because of Mrs. Moore." I decided not to call her Genevieve. Hopefully that would help ease her mind. "When I was in the coach's office before the game, Coach Miller was talking to Riley about his first quarry party as captain of the football team. Coach Miller told him that his rite of passage challenge was to bring up an old car tire from the bottom of a quarry lake that was about five feet deep and to see who could get it to the shore first. He talked about how cold and dark the lake was and how he beat Red Nelson easily. And he did this when he was only a sophomore.

"But after he finished, he concluded with, 'It's a shame that some traditions have to die.' I felt like I was responsible for ending the rite of passage—me, not Oliver. As stupid as it sounds, I didn't want to disappoint Coach Miller. He was a sophomore, too, just like I was last year. I didn't plan to do it, but when Riley's wife asked about our traditions, it reminded me that I was partially to blame for ending this one. So that's the reason why I did it. I'm so sorry, Elle. I would never intentionally try to hurt you."

I couldn't look at her. I felt disgusted with how easily the lies came out of my mouth. Elle didn't say anything at first, which was good. I didn't think I could look into her eyes yet for fear she would discover the truth. She took a deep breath and sighed. I braced for the worst.

"I don't like you being alone with Genevieve." What? Elle was more upset about her than the actual rite of passage.

"She is like an aunt to me, or a much older sister; plus, she's married to Riley. Elle, I love you, no one else." I reached out and grabbed her hand.

Elle smiled. She liked that answer.

"Does that mean you forgive me for acting like an idiot?"

"Yes, of course."

She gave me a big hug. Her hands made their way up my back to my head. Even though her hands brushed over my scrapes and bruises, the movement sent chills through my body.

"Elle, I hope I don't have any reason to be upset with Bryce, do I?" I said, realizing that I was jealous, too. This type of jealousy was something that I had never really felt before. I used to be jealous of other people living normal lives while I was forced to hide. I was even jealous of Oliver last year, because he was expected to stand out and I was told to blend in. I didn't like how this new jealousy made me feel.

"No, actually, you have him to thank. He defended you the whole ride home. He wouldn't let Livi or I say anything bad about you. He said you are a good person and there had to be a good reason for what you had done. And as it turns out, he was right. Livi wasn't comforted at all. She knew he was right about you, but Eric, well, Eric is Eric. There's not much he could say to defend him after his over-the-top behavior."

She was right about Eric, but that's what makes him so great. If I didn't have him as a friend, we might not have been able to get the crowd away from the stage. He was one of the main reasons why we succeeded in saving all of those people, and no one will ever know.

I heard the TV in the family room turn off. I stole a kiss and was up and out of the window right when the door opened. Walking back to the truck, I still felt the lingering effects of jealousy.

Riley was sitting alone in our family room when I came

in. He stood quickly like he had been waiting for me to get home.

"Riley, is everything okay?"

"Yes, everything is fine. Well, kind of. You have to take what I am about to say as someone who cares about you and your well-being, and realize that I'm not trying to be overbearing. But you have to make sure that you talk with all three of us after things like the attack tonight. We needed time to think of what our next step should be, if any. Someone could have followed you to Elle's house, expecting you to do that, and we wouldn't have been able to protect you. We have to work as a team now for everyone's safety. The way you and Genevieve worked together tonight was a perfect example of how it's done."

He was right. "I understand, Riley."

He nodded and walked by me out the door.

FIELD TRIP
CHAPTER TWELVE

Through the end of August and most of September, there wasn't much talk about anything Thusian-related. Not because we didn't want to, but just because there weren't any new leads. Riley and Cora spent a lot of time going back and forth from the site of the last quarry party, looking for any evidence. Each time they found nothing. They even went back to the broken dock to see if there were any clues from last year's party. Despite not finding anything, Riley was still determined to keep looking, and that meant Cora would be too. It seemed to me that he was just trying to spend more time alone with her, and it was working.

As determined as Riley and Cora were, Genevieve was not. She had no interest in going to look for evidence. She said, "I don't need evidence to know that they did it, so I don't see the point of looking." I hated the fact that I agreed with her on this because it did seem like a big waste of time.

Everything with my group of friends had returned to normal. Livi eventually forgave Eric, but now he was by her side even more, which I didn't think was humanly possible.

Once Eric took over as Varsity quarterback, things should have changed for him. The quarterback position held a certain status at our school, but he was in no position to take advantage of it. Livi had him on a short leash, and by the looks of it, he was fine with it, just happy to still be with her.

We did have a new addition to our group, Bryce. He had joined our group of friends permanently—our six was now seven. Even though he didn't have a girlfriend, he fit in pretty well. Part of me kind of felt sorry for him because he was a new student, and I could relate with how difficult it was to move a lot. I found myself going out of my way to include him in things, but deep down inside I still felt some jealousy toward him. Every time he talked to her, I would listen closely to see what they talked about. It was driving me so crazy that I had to do something about it, but what? Maybe I could try to make Elle jealous also.

"Amber, do you know McKenna? She's in our grade," I asked during lunch.

"Yeah, I have English with her," Amber said.

"Did you see her hair this morning? I think she curled it. She looks pretty that way, don't you think?"

Why did I just say that? The whole lunch table stared at me. Eric's mouth was half open with his sandwich hanging out.

Elle had stopped talking to Bryce and said, "Nicholas, it did look nice. Come to think of it, she always looks pretty."

Her eyes met mine. I looked away, feeling embarrassed and ashamed. My attempt to make her jealous backfired miserably. Now I felt bad for what I had said, and on top of it

I was still jealous of her talking to Bryce. What was I doing? I didn't know how to play these games. This relationship stuff was becoming complicated. Why couldn't we be sitting under the stairs in our own little world right now, sheltered from everything but my love for her?

"The football team sure is on a roll," Livi said, breaking the deafening silence.

"They are on a serious roll thanks to Chad, Eric and Bryce. This team could easily beat some college teams," I said, trying to force the ugly feeling of jealousy aside by praising Bryce too.

"We can't forget their coaches," Elle said, leaning up against me. My stomach did somersaults. I guess she didn't care about my stupid comment, which was a relief.

The football team was unstoppable. They weren't winning by small margins like last year. Our offense now would easily put up 45 points on any team that we faced, and our defense was holding teams to seven points or less. The Winsor Cougars were ranked number one in the entire country. Chad, Eric and Bryce were all likely to be First Team State and National. Several Division One schools were looking at both Bryce and Chad, and even Eric got some looks from scouts.

"So, are you guys going on the field trip to the Saint Louis Art Museum?" Livi asked our lunch table. "Eric and I are."

"Chad and I didn't get lucky enough to go this year," Amber said.

Livi looked upset but perked up when I said, "Elle and I are going, and Bryce too, right?"

"Yes," Bryce said, taken off-guard. He had been staring at a table full of girls who were eyeing him as usual.

"Well, great then. Eric and I will save you seats on the bus tomorrow morning."

Eric nodded.

After the night of the quarry party, Livi always spoke for Eric. I guess that was part of his punishment, and knowing him, that was far worse than anything else that could have been done to the "greatest show on earth."

The next morning, Eric and Livi were taking up three seats in the back of the bus. Bryce got on a minute after Elle and me with only half of his shirt tucked in. He was also sporting black sunglasses. It was sunny out, but sunglasses on the bus were really too much. The five of us all sat together. The two girls sat with each other, already chatting away. Eric sat behind them, listening to Elle and Livi. Bryce and I sat across from Eric. Bryce was on the inside, looking out the window. I nudged him, making him look over at Eric.

"Man, he is whipped."

Bryce laughed. "Yeah, I'm kind of jealous."

"Of Eric and Livi?" I asked, puzzled.

"No, it's not that I like Livi, but I am envious of their relationship, and yours too." Bryce looked down into his lap.

"Bryce, my friend, I'll see what I can do about that. You are a big time football star. Finding a special someone shouldn't be too difficult." I was beginning to sound like Eric.

He smiled.

Now that I knew he didn't want to be with Elle, that he just wanted a girlfriend, I felt better and my jealousy disappeared. When I glanced out the window, I caught a glimpse of a dark circle that protruded out from behind Bryce's sunglasses.

"Hey, I don't remember you getting that at the game Friday," I said.

He slowly removed his glasses, exposing an ugly black eye.

I stared at him, not sure how he could have gotten it during the game; I'm sure I would have noticed. "What happened? That thing looks nasty."

Bryce sank down in his seat and whispered so only I could hear, "I really don't want to talk about it. It was just an accident," he said, regaining his composure and putting his glasses back on.

"Are you sure you're okay?" I whispered, so no one else could hear.

Bryce nodded his head yes.

I guess whenever he wanted to talk about it he would, but I would definitely be keeping an eye on him to make sure there weren't any other unexplained injuries.

The bus dropped us off at Memorial Presbyterian Church on Skinker Boulevard, because they weren't letting traffic into the park where the art museum was located. The Presbyterian Church was magnificent. Its tall stone walls and slender windows seemed to reach up into the clouds that filled the deep blue sky. It was exactly how I imagined the outside of the Thusian Vault would look.

After walking down the street, we were finally at the park entrance. The five of us and a couple of others had drifted back behind the rest of the group. We were walking down the middle of the road toward the art museum. I could see it off in the distance.

Riley's class was also attending the field trip. I'm sure if his classes weren't originally going, he would have found a way to come, or had Cora or Genevieve come as a chaperone.

Melissa and Erin had joined our group and were right next to Bryce, of course. It was funny to see them around him. It reminded me of last year and how they wouldn't leave me alone, but he didn't seem to mind all the attention he was getting. Finding him a date would be a piece of cake. Elle and I were in the center of the two groups—Bryce, Erin, and Melissa on our left and Eric and Livi on the right. Squealing tires from behind us startled me, instantly slowing everything around me. The fire in me exploded. I turned to see a St. Louis public transit bus barreling down the middle of the street toward us with a long blurred streak off the back of it. It was moving fast. I reached out and pushed Livi and Eric toward the curb. I went to grab Elle, but she already had my shirt in her hand pulling me out of the way. I had to get to Bryce, but he was already moving to the other side of the road with Erin and Melissa both under his arms. Time resumed to full speed when we were all out of the way, and the bus roared past, not hitting anyone.

Riley was standing next to me. "Is everyone okay?" he asked, looking directly at me. I looked around at the others. Eric and Livi looked fine, but Melissa and Erin looked shaken up. Both Bryce and Elle looked like nothing life-threatening had just happened.

"Make sure you kids stay out of the road this time. I don't want any of you missing the excitement of the art museum," Riley said sarcastically. We all caught up with the rest of the group.

Riley hung back with me. When Elle was just far enough away, he said, "I think that bus was trying to hit you."

"I think so too. Did you see what happened?"

"No, I missed it," Riley said.

"Bryce picked up Erin and Melissa and got them out of the way, and Elle grabbed me to pull me out of the way. They didn't move as fast as me, but they did move quickly."

"Are you sure?" he asked.

"I'm sure. We have two candidates."

"Thank goodness. I was getting worried," Riley sighed.

Elle and I walked through the museum alone. She led me to exhibit after exhibit. I was consumed with which one of them could be the 4th. I was definitely drawn to Elle, but was I drawn to Bryce, too? I did go out of my way to include him in our group and now I was trying to get him a date. I guess he could be the one.

"Hello, Nicholas, are you in there?"

I was staring at a brightly colored painting of four little girls playing. "Sorry, I'm just preoccupied," I said to Elle.

"With?"

"The whole bus trying to hit us thing. It seems like that sort of thing follows me around."

She took my hand. I had to test her to see if she was the one or not, but I couldn't think of how to do it. I couldn't just ask her, "So do you slow down time or do you have super speed or strength?" I would have to be subtle because she could see right through me. Her blue eyes had no problem getting whatever they wanted from me. I would have to bury my feelings for her somehow so they wouldn't cloud my judgment.

"Nicholas, don't be upset. You aren't to blame for any of that stuff," she said.

"I know, but I've been having these horrible nightmares and the bus coming after us reminded me of them."

"I'm so sorry." She leaned closer to me, so no one could hear what we were saying. "Tell me about it."

"I feel like I'm being smothered, like this horrible dark weight is trying to crush me. And then right when I can't take it anymore, I wake up."

"Nicholas, that's awful. You shouldn't worry about those silly dreams." She leaned in closer to comfort me. Her soft hair brushed my face. My mind went blank.

"If you want, I could come over and be with you, instead of you coming to my house every night. I'm sure Cora wouldn't mind."

She was right, Cora wouldn't mind. Her offer made my heart pound. She was distracting me from my task. I had to ignore her offer, as difficult as it was, and continue with my test.

"So have you had any of those types of dreams?" I was surprised that I could get the question out.

"Bad ones? Of course, you're not alone," she responded, rubbing my hand for reassurance.

"So what are your nightmares like, Elle?" I asked, still focusing hard.

"I don't really remember. At a young age I began to block them out and now I only remember the good ones. So if I wake up a little tired and with no memory of my dreams, I assume I had a bad dream that night."

That was not helpful at all. She could be having the same sort of dreams and she wouldn't even know it. Great, now I was back to square one.

**

That night, Cora and I went to Riley and Genevieve's house for dinner, which was becoming normal. The four of us were seated around their table. Cora, Riley and I were discussing what took place with the bus. Genevieve was just listening. She and I hadn't spoken to each other since the quarry party when I yelled at her.

"Cora, what do you think?" Riley asked.

"Well, I'm not really sure. I personally love Elle, but Bryce seems pretty nice from what Nicholas has told me."

"I don't care for either of them," Genevieve said, breaking her silence. "I thought we were supposed to be drawn to them as the three of us were drawn together, but I don't feel anything for either of them. I have stronger feelings toward Cora, and that's not saying much." She grinned and crossed her arms.

"Genevieve, you know it's a gradual thing. You said the same thing when we started looking for Nicholas," Riley said.

"Nicholas, what do you think?" Riley asked, turning his attention to me.

"I am drawn to Elle for obvious reasons," I said. Genevieve coughed. I pretended like she wasn't there. I didn't feel like getting drawn into another childish argument with her. "And Bryce has become a pretty good friend, so I'm not sure. I did try to see if Elle had the bad dreams that we get when we begin to get our talents, but she has learned to block them out, so I didn't get much further. Is there a possibility that neither one of them is the 4th?" I asked.

"Of course, but it seems most likely that one of them is. On a different note, Cora, if it's okay with you, I would like for you and Nicholas to stay here all day on Saturday. With it being October 10th, the six-year anniversary of the earthquake, I don't want to take any chances. Genevieve and I were there last year at the graveyard," Riley said.

"Wait a minute. You were watching me at my parents' graves?" I asked, feeling violated. They had intruded on another private moment.

"Yes, we were in the cemetery, but we weren't that close to you. We pretended to be cemetery workers putting flags on the graves. One minute you were there and the next you were getting into the truck, leaving in a rush."

Before I had a chance to say anything more about it, Cora took over the conversation, protecting me from reliving those feelings again.

"We can't come over on Saturday; we're having company

that day. Chase has been trying to come visit us for some time now, but I have been putting him off. He finally said he was coming this weekend whether we wanted him to or not, so I agreed to it."

Riley's mood changed dramatically. He looked upset, on the verge of anger. Lines appeared on his forehead and his fists balled up on the table. This surprised me, because he never showed much emotion.

"Fine," he said. "We will be here at the house if you need us, and please remember to be careful and don't trust anyone." He looked right at Cora.

RILEY'S STORY
CHAPTER THIRTEEN

Early Friday morning before school, I was sitting in the small reading area inside the family room bay window, which Cora often used. Chase pulled into our driveway, shooting gravel in every direction and nearly killing two robins that were looking for worms close by. He was dressed in a black pinstriped suit, rolling a small metallic black suitcase behind him like he was going on some business retreat. Parked in our driveway was a small, yellow, foreign sports car made by someone whose name I probably couldn't pronounce. His car most likely cost more than our house.

"Nicholas! How is my favorite patient?" he asked as I opened the front door for him.

"Good. Where's the helicopter?" I was joking, of course, but he answered all the same.

"In the shop getting tuned up, so this car will have to do for the weekend. It moves just as fast, though."

He let go of his suitcase and moved quickly past me, nearly knocking me over. He grabbed Cora, who had come into the hall from the kitchen. He gave her a great big bear hug, spinning her around, like a scene from some cheesy romance movie.

"And how's my vivacious main squeeze?"

Cora wiggled free. "You wish, Chase. It's good to see you," she said with a big smile. She leaned in on tiptoes and gave him a peck on the cheek.

"Back at ya, baby doll. So what's on the agenda for today? It has been way too long. We have some serious catchin' up to do."

"Well, it's Friday and I'm heading to school," I responded. "Could you move your car? I don't want to be late."

"Are you kidding? I don't get to see you guys that often. Skip school and hang with me and your aunt today, unless Cora wants me all to her lonesome."

As if on cue, a voice came from outside our house. "Well, goodness gracious, this must be the ever-so-talented, incredible and terribly attractive Dr. Chase Letterby." Genevieve was walking up the stairs to the porch. She walked right into our house through the open door like she owned the place, and positioned herself between Chase and Cora. She extended her hand to have him kiss it like he was King Arthur and she was Lady Guinevere. He took it and kissed it, lingering for a moment as he stared up at her.

"I don't think I've had the pleasure of making your acquaintance," he said, dropping his voice even deeper than it already was.

"I'm the Kellers' new neighbor. Well, my husband and I."

Chase didn't look too bothered by the mention of a husband. I am sure that to him, it was just a technicality.

"Cora and I have become such good friends and she has talked about you on many occasions. But she never mentioned how big and strong you are."

"And she never mentioned she had such a breathtaking neighbor, either," Chase said.

I didn't know if I could take much more of this. The flirting was too much. Genevieve was up to something, but I didn't care to find out what. Cora stepped up next to Genevieve, forcing Chase to drop her hand and break their gaze.

"This is my friend Gen-Genna Moore. Her husband is Coach Moore, the Winsor football team's assistant coach."

Cora had changed Genevieve's name, hoping to throw Chase off of the fact they were really Genevieve and Riley, the two I had mentioned at the hospital last year after Xavier's attack. I think he was too wrapped up in her to put those two things together, but it was still good thinking on Cora's part. I marveled at how such a brilliant doctor could be tricked so easily.

"My husband and I were hoping that the three of you could come and spend the day with us on Saturday. We could go to Oktoberfest and then I could make a dinner you will never forget." Genevieve was looking right into Chase's eyes, like she was putting a spell on him. "I have the best recipe for chicken cordon bleu." He didn't blink. She had him.

Cora had told both of them that Chase was coming over. I thought they were going to stay at their house. Did Genevieve ever listen?

"No, I don't think we can. I haven't seen Chase for a while

127

and we have to catch up," Cora said, trying to snap him out of it.

"Nonsense, Cora. Let's go. It will be fun," Chase spoke. Again, Genevieve got her way, annoying both me and Cora. Chase was in her trance, helpless to fight against Genevieve's control.

"Okay, we'll go," Cora said, clearly frustrated because she knew it was no use fighting Genevieve.

During school, I mentioned to Elle about going with me to Winsor's Oktoberfest on Saturday at old Lunken Airport. I could tell she wanted to come, but didn't want to go with the group I had mentioned would be going. I am sure it mostly had to do with Genevieve. She knew it was the anniversary of the earthquake and my parents' deaths, so she swallowed any objections she had and agreed to go.

**

"Men, tonight's game gets us one step closer to the state championship," Coach Miller said to the crowded locker room. All eyes were on him except mine. I was thinking about Genevieve and how she manipulated Chase to get what Riley wanted us to do. They were taking over every aspect of my life, with little hope of escape. I hadn't heard a word Coach Miller had said, so I re-focused.

"Eric, you and Bryce are going to have to work hard today. Their pass rush is top in the league. They aren't going to make this easy. We'll have to fight for every yard. Let's show them whose house this is," Coach Miller said.

Then he went down on one knee. "Now let us pray." We all bowed our heads while Coach Miller said a silent prayer. After he finished, we all followed him out to the field.

During the game, Eric managed to throw the ball to Bryce a few times. When he got it, no one was a match for him. He would weave in and out of the players like they were standing still. I missed being in the game; the excitement of it was incredible. Bryce and Eric were unstoppable. Every time Eric got the ball to Bryce it would result in a touchdown. We were killing them, already up by 35 points at the half. The crowd was cheering so loudly that I couldn't hear what the announcer was saying over the PA.

"Kelly, Hess, Archer, Hallum, Otto, Beverley, get out there," Coach Miller yelled. We were running out of players for Coach Miller to substitute into the game. He was using everyone. This was the first time ever that Coach Miller used this many back-ups in the game. At least that was what Coach Hoff told Riley during halftime. With Bryce and Eric out there on offense and Chad on defense, it didn't matter who was playing the other positions.

After the game, Coach Miller stood at the entrance of the locker room and shook the players' hands as they came in, congratulating them on a good game, because everyone ended up getting to play. The locker room was filled with loud music and celebrating. I escaped to go find Elle.

Elle insisted on coming over to my house after the game. I wasn't sure what she told her parents she was going to do, because her dad was having her stay home more and more. It was really starting to bother me. What did he have against me?

"Elle, why has your dad been trying to keep us apart?" I asked, sitting on our front porch, wrapped in a thick, warm blanket with her.

"He thinks I need to be focusing on my future more," she said, doing her best impression of her dad.

"What if he's right?"

"Are you saying that you don't see us together?" She pulled away from me.

"Elle," I grabbed her and pulled her back to me. "No, I meant that I have been scared about our future for a while, you know, with you going off to school. Maybe you will meet some college guy who will replace me."

She brushed my cheek with her hand. "Nicholas, no one could ever replace you." My doubts about our future were suppressed for the moment. She always knew what to say.

"Nicholas, I still can't believe what happened to Mrs. Lemmins and Chase earlier at the game," she said with a giggle.

"I know. It was crazy."

I was lucky enough to see all of the events unfold from the field. The game had ended. Chase was walking out of the stands with Cora and Genevieve, signing some autographs of course, when Joy Lemmins caught sight of him. She was a few rows above him. They had just started walking down the steps when Joy Lemmins rushed down the bleachers, taking two steps at a time, trying to catch up to Chase. She tripped, falling head first into him. He turned right when she hit him, knocking him off his feet and pinning him to the bleachers like a wrestler. He couldn't get free because she was unconscious. Cora swore she was faking it, because she thought she could hear Joy Lemmins whispering, "I'm lying on Doctor Hotty Pants; this is the greatest day of my life."

It took a couple of minutes before three men from the crowd could help lift her off of Chase. The paramedics at the game rushed into the stands to help. By the time I got to them, she was already strapped down on the gurney. They tried to put her in the ambulance, but she refused to let go of Chase's jacket. She had a death grip on it. She kept mumbling about how she must be taken care of by Dr. Letterby. When he finally agreed to go to the hospital to check on her, she promptly let go of his jacket and beamed a big smile. Genevieve and Cora were right next to Chase, watching everything and laughing. I guess in the end, Chase was no match for a determined Joy Lemmins. Forget about the Seekers, she was far worse. She got what she wanted, Dr. Hotty Pants.

Later that night after Elle left, I wasn't able to sleep at all. My thoughts were consumed with the anniversary of the 10-10 Earthquake. Also, I was worried about Genevieve and Elle both being with me the whole day, which probably meant trouble. As difficult as it was to fall asleep, I eventually drifted off. I was instantly surrounded by the familiar black nothingness. *I am asleep,* I told myself, *and this will all end soon.* Maybe like Elle, I could learn to block out these dreams, but tonight I just had to survive.

After a long night of fighting with the darkness, I finally awoke sick. This was the sickest I had been in a long time. I looked for my Tic Tacs but didn't see any in my room, so I got up and walked slowly out into the hallway to see if Cora had some. To my relief, there was a fresh pack on the table just outside my room. I quickly emptied part of it into my mouth. The cool vanilla and mint flavor helped to take the edge off of my sickness immediately.

I had to see Elle because I needed to get some of the relief that only she could provide. She was my medicine, the only one who could heal me completely, so I got ready quickly.

"Cora, I'm going to pick up Elle. I'll be right back."

Before she answered, I was out the door. The bed that she had made for Chase in the family room was untouched. Where did he sleep if not here? His car wasn't in the driveway either.

I went and got Elle, and by the time we got back, Chase's car had returned. Everyone was standing in our foyer.

"Good, I'm glad we are all here," Cora said. "Chase can't go with us today. He has to go back to the hospital to check on Joy Lemmins one more time, and then he has to head to London to perform an emergency surgery."

"And yes, it is a royal secret," Chase said as he sauntered out of the kitchen. Genevieve smiled big, keeping up her part of the charade. Riley and Cora didn't even bat an eye.

"So I thought it would be nice if we girls went to Oktoberfest, and the guys spent time at home watching football," Genevieve said.

"No, I don't think that's such a good idea. Elle doesn't want to spend the day with you two without me," I said.

"Elle, you and Nicholas will have plenty of time together. Plus, Elle has to get used to doing some stuff with your family and friends, especially if you guys are going to stay together for the long haul like Riley and me," Genevieve said.

The nervousness I felt from Elle was intense. I wasn't sure if she was worried about spending the day with the "girls" or about our future together. She gave me a kiss on the cheek and said, "I'll be fine."

Genevieve took Elle by the arm and led her out the front door. Cora gave Chase a quick goodbye hug, leaving the three of us guys standing there.

"Well, I guess I better get back to that loon at the hospital," Chase said after a brief moment.

"Is she going to be okay?" I asked.

"Of course. There's nothing wrong with her, but every time I tried to discharge her, she made up a new symptom so I would have to keep running more tests. I would have passed her on to the Bethesda South staff, but she refused to talk to anyone but me. I finally convinced her that I would make house calls if she agreed to leave the hospital today. Needless to say, I won't be coming back to Winsor for a long time. She needs help and not the help I can give. She needs to be locked up."

Riley nodded his head profusely, as if he knew exactly what Chase was talking about. I think he'd had a couple of run-ins with her at school. Chase took his suitcase out to his sports car, hopped in and was speeding down the street in a matter of seconds.

"Did you know that Genevieve was going to do all of this?" I asked Riley. "You both knew Chase was coming into town."

"No, but when she wants something, she usually gets it. If it makes you feel any better, I think she just wanted an excuse to get out of the house with the girls. Even if it's not with her choice of company, she is tired of being cooped up with me for all of these years. I can't really blame her. I'm not the most talkative person. So what do you want to do today?"

"Watch football. I want to see the University of Cincinnati play Rutgers," I said.

"Okay, but let's do it at my house."

"Sure," I agreed.

For most of the afternoon, we sat on the super-sized couches in their basement, watching football and eating leftover pizza. Their basement was still mostly covered in plastic. Riley explained how he was building a panic room and some tunnels to get out of there, if needed. But it wouldn't be completed until after spring because he was waiting on some more parts to get in from the manufacturers. It still amazed me how little furniture they had. They only had the necessary pieces in each room. It would make packing easy and quick. Cora and I knew that firsthand. But at least we had some personal touches to make our house feel like home, not plain like this.

It felt so good just sitting and watching football. It was relaxing, another slice of normalcy that I craved.

It was getting close to dinner. My stomach was beginning to rumble.

"So when do you expect the girls to be home?" I asked.

Riley didn't answer at first. Then he responded, "Not sure."

He sounded like something was wrong. I knew it couldn't

be the football game, because he had told me earlier he didn't care who won.

"Riley, are you okay?" Right then he turned off the game. I sat up. He was now slumped-over, sitting on the edge of the couch.

"Nicholas, you and I have more in common than just being Thusians. I also lost my ma and da six years ago today." When he mentioned his parents, a thick, rich Irish accent resurfaced.

I had made it pretty far into the day without discussing or really thinking about the past. I should have known it was only going to be a matter of time before I would have to talk about it.

"You lost both of your parents the same day, too?" I asked.

"Remember, Nicholas, that Genevieve and I had our Realization of our talents the same day, and in a very public way too. Both of my parents died during it."

He took a deep breath, and then continued. "I grew up in a small fishing village just north of Dublin called Howth. My parents owned a pub there named Abbey Tavern. It had been in our family for generations, a real solid establishment that had loads of traditions and good food. I, of course, was going to take it over when my parents retired. From an early age I knew all about the Thusian way of life because my parents had told me everything. They were proud of our heritage and acted as historians of sorts for the Thusians. They and a few others kept the history alive after the Keepers were gone, often using the pub as a meeting place."

He continued, "Our pub was always busy. If you wanted a

pint and some fish and chips, it was the place to go. One day during a busy lunch hour, a man walked in. He didn't look any different than the rest of the people that frequented our establishment, but he seemed suspicious to me. Something was off. I waited on him, but nothing. He seemed normal enough, but that bad feeling in the pit of my stomach wouldn't go away.

"He finished his pint of Guinness, paid and walked outside. His car was parked on the street right in front of the pub's large glass windows. As soon as he got into his car, everything slowed down around me. At first, I didn't know what was going on, but everything my ma and da had told me over the years clued me in to what was happening to me. My body just took over like it knew what to do on its own. The man's car exploded. I'm still not sure if he knew it was going to happen, or if someone planted a bomb in it. Either way, I could see the fireball heading toward the windows. I pushed a young couple who was right next to the window to the ground and picked up their small, round table and used it as a shield. The blast sent me and the shattered table back to the other side of the pub. When I was hurtled backward, I knocked several other people to safety while flying through the air. The blast shattered all of the front windows and destroyed a good part of the front of the pub, leaving black scorch marks everywhere. I was unhurt—just a couple of gashes, but nothing bad. The people around me weren't hurt, just dazed. The table I picked up had absorbed most of the blast and most of the flying glass.

"For a moment after the explosion, everything was quiet

and still, like people mourning at a funeral, but then the screaming and yelling began. People everywhere were hurt. It was horrific. I looked at the bar where my parents had both been working at the time of the blast, but they were gone. I frantically searched for them." Riley paused, his voice full of grief. His Irish accent became even thicker.

"My da had done the same thing I had done with the table bu-but, but at his age he was not able to take being thrown back with such force. When I pulled the table off of him," Riley fought back tears and continued, "my ma was right next to him lying there. My ma must have seen him pick up the table to shield everyone from the blast and tried to help him hold the table in place against the explosion. The car that blew up was right in front of the window by the bar area, so most of the force came right at them."

Riley sat back with his hands over his face and began to sob quietly. His grief reminded me that I, too, was alone. My parents, like his, had died protecting others. A voice in my head said, *They died because they were destined to. This is what Thusians' lives are for, to sacrifice for others, our Final Sacrifice.*

They died because of this curse that we both bear, I shouted back at the voice in my head.

We spent the remainder of the time in silence. Later, I asked about Genevieve's story. He told me that it was for her to tell when she was ready. The girls got home right before 6:00 p.m. They must have known that we would end up over here, because they had all of the shopping and food bags on the kitchen table when we came up.

I took a couple of the hamburgers and some fries and put

them into one of the empty bags. My mind was abuzz from everything. I had to escape. I took Elle's hand and led her outside. I walked her to my truck, opening the passenger door for her to get in. She didn't look like she was upset after the time she spent with Cora and Genevieve, which was a relief.

We didn't talk on our way to her house. She sat in her seat, looking out the window, holding my hand in her lap. Her long fingernails gently scratched the top of my hand, moving back and forth, sending reassurance through me. She sensed my pain and without words she was taking care of me. She was what I needed.

We arrived at her house and went down to her basement. We sat and ate dinner, watching the TV, which was already on when we got down there.

The evening news came on and the reporter said, "My name is Rachel Roberson and tonight we are remembering the victims of the 10-10 Quake."

Before the reporter was able to say another word, Elle turned the TV off.

"I hate the news. It's so boring," she said, with her small, crooked smile.

After eating, I laid my head down on her lap, taking her hand and pressing it to my lips. She rubbed my head slowly, taking away all of my pain from the day.

I left her house later that night feeling renewed. I was able to stay until midnight because her dad was gone on another business trip. After a long, final embrace at her front door, I walked back to my truck. I got in and started driving home.

"So, do you feel better now?"

I nearly swerved off the road. Genevieve was sitting in my back seat with her arms folded.

"What are you doing in here?" I didn't give her the satisfaction of looking back at her.

"Well, the way you two were on the couch, and that big old goodbye kiss, it looked like you were feeling a lot better."

I had to ignore her—I wasn't in the mood for her antics. "I know we have to do the buddy system thing. But I don't think I was in any real danger on her couch. What do you want? You knew I was fine. Why don't you leave us alone?"

"Believe me, I didn't want to chase you over here, but Riley told me to."

"Do you do everything Riley asks?" I said, holding back the anger welling up inside me.

"No, we work together. You would understand that if you started to act like we were all on the same team for once. Leaving without telling anyone was childish. You are supposed to let us know. You know she's not that important in the grand scheme of things. She's not the 4th."

I swerved off the side of the road and slammed on my brakes, sending her into the back of my seat. I couldn't take it anymore. She had crossed the line. I turned around to look straight into her eyes.

"First of all, you will not talk about Elle ever again. Do I make myself clear?" I was yelling. Her face drained of all color. "And secondly, you might be right about her not being the one, but maybe you are not looking at her fairly because you are jealous of her."

Her face became even paler.

I turned back around. I was so angry, but the anger wasn't fueled by any type of fire or Thusian response. We arrived back at my house and I pulled into the driveway.

I stood holding the door open, waiting for Genevieve. She got out of the back and took both of my hands. I wanted to jerk away but her warm, soft hands gripped mine tightly, keeping me from recoiling.

"Nicholas, you are right about what you said. I didn't give her a chance because I am jealous of what she has. She could be the one we are looking for and I wouldn't know it."

She looked at me, and her eyes were damp with tears.

"I promise I will never let you down like this again. I'm so sorry for making you feel this way, especially today."

She turned and walked toward her house.

I stood there stunned and puzzled by what she had said. What did she mean she's jealous of what Elle has?

ANGER
CHAPTER FOURTEEN

Genevieve was true to her word. She never gave me another reason to be angry with her or to doubt her motives after that night. The next couple of times that she saw Elle, she went out of her way to talk to her, to make Elle feel like Genevieve was more like a family member than competition. Because of that, Elle became more comfortable around her, which was a big weight off my shoulders. And that helped me a lot, because Riley and Genevieve were always at our house now.

With the changing colors of leaves came Homecoming. I was picked to possibly be on the Court once again, along with Elle, Chad, Amber, Eric and Bryce. It was everyone at our lunch table. The only exception was Livi, but she didn't care. She was too busy helping Eric campaign for Junior Duke. She had put up posters of him everywhere and handed out cookies with his picture on it. I was so glad that he got nominated, because he normally was the one trying to get me elected. I hoped that Eric would win this time. After all the attention last year, it would be a nice change to not be in the spotlight. I was looking forward to just being part of the crowd, but not having to hide.

"Elle, what color dress are you wearing to the dance?" I asked in between bites of an incredible apple dumpling that Cora had made for me for lunch.

"I'm not wearing a dress. I was thinking I'd go in shorts and a t-shirt. Do you think that's okay?" Elle grabbed her fork and took a piece of the dessert.

"You would look stunning in anything, my dear, but I think Cora would be devastated. She can't wait to coordinate my suit with your dress."

"Well, we can't rob her of that pleasure. I will be wearing a light pink and black dress. But that is all I'm telling you. The rest will have to be a surprise."

I looked around our table. Everyone was talking about Homecoming, including Erin, who had become a regular at our table now. Knowing her, she was hoping Bryce would ask her to the dance. I said I would help Bryce get a date, but Erin wouldn't have been my first pick. When Erin saw something she wanted, she was aggressive in going after it. And after he saved her from the runaway bus, she followed him around like a lost puppy.

I leaned over to Bryce. "So are you going to ask anyone to the dance?" I whispered to him.

He shrugged his shoulders.

"I think you should ask Erin. She is dying to go with you, if you haven't noticed. She has turned down two other guys, hoping you will ask her."

Bryce looked up, hoping no one had heard what I said.

Elle had and whispered, "Bryce, yeah, do it. It would be fun. We can double date."

"Okay, Elle, I will," he said.

Bryce looked at Erin across the table. He cleared his throat. "Erin," his voiced cracked a little in the middle of her name, "will you do me the honor of being my date for Homecoming?"

She hopped up from her seat and ran around the table like she was playing a game of Duck Duck Goose. She tackled him with a big hug, saying loudly, "Yes, I will go with you!"

Bryce's cheeks turned a deep shade of scarlet. He was so embarrassed by her reaction. The lunchroom went quiet, including the table of girls who watched him every day. They were clearly not happy with his choice. I bet he wished he could take back the invitation right about now.

Eric jumped up and stood on top of his chair putting his hands up. "Can I have everyone's attention? Please, please, everyone can I have your attention?" Eric yelled. "Bryce, the most eligible bachelor at Winsor, now has a date for the dance. So sorry, ladies. Better luck next year. Erin is the lucky winner of the Bryce Adams lottery." Eric then took a bow and sat back down like nothing happened. The lunchroom applauded. Livi punched him.

Bryce slid down in his chair almost all the way under the table. Some more of the girls' faces around the lunchroom showed that Eric's announcement crushed their dreams of being asked. I guess the announcement was needed after all.

Bryce and I got up from lunch a short time later. We

walked down the hall toward our classes which were right next to each other.

"So, do you want me to pick you and Erin up or do you want to meet at the restaurant?" I asked.

"To be honest, I haven't given it much thought. I didn't really think I was going," Bryce said.

"No problem, I will pick you guys up." I put my hand on his shoulder. "Don't worry about anything. I was in the same position last year. Everything works out for the best. You'll have a good time, I promise."

"Thanks, Nicholas. I am lucky to have made such a good friend like you."

**

The night of the Homecoming game arrived, and like last year, I was standing next to Amber on the 50 yard line waiting for them to announce the winners for Homecoming Court. The parade was identical right down to the same red convertible that I rode in last year with Amber, and we even had the same beautiful autumn weather. But this time, Eric made it a lot more fun. He threw beads and candy out of the car like it was Mardi Gras and occasionally jumped out to go and greet the people watching the parade. I even thought I saw him kiss a baby or two.

"And now for our Winsor Junior Duchess: Ms. Amber King."

"And for our Winsor Junior Duke . . ."

Please let Eric win, I thought to myself over and over.

"I can't believe this," said the announcer. "We have a tie—Nicholas Keller and Eric Iery." Eric ran over to me, picked me up over his shoulder and ran us to the winner's area. The student section was going nuts, chanting both of our names. How did we tie? I couldn't believe it. Amber was laughing at Eric's craziness along with the other winners. In the stands, Cora and Genevieve were cheering for us and shaking green and gold pom-poms right in front. The announcer tried to calm the crowd down with very little luck. Eric did several awkward cartwheels and a bunch of somersaults. He was in his element and the crowd was eating it up. Finally, Joy Lemmins chased him back into line. Again the announcer tried to calm the crowd, with more success.

"Okay now, okay, settle down. And now for your King and Queen: Bryce Adams and Elle Canan."

Elle led Bryce up to the line with the rest of us; they were right in the middle. I looked back to see Chad clapping for Bryce, even though he lost. Last year, Oliver was in that very same spot but handled it totally differently.

The halftime festivities were short-lived because we were losing, 3-7. Our defense was holding the Sycamore Aviators, but we were struggling on offense. Their only points came from the opening kickoff, which they returned for a touchdown. I was yelling to Chad the different things I saw on the field. The game was still going in slow motion for me during every play as if I were out there. With this help, Chad was able to adjust to what I was telling him. He made big play after big play on defense. Eric and Bryce had connected several times, but the other team was putting two or three guys just on Bryce.

The end of the game was only two minutes away, and we were still down by 4 points. If we lost this game, our chance to repeat as state champs would be over. We got the ball on our own 15 yard line with 85 yards to go. The first play was a pass to Bryce right in the middle of the field. He caught the ball and ran toward the sideline, away from the Sycamore defenders that were swarming around him. He got the first down and went out of bounds to stop the clock when one of their players hit him in the back, sending him to the ground hard. It was a late hit, but no penalty flags were thrown. The crowd booed profusely at the refs. Bryce wasn't hurt. He jumped up and ran to the huddle like nothing had happened. Eric got the next play from Coach Miller. It was another passing play to Bryce. Bryce lingered next to Eric for a moment. Eric nodded his head and Bryce ran to his spot.

Eric hiked the ball and Bryce went sprinting behind him. Eric pitched the ball back to him instead of passing it. Then Eric ran out in front of him, leading the way. Eric dove into two Sycamore defenders, knocking them back out of the way. Bryce got by them and was now streaking down the sideline. He was on his way to scoring and the crowd cheered wildly. But then he began to slow down ever so slightly, roaming back toward the middle of the field. A defender caught up to him and Bryce stiff-armed him, knocking him to the ground. The next closest defender caught up to him too, and then Bryce slowed down even more. The defender shot past him and was now in front of him; it was the same player who had hit Bryce in the back on the play before. Bryce lowered his shoulder and hit the defender hard, throwing him backward. The defender's helmet flew off, and Bryce walked into the end zone over the flattened Aviator.

The crowd cheered, then hushed. The defender wasn't moving. Everything was silent. The trainers and paramedics rushed onto the field. They had him strapped to the board and off the field quickly. Whatever was wrong seemed serious. They were rushing him to the hospital.

We ended up winning the game 10-7 on Bryce's touchdown run, but it was not as great because of the uncertainty about the Sycamore player's condition. Later in the locker room, Coach Miller informed us that he had sustained a slight concussion and had some bruised ribs, but that he would make a full recovery. The team's excitement grew after hearing the news, because that win sealed our number one seed in the tournament for the state championship. Bryce didn't look excited at all.

"Good game, Bryce," I said, walking over to him. He was blankly staring at his locker. He still had on all of his football pads.

"Not really," he said, still not showing any excitement.

"What's wrong with you? You scored the game-winning touchdown."

"I could've hurt that guy badly. I don't know what came over me. I was so angry about getting hit out of bounds after the play, something just clicked. I wanted some payback. That's why I slowed down, so I could hit him. My anger got the best of me. Nicholas, please don't tell anyone what I just told you. I'm ashamed of how I acted. I should be kicked off the team."

What Bryce said sounded like what I had said last year. He was showing characteristics of the 4th. I remembered how I felt after breaking that quarterback's arm last year. My anger, too, got the best of me.

"Don't worry, Bryce. I won't tell anyone what happened. Actually, you should feel lucky that you scored. Because if you slowed down and caused us not to win the game, I think Coach Miller would have made sure you were in the hospital next to the Sycamore player."

He smiled. "Thanks."

"Don't thank me yet. You are probably going to want to kill me because I told you to ask Erin out. She is a little bit on the aggressive side."

"I know that," he said.

"Trust me, you haven't seen anything yet."

ARABIAN NIGHTS
CHAPTER FIFTEEN

Cora had put her finishing touches on Elle's corsage. A very simple pink rose connected to some white and black silk ribbon, which iridescently shimmered around the flower.

"Cora, Elle's going to love it."

Riley and Genevieve walked in the front door. Riley had on a suit and tie and Genevieve was wearing a white long dress, not as provocative as some of her other outfits. With her darker skin it made her look incredibly wholesome.

"Why are you guys dressed up?" I asked.

"We are chaperones for the dance tonight," Riley said. I noticed that Cora was also wearing a dress. It wasn't odd for her to be dressed up, but tonight it was different.

"Cora, don't tell me that you are chaperoning also."

"Nicholas, don't blame Cora. It's partly my fault," Genevieve said. "I couldn't let Riley go by himself tonight. That Joy Lemmins has been asking if his wife was coming to the dance for weeks now. I guess Chase Letterby wasn't enough for her."

"I think she was hoping to get me by myself. So that means that Cora had to come with us because of the buddy system," Riley added.

"I'm sorry I didn't tell you earlier, Nicholas," Genevieve said.

She sounded so sincere. I couldn't be mad at her. And lately I had begun to trust her. All of my disgust with her had vanished.

"It's fine. I don't mind. Plus the two of you can possibly meet Bryce and tell us what you think. Riley and I already know him well enough."

Last night, I told them what Bryce had said to me. We all agreed it seemed like he was the one we should focus on from now on. But Riley reminded us that we should still be on the lookout for other possibilities, because we could be wrong, which was something we couldn't afford.

Genevieve cornered me outside away from the others before I left to get Elle.

"This is for you." I put my hand out and she dropped a large silver coin into it. The coin was double the size of a quarter.

"What's this for?"

"It's a gift. I have wanted to give it to you for a while now, and tonight seemed like the right time."

I examined both sides of the coin. They were blank.

"There's nothing on it."

"There is something on it, but you will have to look a lot closer."

I slipped the coin into my pocket, thanking her for the gift, still not knowing the meaning of it. I would take a better look later.

The three of them loaded into Cora's truck and left for school. Cora didn't ask to take pictures this year, but I was sure Mrs. Canan would take plenty. Cora probably already talked to her to arrange to get copies.

Elle was standing out in front of her house when I arrived. She looked more beautiful than words could describe. The sun setting behind her made her hair come alive with different rays of light piercing through it. I fell in love with her all over again. The euphoria that engulfed me was intense. I felt free. No boundaries, no worries, just Elle and me.

"Elle, you look absolutely amazing." I could barely get the words out. She flashed her crooked little smile. Her dress was sleeveless with what looked like tiny, shining pieces of polished coal flowing down to her waist and then transforming effortlessly into pink silk or satin that went to the ground with a little flare out at the bottom.

"Nicholas, you look very handsome," Mrs. Canan said. "You both look so cute together and match perfectly."

Somehow Cora knew the exact shade of pink Elle's dress was going to be. My pink tie and vest matched it perfectly with a black and silver pattern going through it. My black Oxford suit also looked like the same shade as the black in her dress with a little of its shine.

"This is for you." I handed her the corsage. Her mom took it out of her hand.

"Cora has simply outdone herself. It's magnificent," Mrs. Canan said, taking it out of the box. "Here, Nicholas, let me get a picture of you putting it on Elle's wrist. Cora will love this picture. She wanted me to take a lot of pictures of the two of you."

I was right. Mrs. Canan took hundreds of pictures of us in different poses.

"Where's your dad?" I whispered to Elle in between poses.

"He's gone on business again."

I hadn't seen her dad much lately, which was fine by me. But I knew Elle hated that he was gone so much. She missed him. I couldn't imagine what it would be like if one of my parents was always gone on business or always traveling like Bryce's dad who was in the military.

"Mom, we have to pick up Bryce and Erin still," Elle said.

"I think I got enough pictures. You both have a good time," Mrs. Canan replied. "Say hi to Cora for me."

Elle looked at me.

"I'll tell you in the truck," I whispered, opening the door for Elle.

"So what did my mom mean when she said to tell Cora hi?" she asked as soon as we both got into the truck.

"She is a chaperone this year, along with Riley and Genevieve."

Elle didn't say much at first. Was she bothered that Cora was going to be there or was she upset about Genevieve?

"I didn't know they needed chaperones that badly," she said.

I explained to her how Joy Lemmins had been stalking Riley, and after the Chase incident, they didn't want to take any chances. Genevieve didn't want Joy Lemmins anywhere near her husband. That made Elle smile big. I guess the thought that Genevieve didn't want Riley alone with Joy made her feel better.

This year, Eric wasn't coming with us. He was planning to make some fancy dinner for Livi instead. Chad and Amber were also going solo. So it was just going to be the four of us: Elle, Erin, Bryce and me. At Erin's house we took some more photos for her parents, but it was quick. Erin's parents both shook my hand repeatedly, thanking me for what I had done during the earthquake, which was awkward. Bryce's dad was out of town so he was absent. Bryce looked extremely uncomfortable, fidgeting with his black bow tie constantly. Maybe it was because Erin was all over him. On top of Erin being handsy, she was also ignoring Elle completely for some unknown reason, like she wasn't even there. She couldn't still be upset about last year's Homecoming. Maybe she felt like Elle stole me away, but in reality, I was Elle's from the start.

We decided to go to a nicer restaurant instead of going to McDonald's again. We went to a fondue place called the Melting Pot, which Cora had suggested to me. It was low lit and very private. When we were seated, Elle and I accidentally sat across from each other in the booth. Erin quickly sat down next to me, making Bryce sit next to Elle. In the center of the table was a pot of oil and several metal skewers to cook our food with. The waiter described what we could order and how to cook it. We all ordered a little bit of everything off the menu. It was odd that we had to cook our own food.

Elle tried to make small talk with Erin and Bryce, but Erin didn't want any part of it. She would only respond in short answers. Bryce tried to keep the conversation going, but you could tell he wasn't used to the small talk thing. Luckily, Erin got up to go to the bathroom and surprisingly asked Elle if she'd like to go with her. This would give me some time to talk with Bryce alone, and hopefully the girls could work out whatever was going on between them.

"So, Bryce, what do you think of Erin?" I asked.

"You weren't kidding. Erin is aggressive. She's cute, but I think she's a little too much for me to handle."

I had to figure out how to ask him about his dreams or find out more about what clicked inside of him when he hurt that guy in the football game.

"So, Bryce, how have you been sleeping?"

Bryce gave me the weirdest look. *Real smooth*, I thought to myself. I sounded like a crazy person asking that.

"I mean, since you moved here, because whenever I used to move to a new place I would have these horrible dreams."

I must have made him feel a little better about the question because he answered it.

"Come to think of it, I have been having these weird dreams, I think. But I don't really remember much of them."

Before I could ask more about it, Erin and Elle came back.

Elle and Erin were both smiling. Elle sat next to me this time and Erin sat down next to Bryce. It looked like whatever was bothering Erin before got worked out somewhere between here and the ladies' room.

"So, what were you boys talking about?" Erin asked while sticking a piece of chicken and putting it into the oil.

"Nicholas asked if I have been having bad dreams," Bryce said. Both of the girls gave me the same look Bryce had given me a minute ago. "He was explaining how he had bad dreams when he moved to different towns."

Erin interrupted him. "I would have had bad dreams too if I were you, Nicholas. I mean, your parents died in the 10-10 Earthquake and then those reporters kept wanting to ask you questions about how you saved those people, when all the time you had to be thinking about how you didn't have a chance to save your parents. Then moving from town to town to hide from the media—that all sounds like enough of a nightmare to me."

The words rolled off of her tongue like she was talking with a friend about what she ate for lunch. Her words stabbed me like a sharp dagger going into my back. Is that what people said about me when I wasn't around? Did they feel sorry for me? Was I just some charity case?

Elle looked angry, like she could jump over the table and strangle her, but Bryce spoke before she had the opportunity.

"How dare you speak about what Nicholas went through as if you understand! You don't, none of us do. For such a cute girl, you can say some pretty ugly things."

The whole table sat in silence. The crackling of the oil cooking our food was the only sound I could hear.

"Nicholas, I am so sorry," Erin said in a pleading manner.

"I treated you like you were some sort of juicy piece of gossip. I am truly sorry. Bryce, please forgive me, too. You just make me nervous because I like you a lot. I tend to talk a lot when I am nervous. As you can see, I am doing it now." She put her napkin over her mouth like it was the only way she could shut up.

"Erin, it's okay, I accept your apology," I said. "You are right, that is how it happened." I really did mean that it was okay. I was just shocked by it.

Everyone still looked upset, so I tried to lighten the mood.

"But Erin, if you talk about me again, please add in that I saved a van full of nuns and orphans from a fire, while I was saving the people during the earthquake."

It did the trick. Everyone began to laugh. The rest of the dinner was better, full of conversation and fun.

By the time we got to the dance, Bryce and Erin looked to be really hitting it off. He was turning out to be a really good guy, especially after defending me at dinner. I was beginning to see Bryce a lot differently. It was so ridiculous of me to be jealous of him and Elle. I could now see how he could be the 4th.

I pulled into the school lot. We were immediately directed to a newly graveled path that led onto one of the practice fields to park.

"What in the world?" Bryce was pointing back to where the school parking lot used to be. There were mounds of sand everywhere, making it look like there was a vast desert oasis between us and the school.

"I thought the sand would be the right touch for the Arabian Night theme," Elle said.

"You knew about this?" I asked Elle.

"Well, of course; I planned it, but I didn't want to tell anyone about it. I wanted it to be a surprise." She squeezed my hand.

"It sure is a surprise. You guys took the theme really seriously," Bryce said, still staring at the sand.

"We were getting tired of the same old Homecoming themes. Just wait until you get inside. I'm really excited to see it myself, because I was just responsible for helping get the sand and the transportation set up from the parking area."

We parked and got out of the truck, walking toward a large colorful tent that looked like it was taken straight out of some Hollywood movie set. Inside, there were dozens of small tents mounted on what looked like golf carts with larger tires. We got in line for the tents on wheels. They would pull up and pick up a group of people, taking them to the dance, I guessed. When it was our turn, a man dressed in a genie costume opened the tent flap and we all got in. There were several large pillows in there to lounge on. Once in, Elle said, "How do you like our magic carpets?"

Sure enough, we were sitting on something that could have passed as a magic carpet. We began to move. Elle opened both sides of the tent to reveal the desert landscape. We passed people on camels that were placed around more colorful tents. If I didn't know we were in Winsor, Illinois, I would have sworn we were in the Sahara Desert. We arrived at the school after a ten minute journey through the oasis. The entire entrance to the school was covered in colorful fabric, hiding the school's exterior completely from our view. The sand continued to the entrance of the school, and right down the middle was a reddish stone walkway for us to step on. Lighting the pathway were large oil lamps that were held by an L-shaped pole and hook. Surrounding them were cactuses with vibrant colored flowers. The four of us walked slowly down the path. Like everyone in my group, I was trying to see everything I could. Even Elle looked amazed, and she had helped with the planning.

We opened the fabric flap to go into the school. The red stone continued into the school, weaving in and out of the mini sand dunes down the hallway.

"Nicholas, is this type of thing normal here?" Bryce whispered.

"Unfortunately, it is."

He smiled.

The lunchroom looked like the inside of a large silk tent. Red, gold and purple silk fabric stretched to the ceiling. All around the outside of the dance floor were different sitting areas covered in pillows. It took me a couple of minutes to take in all of the Arabian-themed décor. It even looked like they actually had a real snake charmer.

"So, what do you want to do first?" Erin asked.

"Let's get our pictures taken so we can get it out of the way," I said.

We walked into the gym, which looked the same as usual, but with a couple of themed areas for photos like last year.

"Nicholas," Elle stopped me and turned me to face her.

"Right here is the first time I knew that I loved you. When I saw you last year getting your pictures taken with Erin, I knew right then that no one else should be with you but me. I was so jealous. I thought I had lost my chance to be with you. I decided then that if I ever got the chance to be with you, I would grab on to it and never let go."

"You knew then? Why did you wait so long?" I asked with a smile.

She tilted her head to the side and smiled a very mischievous grin. "I had to play hard-to-get, even though you really didn't have a choice. When I want something, I get it."

I pulled her close and gently kissed her. The energy between us could have lit up San Francisco.

After pictures, we walked around the outside of the dance area. We wanted to see what the restaurant looked like this year, so we peeked in. It was just as amazing as everything else. Instead of tables, there were private tents placed on top of mounds of sand. There were stone paths that led to each tent. Instead of waiters and waitresses, it looked like there were belly dancers and genies. They had a little more clothing on than you would expect, but it was still something you wouldn't usually see in a high school. I was sure the guys loved it in there.

"Let's go dance," Erin said, dragging Bryce to the dance floor.

His expression turned to horror; it was priceless. Elle and I laughed at Bryce as we followed them out to the dance floor. When we got to a certain point near the middle, I could see that a large circle had formed. When we got to the edge of it, I saw Eric, of course, dancing in the middle. I should have known it would be him. The crowd around him was clapping to the beat. He had his suit jacket off and his tie up around his head like it was a headband. He was a surprisingly good dancer. Then he stopped and pointed at Chad, who strutted into the center of the circle and started to dance. The crowd began to clap and chant his name, "Chad, Chad, Chad." He wasn't the best dancer, but that didn't stop him from doing every funny dance move he could think of. He was just as entertaining as Eric.

I lost sight of Eric. Then he appeared right next to me and was pushing me into the middle of the circle. Everyone cheered. I was frozen. What was I going to do now? I was hoping that my talent would slow everything down so I could escape, but to my horror it didn't. I was trapped. I looked back at Elle and Bryce. They were both clapping and screaming my name. I was only in the middle for a second, but it felt like an eternity. Then I came up with a plan. I closed my eyes and blocked out the crowd. I put my arms out like I was holding Elle and began to slow dance. The thumping music died away quickly. I opened my eyes, and Elle was standing in front of me. She took my arms and put them over her head.

"Nicholas, you sure know how to command attention." She smiled.

"What?"

"As soon as you put your arms out, the DJ changed the song to a slow one like he was waiting for your cue. No one said anything. They just grabbed their dates and followed your lead, kind of like sheep following their shepherd."

Around me, everyone was slow dancing. It was kind of funny to hear her use that expression about the shepherd and the sheep. I used that same expression last year to describe how the people at the hospital acted around Chase.

"Elle, I just wanted to dance with you."

She smiled.

SUMMONED

CHAPTER SIXTEEN

Over the DJ's microphone came a loud squeal, then several loud taps. "Is this on? Check, check, one, two, three. Well good evening, youngsters, and welcome to the Winsor Homecoming Arabian Nights," Joy Lemmins' voice screeched over the speakers. "If we could now have the Homecoming Court come up to the DJ booth."

Elle and I walked up to the booth. When I first saw what Joy Lemmins was wearing, I almost fell over. She was dressed in what looked like a cross between a belly dancer's costume and a tent. It was like she had taken one of the little tents in the restaurant area and put it on. The dress, of course, was covered in sequins and fake jewels. Her face was covered in a veil matching her dress. What was she thinking? She looked ridiculous.

"I would now like to introduce the Homecoming Court and our King and Queen."

She read off all of our names and we all walked to the center of the room. Eric brought out Livi to dance with him. I was hoping that Amber would have grabbed Chad so that I could dance with Elle, but he was nowhere to be found. The music began. Amber and I started to dance, and so did Elle and Bryce.

"Wow, two years in a row. What are the chances? I hope this year you can avoid getting punched," Amber said.

"I think I'm safe."

Elle and Bryce were dancing right next to us. They were laughing about something. I wanted to dance with Elle instead, but I knew she would be back in my arms in a couple of minutes so I would just have to wait.

"Oh, Nicholas, before I forget, I have something for you." She fished around in a small purse hanging from her wrist. She pulled out a round, smooth rock with some symbol carved into it. "This is for you."

"What is it, Amber?" I asked, examining it as she put it into my hand.

"I thought you'd know. Mrs. Theasing—you know, the Theasings who give all the money to the school—gave it to me and told me that you needed it for tomorrow."

"Ester Theasing?" I asked.

"Yes," she nodded.

This had to be a Thusian thing, but what? I played along.

"Oh yes, of course, thanks. I think it's something my aunt loaned her for one of her book clubs. They were talking about ancient types of currency and Cora had a couple of pieces to show. Not sure why she gave it to you, but I'm sure Cora will be happy to get it back." I paused, taking a deep breath. "So, how do you know the Theasings?" I asked.

"Mrs. and Mr. Theasing are boosters for the football

program along with my parents. They are always over at the house. Mr. Theasing is my dad's boss too."

I dropped the stone into my pocket. It hit the coin that Genevieve had given me earlier. I now had in my possession two items, and I had no idea what they were for or why they were given to me. I had to find Cora, Genevieve, and Riley to find out what this rock was all about. I had been at the dance for a while, but still hadn't seen any of them.

I was now back in Elle's arms. Elle was talking about Bryce and Erin and how cute they were, but I couldn't focus. Something that Amber had said kept playing over in my mind. *You needed it for tomorrow.* What did she mean? I did catch something Elle said about how funny she thought Bryce was, which struck a nerve. I didn't have time for jealousy. *Enough, Nicholas,* I told myself.

"Are you listening to me?" Elle said.

"I'm sorry, I am a little preoccupied."

"You better be preoccupied with me, buddy," she teased, smiling and staring deep into my eyes. She pulled me closer to her, pressing her body firmly against mine.

"Ouch!" She pulled away. "What's that?" She was rubbing her leg where the stone and the coin were sitting in my pocket.

I fished out the coin that Genevieve gave me. I couldn't tell her that Genevieve gave me a present, because that would lead down a path of more trouble.

"Sorry. It must be the coin that Riley gave me."

She took it out of my hand and looked at both sides. "It's blank. What's it for?" she asked.

"Not sure. I think it's a good luck charm of some sort for my date with you tonight."

She handed it back to me and I slipped it into my pocket.

"You don't need luck with me." She laid her head on my shoulder, kissing my neck, which sent a tingling feeling throughout my body.

We danced to a few more songs and then walked to the dining area with a large group in tow. Instead of the four of us, we had become eight. Eric, Livi, Chad, and Amber had now joined us. We got in line. From where we were standing, I looked for Cora and the others, but I still didn't see them anywhere. I stopped thinking about the stone and what it meant because there was nothing I could do about it. I wanted to have fun at the dance with Elle and my friends while I could.

"No way, Coach Moore, what are you doing here?" Eric said. Riley was standing in front of us, dressed in one of the genie outfits.

"My wife and I volunteered to help and this is where they put me." He looked ridiculous. "If you would all follow me to your table?" Riley walked off so quickly down the desert path that we fell behind.

"Oh yeah, this is how I wish the lunch ladies would normally dress here," Eric said and motioned straight ahead. In front of us there were two women dressed in tight, purple belly dancer outfits, both bent over putting food into two tents side-by-side. The waitresses heard him and turned around. To my surprise and shock, it was Genevieve and Cora.

165

"Do you want to take that back before I shove a genie bottle down your throat?" Genevieve said.

"I am so sorry, Mrs. Moore. I didn't know it was you, or you Ms. Keller." He looked at Cora and then back at Genevieve, then back at Cora, his mouth open in complete shock.

"Eric, do I have to talk to your mother about how you speak about women?" asked Cora.

"No ma-ma-ma-ma'am."

"Good, now move along and stop your staring," Genevieve said, pushing by us.

Chad punched Eric, laughing. We settled onto a fluffy large mattress that was surrounded by pillows and covered by a multi-colored tent on top of a large mound of sand.

"Eric, that was awesome. I can't wait to tell the guys on the team," Chad said.

"I'm sorry, but I couldn't help it. You all saw them." He didn't get any sympathy from the girls, and Bryce and Chad knew not to make any sort of eye contact with him. "Come on, Nicholas, you saw them. I know it was horrible seeing your aunt, but come on. You saw what Mrs. Moore looked like—freakin' incredible, right?"

He was going down a slippery slope. And if he was looking for some help, he was definitely going about it the wrong way.

"Nicholas?" he pushed, hoping I would respond.

"Sorry, Eric. Seeing Cora that way blinded me." Everyone laughed.

Livi spoke up. "Eric, you do have an excellent eye for beauty. You picked me, right? So go ahead and say what you want. If you think I'm as hot as Mrs. Moore, then that's all right by me." She leaned over and kissed him. I was shocked. Livi must have finally given up trying to change Eric, figuring she would just have to make the best of it.

Luckily, Cora and Genevieve weren't our waitresses. We all ate some dessert and settled into different corners of the tent. Elle and I were lounging up against one of the large, gold pillows, which engulfed both of us.

After fifteen minutes of no talking, she leaned over. "Why didn't you say anything about how Genevieve looked when Eric asked?"

Why was she asking me this? Her obsession with Genevieve was beginning to make me crazy. What was I supposed to say? *Eric, you're right. She looked hot.* That would've been stupid and not quite true. I really didn't see her that way; I saw her differently. Sure, I saw what he was talking about, but that's where it stopped.

"Elle, it's because I don't look at her that way. She's more like Cora to me. How many more times can I tell you? It hurts to think you doubt my love for you."

She didn't answer me. She still didn't look convinced, but it was good enough for the moment. I felt like asking what she and Bryce were laughing about when they were dancing, but that would have been petty. These jealousies were getting out of control for both of us.

By the time we left our tent, the dance was over and Cora

and Genevieve were gone from sight, which was a relief. Riley was still at the entrance. He was taking down some of the decorations around him.

"Nicholas, could I talk to you for a minute?" Riley asked.

Eric walked by and whispered, "Do not say anything about how hot I think his wife is."

I ignored him. Elle was right next to me. She was refusing to leave my side.

"Cora wanted me to ask you what time you were planning on coming home," Riley said. "She wanted to remind you that you and she have to leave early in the morning to meet with those people about the stone monument."

What he was saying was news to me, but Riley had to be talking about the stone in my pocket. I had to play along.

"I'm going over to Elle's with everyone else as planned; I won't be home too late." It sounded weird that he was asking, so I had to throw in something else to make it believable. "I told Cora already that I would call her later."

He must have understood how strange it was for him to talk to me about when I was coming home. "Cora's going out with Genevieve and me later, so she might not hear her phone ring. They're changing out of their costumes, so she wanted to make sure you knew that."

"Okay. Thanks," I said.

"Have a good night and please be careful," he said, which sounded like a warning.

Elle and I walked by Joy Lemmins, who was making her way straight for Riley. I turned around and Riley was gone, vanished into thin air. His Thusian talent must have known danger was coming.

I had to lie to Elle later about the stone monument. I said it was something for my parents' graves. I hated telling her all these lies, but Riley left me no choice.

When I got home from Elle's later, Cora, Genevieve, and Riley were waiting for me at the kitchen table. The women still had on their belly dancing tops but were now wearing sweatpants. Riley had completely changed into his normal clothes.

"What's going on?" I asked.

All three of them held out their hands, revealing stones similar to the one I had gotten earlier. I took mine out of my pocket and revealed it to them also. Their faces looked grim.

"Riley just got done explaining the meaning of the stones," Cora said. "We have been summoned by the Thusian Divine Council. You and I have to appear in front of them tomorrow at 7:00 p.m., and Genevieve and Riley have to be there at 6:00 p.m."

I examined the stone more closely. The symbols on it were actually roughly carved numbers.

"Mine has a seventeen on it," I said.

Riley answered, "It's a one and a seven. The first number is the number of days from when you get it to the meeting, and the second is the time of the meeting, always in the p.m."

"Why didn't she just tell us or give it to us in person?" I asked.

"The Council has summoned Thusians this way from the

beginning. Back then they weren't allowed to talk or associate with each other for fear of someone finding out about them," Riley explained. "This tradition of using non-Thusians to deliver messages has been kept alive all this time."

Cora looked frightened.

"What's wrong?" I asked.

Riley answered for her. "Normally they give one or two weeks' warning to people they want to talk to. But since they only gave us one day, it must be serious, like they have been watching us and they don't want us to try to escape. I'm afraid they might be on to us. We can't let the Council know what we're doing no matter what. We need to get our stories straight tonight because if we don't, they will put an end to this . . . or us. Then Xavier and his Seekers will be unstoppable."

COUNCIL
CHAPTER SEVENTEEN

The trip to the Thusian Vault was very much like the last time. I slept most of the way, while Cora drove. She was tired but she refused to let me drive at all. We had spent most of the night working on our stories: Riley's parents were close to my parents and grandparents. Since my parents had been on the Council and Riley's parents had been historians and active Thusians, there was no way for them to prove otherwise. Plus, that would explain why Riley and Genevieve moved in next door. The two of them had their own story about how they met and married. As for Cora and me, our story was actually the only true part, so we didn't have to lie about it.

When we got closer, I began to worry, not for us so much, but for Genevieve. Riley had a lot of secrets, so I was sure he could lie pretty well, but I didn't know about Genevieve.

"Cora, what can they do to us if they find out what we are trying to do?"

"Not sure, but I'm positive Riley is right—they could and would stop us if they really wanted to. It's important that we stick to what we discussed no matter what. They will do everything to try to find out what is going on. Riley said that his dad was summoned once and he never spoke of it after he returned."

It baffled me why the Council wouldn't want us to try to find the 4th. If this was the best way to fight Xavier and the Seekers, you would think they would be allies wanting to help. Maybe Riley's apprehension toward the Council was misguided and we could actually trust them. Maybe they already knew what we were doing, and we were being summoned so they could help us.

I put a couple of Tic Tacs in my mouth and turned my attention to the incredible evening sky that was filled with large puffy clouds floating effortlessly. I was twirling the blank silver coin in my hand, staring at the sky. The cold, smooth silver gave me some comfort as it moved back and forth against my skin.

When we got there, I saw the small guard shack with the same guy as last time standing by the gate to let us in. This time he was dressed in what looked like a black pair of overalls. He was clean-shaven and his hair was combed to the side.

"Good evening, Mr. Weathers. We're here for the meeting."

"Well, of course you are. You're right on time." He raised the metal gate, and we slowly drove through. He said as we passed, "I'm glad to see such a unique group of people gathering here today."

We drove up to the entrance, which was crowded with four helicopters and a bunch of cars and trucks. We parked next to a teal minivan and walked to the entrance in the side of the mountain.

"Remember to stay close to me," Cora whispered. "I will count out the steps before we open the door."

The first couple of steps into the mountain still had some residual light from the outside, but as we started to walk down the decline, it became dark fast. I heard Cora counting aloud, but then she stopped. I put my hands out so I wouldn't run into her. But then I realized I could see her back. The farther we walked, the brighter it became. Up ahead was the door that Cora had opened the last time we were here. The bright white light was pushing through the darkness to guide our way. By the time we got to the door, our eyes had already adjusted to the intense light in the round, white tunnel. We walked down the narrow staircase deeper into the mountain. The fifteen minute descent seemed longer than last time. But this time there was no loud roar of the river rushing inside the Thusian Vault below. The door that led directly into the copper room with the wheels was open. Voices were coming from the vault. Cora walked through the doorway and I followed close behind.

When we entered the large stone cathedral, all of the stone chairs that were cut out of the floor were filled with people. Genevieve and Riley stood at the end of them on the opposite side from where Ester was seated. She was at the head of an invisible table. We could only see Genevieve and Riley's backs. Cora and I stood against the wall next to the entrance. Everyone was silent. At first I thought it was because of us entering the room, but the seated individuals were looking over some pieces of paper they were circulating, all looking dead serious. The diverse modes of transportation outside reflected the people in the seats. From what I could see, all of the women were seated to the right of Ester. The first one had on a business suit and glasses. Her blond hair was pulled back tightly. The next woman was dressed in what you would expect someone to wear when cleaning the house or working in the yard—a pair of sweatpants and a mismatched sweatshirt. Her hair was also pulled back, but several parts of her long, golden brown hair were not tied up. The rest of the women all looked normal. The men sat to the left of Ester. The first man was large and had the darkest skin I had ever seen. His eyes looked like two candles flickering against his skin, and his teeth were brilliantly white. He was dressed in camouflage. The three men that were next to him were all dressed well, wearing different types of business suits. I couldn't see what the last couple of men looked like.

"Riley and Genevieve, the Council doesn't need anything else from you. You need to heed our warning. That is all," Ester said firmly.

Both Genevieve and Riley turned and left, never making eye contact with us as they walked by. I became uneasy. I searched in my pocket for the lone pack of Tic Tacs left after our long trip to West Virginia.

"Let's take a break to welcome our guests." Ester gestured toward Cora and me. *Guests?* I thought we were here to be questioned. It didn't look like Genevieve and Riley were treated like guests.

Ester motioned for us to step forward. She had a big smile on her face.

"How are you both doing? It's been too long," Ester said, giving us both a hug.

"Nervous," I blurted out.

She laughed. "There's no reason to be nervous, Nicholas. We're going to ask you a couple of questions, and then we would like you both to ask us any questions you may have about the Thusians. This meeting is as much about the two of you learning more about who you are as it is about what we have to ask you."

For some reason I didn't feel relieved at all.

"How are you doing, young man?" Towering over me was the man dressed in all camouflage. I stuck my hand out to shake, not knowing who he was. He looked at it, smiled and grabbed it, pulling me in to his chest. He picked me up, giving me a great, big bear hug. He squeezed tightly, knocking the wind out of me. When he put me down, I was trying to catch my breath.

"Alexander Nicholas Taylor, don't tell me you don't remember me!" His deep voice reverberated through the large stone chamber.

I looked to Cora for some help.

"Walter Reed was a good friend of your father," Cora said.

"Good! I was the best man in your parents' wedding."

I kind of remembered my dad's best friend from some old pictures, but he was smaller than Walter.

"I remember, I think, but I don't remember you being so big."

He laughed like he was doing his best Santa Claus impression. "I was in my twenties then. I work out a lot now, being an Army Ranger." He flexed one of his large biceps, which was easily the size of my torso.

Behind him were two other people waiting to talk to us. Cora just stood at my side.

"I will talk to you later and maybe I'll tell you some of the old stories about how your dad and I used to get into all sorts of trouble." Walter winked at me and stepped aside.

The next person walked up to me. "Nicholas, I know you don't know me, but I knew your mother very well. I took her spot on the Council after her Final Sacrifice during the earthquake. My name is Clare Winters." It was the woman in the sweatpants. "Your mother and I spent a lot of time together when we were younger before she got married. I was honored when she picked me to be on her Death Rite List. I was third in line, but I think the first two people on the list also died fulfilling their sacrifices during the earthquake."

I stood there not knowing what to say.

The man next to her spoke up. "Hi, Nicholas, my name is Virgil, Virgil May." He spoke with a slight stutter. "Y-you don't know me either but I-I was your father's replacement on the Council. I was first on his Death Rite List. It was such an honor. I served with him in the fire d-department in Mt. Vernon. I was there when he saved th-those kids during the earthquake. He truly is a hero and it's an honor to meet you."

Again, what was I supposed to say? And what was this

Death Rite List they kept referring to? For a fireman he seemed pretty frail and awfully timid, not like the other guys I knew from Dad's firehouse. I thought I knew everyone.

"Okay now, everyone please take your seats," Ester said in a very commanding, yet calm voice.

Next to Ester's seat was a cushioned bench that was made of wood. It was carved very ornately like the rest of the Thusian Vault. She waved us over and pointed to the bench.

"Before we get to our guests, we have some other business we need to attend to. Ms. Sidney Reese, would you please begin?" A woman with dark brown hair pulled back tightly into a bun put on some black reading glasses.

"If everyone could refer to the sheets of paper I handed out before the meeting. The museums have yielded over $1,132,400,200 in the third quarter. Of course this is very low, but we plan to show some of our more impressive pieces of art in the fourth quarter, which will increase our income significantly. Also, we are planning to buy back some of the pieces we sold last year. With the economy doing so poorly now, we will be able to buy them back at a fraction of what we sold them for. This will boost our holdings and assets considerably. If you would please turn to page five, you can see our total for the year. We will also be building several more museums around the world, allowing us to expand considerably into brand new markets. If you have any questions about locations or what will be featured in the museums, Virgil will be happy to answer those questions after the meeting. Does anyone have any other questions for me?"

I did. I wanted to know how they owned museums

and how they made so much money from them in just one quarter. The more I looked at Ms. Sidney Reese, the more she looked like a museum curator of sorts, very prim and proper. And Virgil definitely looked like the museum type too, but older and more fragile.

"Thank you, Sidney. Now let's move on to Ms. Michelle Lightfoot's report." Ester motioned to a woman at the far end. Her skin was pale but had a slight tint of brownish-red. She was quite attractive. She was young, maybe in her early twenties or late teens. Her black hair draped straight over her shoulders. Her facial features reminded me of the face on the cover of a book my mom used to read to me when I was young, *Pocahontas*.

"Thank you, Ester." She opened a large book that was bound in what looked like an old piece of patched-together, blood-red leather. The pages were discolored from age.

"The lineage tree of the Thusians is now up to date. I have added and subtracted as many of the new and dead Thusians that we know of. If you have any questions, please let me know. On a side note, we are down to 3,281 known Thusians. We all know that there must be thousands, if not tens of thousands, still out there unaccounted for." She sat down as quickly as she stood up.

"Any questions?" Ester asked, looking from side to side. "If there are no other questions about our current holdings or the Thusian lineage, then let us proceed to our special guests." Ester smiled big, like she was about to introduce the President of the United States.

"Cora, Nicholas, it's such an honor to have both of you here at your first official Thusian Council Meeting. Your family has been such an integral part of the Council over the years. Nicholas, both your parents and grandparents served on this board. Before we begin answering your questions, we would like to ask Nicholas a couple of our own."

Cora stood up. I did too.

"No, Cora, you don't have to leave. You can stay," Ester said.

Cora sat down.

I took a step forward, focusing on Ester, no one else.

She started the questioning by saying, "Nicholas, we all know that your Realization of your talent happened during the 10-10 Earthquake, at such a young age, and I must add, in such a heroic manner." Several members of the Council clapped. "But have you heard about The 7?" Ester continued.

I took a deep breath. I knew what my story was going to be. I had rehearsed it over and over in my head. "The what?"

Ester repeated, "The 7."

"No, I'm not sure what you're talking about."

Ester smiled, apparently liking my answer. "No one, not even Riley Moore, spoke to you about The 7 or finding the others to complete it?"

"No ma'am, no one did," I answered. My eyes were fixed on her.

"Okay then. That satisfies my questions. Very good, Nicholas. Thank you so much for being such a good sport about all of this. Would you like to ask—"

"Excuse me, Ester," a familiar voice interrupted her. "I would like to ask some questions, because I am not remotely satisfied."

The fire in me roared to life. Acid crept up my throat. James Caldwell, the D.A. from Oliver's trial, was standing at the far end of the room; he was one of the men I hadn't been able to see when I came in. I wanted to run down there and rip his head off for what he had done to Elle during the trial. He used our Thusian secrets against me at the trial when he knew that I didn't know he was a Thusian. If I would have known that, it would have ended up differently. He had to pay.

"Nicholas, you know already that my talent is in questioning and reasoning, so you will not be able to lie to me."

I couldn't hold my tongue. His voice sounded so arrogant that it made me burn hotter inside.

"Are you sure that's your talent? It didn't work so well for you during Oliver's trial. And to think you had to blackmail me up on the stand to get the answers you wanted. You knew my secret about how I saved them from the car. You make me sick," I spit out, barely containing myself.

A couple of people gasped. He became agitated; his smug look was wiped from his face, leaving a scowl. A couple of veins bulged out of his neck. He was lucky that there were others around because I would have personally thrown him out of here.

"Have you been in communication with the two

people who just left?" He paced back and forth like he was questioning me on the witness stand.

"Yes, they are our neighbors."

"Have you discussed Thusian stuff with them?" he asked.

"Yes. As you know, my parents and his were friends."

"If they were friends, then why didn't you talk with them before the day they moved next door to you?"

"But I did talk to them before that day," I answered.

"So you did talk to them? When was that?" he asked, like he had finally caught me in a lie.

"In the park when—"

He interrupted me. "So you *did* talk with them about our secrets before you knew they were Thusians?" He looked like he had won a contest, but his questioning didn't make any sense. He must have been trying too hard and got himself mixed up.

"Yes, James, I did talk to them in the park," I held up my hand so he wouldn't interrupt again, "because they were busy saving my life from Xavier and another Seeker who were trying to kill me. Maybe you've heard of him? Come to think of it, the only reason I knew they were Thusians then was because Xavier referred to them as my Thusian bodyguards. And why does it matter if I talked to them?"

"It matters because your two stories don't add up. How could Thusians just one day move next door to each other when they haven't talked before?"

"James, I'm sorry if your small brain can't figure this out, but once and for all, we did speak before they moved next door. They had been searching for me and Cora for a while because my parents were friends of Riley's parents. That's why he and Genevieve moved to Winsor, and it's lucky they were there because they saved my life. And let me be clear, this all happened before they moved in next door. But now I have a question for you, James."

He didn't say anything, looking frustrated.

"During Oliver's trial, why did you pretend you were some normal person who knew about my secrets? Were you afraid that your 'questioning talents' wouldn't help you?"

His hands tightened into fists and he slowly crept toward me. If he wanted a fight, I would be happy to oblige.

"Listen here, you little punk," he hissed through clenched teeth. "Just because some people treat you like you're special, doesn't mean I have to. You are nothing but—"

In a steady, deep voice that froze James in place, Walter said, "James, they are our guests." Walter stood and James slowly retreated back to his seat.

"James, would you still like to ask another question of Nicholas?" Ester asked. He didn't respond, so she continued, "Great then. Nicholas or Cora, do you have any questions for us? Please feel free to ask us about whatever your hearts desire."

I knew exactly what I wanted to ask.

"So what's all this talk about The 7 for?" I thought that question would help substantiate our stories more.

"Would anyone like to answer this question?" Ester asked. "Reed Godfree, why don't you answer it, since you are one of the last Thusian historians we have left."

An elderly gentleman dressed in a black turtleneck and black slacks and a sport coat stood slowly.

"The 7 was put together at the same time as the formation of the Seekers. The Council that developed the Seekers knew that one day they might become too powerful. So that's why, in the beginning, they put together three Seekers and four Thusians to be a smaller council so they could keep each other in check. Just like the Old Council, the group of seven broke up. The three Seekers lured the four Thusians into a trap and killed them all. There have been several attempts over the ages to find the four Thusians needed to reform The 7, but every attempt has ended in tragedy and death. The difficulty of trying to form The 7 is that without a Keeper, the 4th is too hard to find. But if the 4th is found, everyone in the group usually dies in the process of establishing him or her as the 4th, because you can't just put any four Thusians together. It's much harder than that. When the three Thusians start to try to find the 4th, they only have a limited amount of time because when the three Seekers find out—and they always do—they will try to make the 4th sacrifice his or her life, leaving three Seekers and three Thusians, thus creating The Unholy Six."

I didn't like the sound of that at all.

"At that point, the three Seekers would become more powerful than the three Thusians, because evil is more powerful than good. The fight between these two groups of three would cause massive devastation. This group of six has gotten a lot of attention over the years from non-Thusians too and has even been confused with 666, the mark of the devil. But the confusion is understandable. There have been three consecutive times that Thusians failed to form The 7, creating 6-6-6. Millions of people died in that short period of time as a result, and they feared it was the devil's work. The Thusians were almost all eradicated during that dark period hundreds of years ago."

Then he slowly sat down.

"You see, that's why it's important for us not to try to form The 7, because of the risks," Ester said.

I had never heard any of this from Riley. His story was completely different. Why didn't he tell us about them trying to put The 7 together before and failing? And why leave out the details about what failing would mean? We could be responsible for thousands of people, if not more, dying. My thoughts immediately focused on the safety of Elle, my friends and Cora. What if my actions would cause them harm, or worse, death?

"So do you have any other questions for us?" Ester asked.

I just stood there, not sure if I did.

"Okay, if there are no more questions, then I call this meeting to a—"

"Wait, one more," I interrupted. "What is the Death List thing?" I asked, not sure if I would get another chance to ask a question of the Council.

Ester answered, "When people are selected to be on the Council, they each have to name twelve successors because of their possible deaths during their Final Sacrifice. It's called a Death Rite List. This list makes sure that the Thusian Divine

Council will never again cease to exist, and it guarantees that we always have a good mix of Thusians," she said with a smile. I cringed at the idea of needing to make such a long list because most of the people on the list might die.

After the meeting, the entire Council except for James Caldwell came up to us to talk more. Most shook my hand, so impressed with how young I was when I had my Realization of talents. They couldn't believe how many people I had already saved. Most of them told me that they were excited to see what my Final Sacrifice was going to be, which I thought was creepy. They should have just said, "Nicholas, we can't wait for you to die so we can see how it happens in all of its glory." No thanks. Walter came up to me and gave me a high five, telling me he was happy about how I had handled myself with James Caldwell. Cora and I walked out with Ester after everyone else was gone.

"I just want you both to remember to be careful of who you trust." She gave Cora a hug and smiled at me, then walked back into the vault. When we got into the truck, Cora was ready to talk.

"Nicholas, what were you thinking? We were supposed to just answer the questions and then be on our way. That was Riley's plan; we had talked about that a lot last night."

"I couldn't let James act that way. He was looking for something that wasn't there. He was trying to make us out to be liars." Cora gave me a look.

"I know, we *were* lying, but I mean he was trying to make himself out to be the only one who could find out if we were hiding something."

"Nicholas, I know you were teaching him a lesson because of how he treated you, but—"

"No, for what he did to Elle," I shot back.

"That's all fine and good but we, I mean you, have something bigger to do, and you can't afford to mess it up. You heard what could happen if we don't succeed."

"Did Riley ever tell you about that other stuff?"

"Some, but not the stuff about us failing and the consequences," Cora said.

"Cora, I'm not sure I would have agreed to do this if I had known what failing would mean. Too many people could get hurt or killed. Also, Reed Godfree told us an entirely different reason for The 7 to be formed than Riley did."

"Nicholas, it doesn't really matter that their stories don't match. Riley warned us that they might try to twist things around," Cora said. She didn't look at me for fear I would read her, but I knew that she was hiding her fear about us failing. I also found it interesting how much she trusted Riley now, when she didn't want to trust him at all in the beginning. My trust in Riley was wavering because of the conflicting stories. Maybe Riley was right about them trying to weaken our alliance, but I wasn't sure.

CONSEQUENCES
CHAPTER EIGHTEEN

Cora and I slept at a rest stop for a while on the trip home, even though that meant we wouldn't get back in time for me to go to school. The autumn air was damp, making it feel even colder than it was. My body was calling for the warmth of my down comforter. All I wanted to do was get inside, lie down and listen to music until football practice that afternoon, but when we pulled into our driveway, Genevieve and Riley were waiting for us on the porch. I ignored them and walked into the house. I went up to my room and closed the door, locking it. I didn't want to talk to them about what happened. The long ride home gave me a lot of time to question everything even more. The only thing I was sure of right now was Elle—nothing else.

Of course, now that I was home and in bed, I couldn't relax. I waited in my room for over an hour, hoping Genevieve and Riley would leave. I went downstairs to get something to eat, and unfortunately they were still here. I could hear their voices from the steps. It sounded like Riley was worked up about something. I went back upstairs and grabbed a pack of

Tic Tacs off of my dresser just in case, and then headed to the kitchen.

"What do you mean, Cora?" I heard Riley say in a very stern voice like he was lecturing one of the players on the team.

I walked into the kitchen. Both Cora and Genevieve were sitting around the table. Riley was leaning against the counter with his arms folded.

"Why don't you ask Nicholas if you don't believe me?" Cora said.

"Ask me what?"

"I told Riley that we didn't get interrogated," Cora said, "and he still doesn't believe me, even after an hour of me telling him the same thing over and over."

"Cora's right. They kept calling us their 'guests.' Even though that snake, James Caldwell, tried to make me out to be a liar. Besides him, everyone was nice and pleasant," I said while getting an apple off the kitchen table.

"What else happened?" Riley demanded like I was hiding something. I guess they had been questioned intensely. He looked like he was on the verge of losing it. But who cared what happened to him?

"It's not what else happened, it's what else I learned, Riley," I said.

"What's that supposed to mean?" Riley stood straight up.

I walked right up to him. Riley was a lot taller than me, but I wasn't intimidated in the least.

"It means that you didn't tell us the whole story, did you? You forgot to tell us some pretty important parts about The 7, like how they were originally formed, and the part that makes me the angriest—the possibility that a lot of people could die if we fail. If you honestly thought that I would sit back and let you continue to lie to us and put so many people in jeopardy, then you are sadly mistaken. I want to know everything. We deserve it." I poked him in the chest and he pulled away, like my finger was a needle.

Riley stumbled and caught the counter. He leaned up against it and rubbed his hands over his face, exhaling.

"You're right, Nicholas, I was wrong not to tell you before. I will tell the three of you everything, but you have to hear me out." Genevieve looked stunned that he hadn't told her everything, either. She stared blankly up at Riley.

"My story about how The 7 came about is different. The Council probably said that they came up with it to keep the Seekers in check, like its own little council. But that is the lie they fed to all the Thusians. The Council wanted to wipe out everything the Keepers said and did, along with anyone who knew the truth, especially about The 7. As I told you before, my parents were two of the last real Thusian historians. They pieced together, in their research, that some of the Thusians grew jealous of Keeper Wren's alleged power. That's when they stripped him of his authority and formed the Thusian Council. But that wasn't good enough, so they formed the Seekers to eliminate Keeper Wren and to use them like some sort of death squad on anyone else that stood as a threat. The Keepers were not really leaders; they just guided Thusians and knew the traditions and the blood lines. The entire lineage was in their heads. They were like human encyclopedias.

189

The Council wanted this knowledge so they could use it for themselves. So the first historians tried to pass the true history down through the generations because the Keepers were gone. Not the stuff the Council wanted everyone to know, but what really had happened."

"Enough of the history lesson, Riley. Get to the part about The 7 and what will happen if we fail to find the 4th." I was growing angrier and angrier.

"When Keeper Wren was ousted, he foretold that there had to be a balance between good and evil, and that the Seekers would destroy the balance, because Thusians were already fighting against the everyday evils of the world. They didn't need anything else working against—"

"Riley, listen to me," I interrupted, growing angrier by the second. "I don't care about that stuff," I yelled. "We know the whole good versus evil thing already. Why didn't you tell us about the consequences of failing?"

"Because failing is not an option!" he yelled back.

"I think you didn't tell us because if we fail, it would create The Unholy Six and that would allow the Seekers to kill thousands of Thusians, which means tens of thousands of people could die along with them."

"We are the last hope for the Thusians and for the world," he pleaded. "There are even those who think that the Seekers are still good to have around to keep Thusians in check, when the truth is that our inevitable Final Sacrifice is our check. No matter how our numbers grow or shrink, the sacrifices will always balance everything. It's just how it's supposed to be and, yes, if we don't succeed a lot of people will die, but,

Nicholas, what do you think will happen if we don't try? The Seekers will still kill a lot of people. So there is only one way to equal things out and put an end to this: find the 4th. We don't have much time—they are hunting us." He sighed and looked away, exhausted. The emotions were pouring from him. "Nicholas, the only way to protect Elle is to do this," he said.

I calmed down immediately. All of the anger I was feeling was gone at the mention of her safety. I didn't know if I could entirely trust him, but Riley was right about one thing. This was the only way that I could help protect her and everyone else I cared for, no matter whose story was right.

"From now on, you tell all of us everything," I said.

He nodded. "I have one more thing," he added. "When we find the 4th—and we will—he or she will help us get rid of the Seekers and the Council, restoring the balance to how it used to be. Then, finally, they will stop watching our every move. The Council fails to remember that the Thusians' sole purpose is to use their talents to protect and serve the world, not to make money and do who knows what else with that power."

Cora stood up and walked to Riley's side to comfort him. I walked out of the room. Genevieve followed after me.

"You know the 4th is going through their Realization, developing their talents right now. They probably started to develop them last year when we caught up with you," she said.

"And?" I didn't see her point.

"That means our time is running out. They are probably past the whole bad dream thing and weird things happening inside them. They must know they have some sort of strange talents. We should focus on that."

"Genevieve, say we do find them. How are we supposed to tell them that they are part of an ancient group that is supposed to sacrifice their lives for others? Oh yeah, and while they are waiting to die they are responsible for helping us fight this evil death squad. Because I am pretty sure I wouldn't have believed that if you had told me. Our candidates don't have the family history to back up our stories when we do tell them."

"I know that's part of the challenge, Nicholas. I have faith that you, I mean we, can find them and make them a believer." She bit her bottom lip like she was caught in some embarrassing slip up.

I found myself twirling that blank coin in my fingers again as I lay in bed later, waiting to go to practice. Just two nights ago, Elle and I shared the most incredible night together at Homecoming, but as usual the memories had now been overshadowed by something else. Why couldn't I be like everyone else? The picture of Elle at Homecoming swirled around in my head like a ghost of some distant memory. I knew I had to succeed in our search in order to keep Elle safe.

LOSS

CHAPTER NINETEEN

"Nicholas, are you okay?" Coach Miller asked. I was sitting in the locker room after practice, staring at my old locker and thinking. I didn't answer him, still suspended in deep thought, looking at my reflection in the Plexiglas.

"Son, are you okay?" he asked again, but this time more firmly.

"Oh yes, sir. I just have a lot on my mind. Sorry, but I better get going." I tried to escape him, but he sat down next to me.

"So what's troubling you?"

It would have been so nice to be able to tell him about everything, but I couldn't. Like every other situation, I would have to lie to protect him. I was getting ready to tell him some story when he spoke.

"Nicholas, I would like to tell you something about myself, but you have to promise not to tell anyone."

Great. Another secret.

"When I was your age, I started dating a girl named Lillian Grace Gartner. She was my Lilly. She was the most beautiful creature I had ever seen. It was love at first sight. We went steady most of my junior and senior years. You may have heard that I played football here at Winsor. I was offered several scholarships to play in college. Lilly planned on going to the same school as me, but her mom got sick, so she couldn't go away to school. Lilly couldn't leave her. I remember thinking to myself how amazing it was that she was willing to sacrifice going to school for her mother. So her act of sacrifice inspired me to do the same. I stayed home, forgoing college to be with her, which also allowed me to help take care of my father, who was getting older.

"Under the biggest oak tree in the center of our farm, I asked Lilly to marry me one year and two days after our graduation. It took me that long to save up enough money to buy a ring and put money down on a house. The ring wasn't anything fancy, but Lilly loved it.

"Prior to our engagement, I joined the volunteer fire department. One of my friends, Brady Metzger from the football team, asked me to join because they needed help. It wasn't like the fire department we have today here in Winsor. It was just a bunch of guys with one very basic water pump truck and that was it. It turned out that I was a pretty good fireman. My football talents turned out to be just what I needed to do my job well.

"On June 15, two weeks before we were planning to send out invitations to our wedding, Lilly went to our house around 11:00 a.m. to continue working on getting everything ready for us to move in. I was in the field with my dad when

I heard the bell ringing to call the firemen to the station. The closer we got to the fire, the more I started to get a sinking feeling in my stomach. The truck entered Lilly and my neighborhood and stopped outside of our house. It was fully engulfed in flames. I looked back and forth to find Lilly, but she was nowhere. The guys were trying to get as much water onto the house as they could. Without thinking, I ran straight for the front door, which was in flames, knocking it down with my axe. I screamed for her but there was no response. The house was filled with a dark, dense, black smoke. Right next to the back door, I found her with one hand on the door, lying on the ground covered in burning pieces of the house. I kicked the debris off her and scooped her up. I knocked down the back door and got her away from the house. I was immediately mobbed by people who tried to help me revive her. She didn't respond. In her arms she was clutching a photo of our families that she had wanted to keep on our night stand."

I was shocked that he had just shared this with me. He cleared his throat.

"The reason I've told you this is because I know what it feels like to lose someone you love. You saved all of those people while your parents died. I, too, have saved people both before and after she was gone, but I was not able to save the one who meant the most to me. But instead of living each day regretting that I wasn't there in time, I live each day remembering who she was and what she meant to me. Every day I work hard to honor her memory. Nicholas, you and

I are a lot alike, so please learn from this old man. I spent years trying to run from it all too. But don't make the same mistakes, because all the running in the world can never get you far enough away or bring them back."

He patted me on the shoulder and left.

**

Coach Miller's story inspired me. It was my responsibility to honor my parents' sacrifices by finding the 4th, hopefully saving a lot of lives in the process. Coach Miller and I became a lot closer after that. Not only was I part of the coaching staff, but now I was helping plan the defensive strategies. I didn't know all of the X's and O's, but I knew what worked. Coach Miller and I came up with some crippling defensive strategies, which carried us on to win another state championship. There was talk that some of the top colleges in the nation were looking at Coach Miller to take over their programs. He dismissed those as rumors, but we all knew it was true.

In the championship parade, I sat right next to him and Riley. The problem with the parade was that it was covered by all the national sports and news programs because our team was said to be the greatest high school team in the last thirty years. I wore one of the Winsor football sweatshirts and kept the hood up so I could hide my face, and so did Riley. Bryce was featured on every one of the TV sports programs. The clip of him running over that player from Sycamore was being played again and again. If Xavier didn't know who we were focusing on before, he did now. But on the brighter side,

I felt like I really belonged with the team and was really part of this championship, not like last year with my fake injury.

Now that football was over, we were able to dedicate 100-percent of our time to searching. We had to hurry because of all the hype around Bryce. He continued to be our leading candidate. But Elle and a newcomer, Eric's older brother, were now part of the group we were considering for the 4th. Riley said it was important not to limit our options. Eric's older brother Seth was added to the list because he was a Navy Seal. He had been awarded a lot of medals for bravery in the line of duty. I met him after one of the football games. He wasn't what I expected for a Navy hero. He was only about 5'10" and skinny. He had to have some talents to aid him. He didn't exactly fit the profile of the 4th because he had received all of the medals over an eight year period, not over the past year when the 4th would have gone through his or her Realization. However, Riley thought he could have been brave from the beginning and now he might have gained his full talents.

Riley had met him several times and really felt a bond with him. Actually, the only reason Riley liked him was because of what he could do as part of our group. A Navy Seal would be an asset to the team. He would be perfect to lead us in crushing Xavier and the Seekers once and for all. Genevieve and I were on the fence about him, but Cora agreed with Riley, again, which was getting pretty annoying, because she agreed with everything he said. It was like she didn't have a mind of her own anymore. If I didn't know any better, I would have thought that she had grown to care for him. Elle was still in the running too because of my intense connection with her and the way she moved when the bus almost hit us on the field trip. We were down to our final three candidates. We were close now, and we couldn't afford to make any mistakes.

For my birthday, November 23, I didn't want to do much, but Elle insisted on cooking me dinner and taking me to the Esquire Theater, which was showing classic movies. We ended up seeing *Ferris Bueller's Day Off.* The whole time we were watching the show, I kept thinking that Ferris reminded me a lot of Eric—it was so funny. At the end of the night, she gave me a playlist of her favorite songs. I hated my birthday and getting gifts, but this was a nice surprise. Now I could listen to this mix whenever I wasn't with Elle.

The first week in December, Cora insisted that we should have a large Christmas party at Riley and Genevieve's house so we could get a better look at the three candidates. Riley and Cora must have already discussed it because Riley just nodded his head, agreeing with her every word. As time went on, our group was being divided. Genevieve and I were on our own and Riley and Cora were together. For the first time, I didn't feel like Cora was thinking of my well-being. I should have been okay with that, because that's what I had wanted for her for a long time, to be able to live her own life. But the other half of me missed it just being Cora and me. Those days were unfortunately over.

The night of the Christmas party brought thick, dark clouds and some light powdery snow. The four of us worked for three days straight to get their house looking as festive as possible. We made several trips back and forth to the store because none of us had decorations to put up. I was in charge of the lights on the outside of the house. My inspiration was what the school looked like last year for Homecoming. So I wrapped every one of the trees and bushes in the yard with white lights. I lined the outline of the roof with white icicles. And to light the guests' way up to the house, I used large white bulbs along the path. We invited so many people that we had to get a valet service to park the cars. I put out a small stand and wrapped it in white lights for the valets to use. Luckily, there was a field on the other side of their house where they could park the cars. The party was by invitation only. I think we had invited 200 guests and it looked like all 200 were coming. I invited all of my friends from school and Cora invited some of the families she had gotten to know during football and the dances. Riley and Genevieve invited the teachers, staff and others involved with the school. A buzz was created around the party weeks before the event. People were already talking about how it was the party to attend this Christmas. Part of the reason everyone wanted to come was because Chase would be there. His celebrity status made the party that much more desirable to attend.

I stood outside admiring the lights on the house, making sure I hadn't missed any spots. Genevieve walked out the front door. She was wrapped in a large red shawl and stood next to me looking at the lights. She looked stunning. She was wearing a form-fitting, snow white dress. Usually, her dresses were more on the revealing side, but this dress was elegant. The white lights and snow seemed to complement her like they were her accessories for the party.

"You did a great job, Nicholas." She leaned over and put her head briefly on my shoulder.

"Thanks. You look beautiful tonight."

She smiled.

"So are we ready inside yet?" I asked.

"Of course. Cora is determined to make everything perfect. I left poor Riley in there alone with her. I'm sure that he didn't know what he was agreeing to when she wanted to do this party."

"How did you get out?" I asked.

"When she went to check on the food, I made my break. But I have to admit she does this well. It's going to be a very nice evening." She paused. "So what's the plan tonight?" she asked.

"I will work on Eric's brother. You and Cora need to work on Elle, and Riley will handle Bryce. We need to try to get as much information as we can from them. And you will definitely need Cora's help with Elle."

Genevieve put her hand on my shoulder. I looked at her.

"What do you mean by I'll 'need help with Elle'?" she asked.

She had to know that Elle didn't care for her, even though she had been on her best behavior as of late. Genevieve looked at me like she had no idea what I meant.

"Elle's hard to connect with sometimes. I was just saying

that Cora already has a great relationship with her and you will need to use that."

"Nicholas, don't lie to me. You're pretty bad at it."

That was funny, because my whole life has been one big lie. "She's jealous of you. I don't know why, but I think that's what it is." I thought I saw a fleeting smile.

"That's silly," she said and turned away.

Who knows if she was sincere? But I did agree with her, it was silly.

"I know. She has nothing to be jealous of," I said as she walked back toward the house. I couldn't figure her out at all.

Elle arrived thirty minutes earlier than anyone else. She was wearing a beautiful red lace dress with cute jingle bell earrings and necklace. Her sparkling eyes left me momentarily helpless. She grabbed my arm and kissed me on the cheek, bringing me back to this world. The warmth of her lips spread throughout my body. I was glad she was the first to show up, since I knew that most of the night she would be with Cora and Genevieve, not me. I was right because as soon as Cora saw her, she asked if Elle would help get things ready. She looked at me for permission to go.

I smiled and whispered in her ear, "Don't worry, we have all night."

She walked into the kitchen area.

The party guests began to show up. Bryce and Erin came together at the beginning of the party, which I was happy to see. I turned out to be a pretty good matchmaker. Riley moved in on them immediately. Riley's plan was to take

Bryce around, bragging about him to the different people at the party. It would be easy because Bryce and Chad were co-MVPs of the state championship game. Erin would just have to follow him around.

I was getting nervous that Eric and Seth wouldn't show. The only thing that eased my mind was knowing that Eric would never miss the biggest party of the year. He lived for these things. Eric and Seth finally arrived. They looked like the complete opposite of each other. Eric was wearing jeans with a navy blue shirt and a crazy red Christmas tie that blinked and sang. Seth was dressed in a sport coat and slacks.

"What's up?" Eric asked.

"Not a whole lot." I extended my hand to Seth, but Eric grabbed it and shook it.

Seth grabbed Eric's arm and he let go wincing in pain.

"None of that Seal death grip crap. I'm not the enemy," Eric whined.

Seth extended his arm and shook my hand. "It's nice to see you again, Nicholas."

"So Eric, where's Livi? I thought she was coming," I said.

"Nah, I came here as a bachelor. So lookout girls, Eric Iery is on the prowl," he said loudly at the front door. Everyone around us gave him strange looks.

I didn't believe him.

"So, Livi couldn't come?" I asked.

Seth, standing behind him nodded empathically, mouthing the words, "She's sick."

"So is Chad here?" Eric asked.

"I think Chad and Amber are over by the food."

Eric rubbed both hands together and walked away toward the food. I didn't think I was going to be alone with Seth so quickly. I was caught off-guard.

"So, Seth, Eric tells me you're a Seal."

"Yes, I've been a Navy Seal for the last eight years. I'm out of active duty now, and I only serve as an advisor to them."

"What do you advise them on?"

"Sorry, Nicholas, I can't tell you." He smiled, but I could tell that he was serious.

"Seth, I've heard that people in the military often can't sleep or have bad dreams. Is that true?" Wow, that sounded weird. I was absolutely horrible at this interrogating thing. Way to go. He looked at me like I had horns growing out of my forehead. I had to think quickly. "Because, I'm doing a report on that sort of thing for school and I thought I could get a couple of quotes for my paper." He still looked at me skeptically. "If you don't mind?" I added.

He looked at me like he was offended. He leaned in close to me. What was he going to say? I braced myself.

He laughed. "Sure. No problem, Nicholas. I was just messing around. Eric told me you were easy to tease."

What a relief. I asked him a series of questions, some that pertained to being a Thusian and others that were just questions I made up. He definitely was a true hero. But I didn't think he was the one we were looking for. He never had a bad dream that he could remember. Also, when he talked about his heroic acts, he said that his incredible training, team and plan got him through every situation, no matter how difficult.

Seth saw a couple of teachers he had not seen for a while. "Nicholas, it's been great talking to you. See you around." He turned around and walked over to them.

I went looking for Elle. I hadn't seen her in a long time. Standing in the kitchen side-by-side were Elle and Genevieve. They were smiling and laughing. It looked like they had been friends for years. It was good to see them both smiling together. For the first time this year, I felt close to Genevieve. Maybe this was a good thing, especially if Elle turned out to be the 4th. Then all of us would get along perfectly. Seeing Genevieve stirred some emotion in me that was foreign. I ignored it and walked up to them.

"Can I help you ladies?"

"No, I think Genevieve and I have it covered. Why don't you go have fun?" Elle sounded like Cora telling me to go out and play with my friends while she fixed dinner. Genevieve didn't look up at me, but she smiled.

Elle was serious. They continued making food while I stood there. I looked around the room and saw Bryce. Riley's arm was around him, ushering him over to another group of people. From the expression on Bryce's face, he wanted to escape. Erin was not with him anymore. She had found Eric, Chad and Amber over by the large Christmas tree near the table with food.

I walked over to Riley and Bryce.

"Hey, Bryce," I said. The look on his face was a cry for help.

As soon as Riley saw me, he winked. "Nicholas, you're just in time. You remember Mr. and Mrs. Theasing."

I hadn't noticed who he was standing with. What was he thinking? This was not good.

"Nicholas, this is such a surprise," Ester said.

What did she mean by surprise? This was partially our party, too. Or was it a cryptic way of saying that she was surprised we were trying to find the 4th. The best plan now would be to avoid her altogether.

"Can I steal Bryce? I need his help."

Bryce didn't wait for me. He hurried away from them. I followed him all the way to the other side of the room. He didn't stop for anything. When he reached the wall, he turned around.

"Nicholas, thank you. The last hour has been torture. I wanted to enjoy a nice Christmas party with Erin, but Coach Moore trapped me." He was breathing heavily.

"Bryce, I know how you feel. I prefer to stay in the background."

"Yeah, that's where I want to be." He smiled.

"Let's go find Erin," I suggested. He grinned at the sound of her name.

Everyone was having a great time. The party brought back memories of my dad's Christmas parties at the firehouse. My mom would dress up in some really nice Christmas dress and Dad would dress up and wear a Santa hat. My dad always did those types of fun things. The firehouse would be packed with all the families of the firemen. The kids saw Santa and got gifts. Every year I looked forward to going down the firehouse pole. It was so much fun. But it seemed like they would always get a call to respond to a fire in the middle of the party. Luckily, the last Christmas we were together, they didn't. We were able to enjoy the entire party. After that we went to see a couple of houses that had the most incredible Christmas displays. One even had a real Nativity with people and animals. My mom held on to my dad to stay warm and she pulled me in close. They would have loved this party.

"Excuse me. Can I have everyone's attention? Please, can I have your attention?" I couldn't place whose voice it was over the sounds of the party. I pushed through the crowd to see who it was. There was a lot of excitement near the large Christmas tree in front of the big front window. It was Chase. He was surrounded by a dozen women and girls who were watching his every move. I was surprised I hadn't seen him enter the party, because he was always so grandiose.

"Thank you, everyone. I would like to thank Riley and Genna Moore for throwing such an incredible Christmas party along with Nicholas and Cora Keller."

He clapped and everyone followed along.

"It's great to be able to mingle with such ordinary, everyday people like yourselves. I am truly blessed."

He's such an idiot, but they still clapped and cheered anyway.

"Please raise your glasses and toast our hosts and hostesses. Merry Christmas and Happy Holidays," he said loudly in a deep voice.

Everyone began wishing "Merry Christmas" and "Happy Holidays" to anyone who was near them. It was like a scene out of *A Christmas Carol*; we were just missing Tiny Tim.

Chase lowered his glass, but he didn't look like he was done speaking. Like Eric, he loved to be in the spotlight.

"Can I please have everyone's attention one more time? His eyes scanned the room. "Cora Keller, could you please come up here?" The crowd searched for her, following his eyes.

"She's right here," someone yelled from the corner of the room.

"Folks, can you please give her a round of applause to get her up here?" The party started clapping. Everyone parted out of her way as she walked up to Chase. He grabbed her and pulled her close. Her face matched the red of his Christmas blazer.

"Cora and I have known each other for a very long time. She and Nicholas are as close to a family as I have ever had."

Yeah right. I bet his mirror is all the family he needs, I thought.

"Cora is such an incredible woman," Chase said with his large arm still around her. He reached into his pocket and pulled out a small black box. That couldn't be an engagement ring. Cora glanced up, petrified. Riley, who was next to them, looked angry, but before Chase spoke again, Riley disappeared into the crowd.

Chase, still holding on to Cora, got down on one knee. The crowd gasped. I couldn't believe this. Could she have really become that close to him over the summer?

"Cora Keller, would you do me the honor of marrying me?" He opened the box. The diamond was enormous. The light reflecting off it made the room look like it had a disco ball in it. The women around him began to cry. I don't know how I missed seeing Joy Lemmins, but she was right up front, close to Chase. She was not even invited and yet there she stood, looking like a bright silver Christmas ornament. Every part of her that could sparkle did. Her reaction was not like the others'. She looked like a desperate woman. Her head was swinging back and forth, looking from side to side, like she didn't know what to do. Then she smiled, closed her eyes and fell straight forward, landing just inches away from the kneeling Chase. She hit with a loud thud. Her beaded hat exploded, sending small silver beads over the entire floor. Chase immediately turned to see if she was okay. That was Cora's chance. She slipped out of his grip and disappeared through the crowd.

"Nicholas, come here." Chase spotted me. "Go find Cora. I need to attend to Ms. Lemmins, then I will come for her."

Joy had figured out that he would always take care of someone that needed medical attention, no matter what. He had to because of the Thusian in him. It was his sacrifice, and now for the first time, it looked like it was a curse for him too. Even if he didn't want to, he had to help. Luckily for Cora, Joy was demented enough to put herself through countless injuries in order to spend time with Chase.

NO

CHAPTER TWENTY

Chase, of course, had to take Joy to the hospital, to her delight. Cora and Riley were nowhere to be found. Most of the guests left after Joy hit the ground. Elle and I were picking up all of the garbage that was left behind, and Genevieve was busy cleaning dishes in the kitchen.

"Nicholas, you're the best. You really know how to throw a party," Eric said, staggering down the hall with his jacket thrown over his shoulder, pretending to be drunk. "The entertainment was stuuuu-pendous."

Seth laughed. "Very funny, Eric," he said, "but if I ever find out that you have been drinking underage, I will break you in half." He grabbed the back of Eric's jacket like he was taking out the trash.

"I don't drink. I'm not that stupid," Eric said, trying to pull away from Seth. Seth tightened his grip and dragged him out the front door. They were the last to leave because they were trying their hardest to get Genevieve to pay attention to them, but with no luck.

"Where's Cora?" Elle asked.

"Not sure. I am giving her some room, you know."

"I can't believe that Dr. Chase Letterby asked her to marry him. There are going to be a lot of broken-hearted women around the world if she says yes." Elle smiled.

"She's not going to say yes," I said quickly.

"How do you know?"

"Just a feeling." I really didn't know, but I knew she didn't feel that way about him. Well, at least I was hoping that was the case. I didn't want her to marry him because she deserved so much better. But maybe this was her only way to escape the danger that I was putting her in. Chase would definitely protect her, and probably take better care of her than anyone else. Chase was arrogant, but he did love her.

Elle ended up leaving not long after Eric and Seth. I walked her out to the car.

"As soon as I check on Cora, I will come over," I said.

I walked back into the house and down the hallway. I heard voices from one of the bedrooms. It was Riley and Cora. I opened the door. Cora had been crying and Riley was standing off to the side, not trying to comfort her at all. His arms were crossed and he was looking down at the floor.

"What's going on in here?" I demanded. Riley brushed by me. "Cora, are you okay?" I went over to her.

She rubbed her eyes and took a deep breath. "Nicholas, don't worry about me. I'll be fine." She stood up and tried to walk past me. I caught her arm. I had to tell her that she could marry Chase if she wanted to. She had given up Marcus, the love of her life, to keep me safe. If she wanted this, then she had my blessing.

"Cora, I want you to marry Chase if that's what you want. I can't ask you to give up this chance for me. You deserve to be happy."

With a big tearful grin, she laughed and wiped away a few stray tears. "Nicholas, don't be ridiculous. I don't love him."

"Then why are you crying?"

She paused. "It just reminded me of my past."

We didn't say anything else after that. I just held on to her, giving as much comfort as I could. I began to wonder what Riley had said to her, but right now was not the time to ask.

Genevieve and Riley had finished cleaning up the rest of the party's mess by the time we came out. I sat down on the family room couch, and they both came over and sat down with me. Cora emerged a few minutes later, looking a lot more composed. Everything in the house had been moved back into its place. The only evidence of a party was the punch bowl on the table in the kitchen, some decorations and the Christmas tree. All the inside lights had been turned off, so now only the outside lights were illuminating the interior with their wonderful winter glow.

"That was an interesting party," Genevieve said, looking at Riley and Cora to see their expressions.

"It sure was. So, Cora, are you going to be Mrs. Doctor or not?" Riley asked rudely.

Cora stood abruptly and walked up to him, blocking our view of his face.

"It's none of your business what I do," she said calmly. Genevieve grabbed her arm, just in case her calmness turned to rage. Cora took a deep, angry breath and jerked free from her grip, then sat back down.

"I don't know what has gotten into everyone. We were supposed to be checking out the three candidates and reporting back about what we found out," I said. "But instead we are talking about Chase. Of course she's not going to marry him. If you don't know that by now, Riley, then you don't know Cora at all. And even if she did, it's none of your business."

"Nicholas, you are absolutely right. I am sorry for the way I have treated you tonight, Cora. You didn't deserve that and of course I know that you wouldn't marry him. But, Nicholas, you're wrong. It *is* my business what she does." He turned and looked directly at her. "We might be searching for the 4th, but you will always be part of our group in my eyes," he said.

Riley and Cora just stared at each other. I couldn't figure out what was going on. I guess Genevieve didn't care anymore, because she was now sitting sideways on the couch, exposing most of her legs and her neon orange gym shoes.

"Nicholas, you go first," Riley said.

"Before I forget, I want to know what you were doing parading Bryce around in front of the Theasings. You told us not to trust anyone and there you were doing something so stupid like that. Are you trying to get us caught? I'm starting to think you are the one we can't trust."

He didn't even acknowledge what I said. He just sat in place, looking out at the lights. It made me angry. I yelled, "Do you hear me, Riley?"

That got his attention. He still didn't say anything, but

he nodded his head like he knew what he did was wrong. There was something else going on with Riley. He was just not letting on to it. Everything about him was just off, like he was hiding something again.

"Seth is not the one we are looking for," I said. "Seth doesn't suffer from any bad dreams at all. He actually always has good dreams. And all of his heroic stuff was due to his training and his unit's plans. Whenever one of my talents comes out, it's not always controlled or planned. He may be a Thusian, but he's not the 4th."

Genevieve spoke next, sitting back up. "Elle could be the one we are searching for. Cora and I learned that she hasn't been sleeping well for some time. She doesn't remember her dreams, but she still doesn't sleep well. This might be because of the accident last year, but it sounds just like my Realization. I didn't remember any bad dreams, but I knew I hadn't slept well either. I also found out that she is a pretty great person. It would be a shame if she's not the one," she concluded, looking at me. "Do you have a problem with that, Nicholas?" Genevieve asked.

"What are you talking about?" I responded, puzzled.

Genevieve looked mad. "You have a grin on your face like I said something that amused you."

I must have been smiling outwardly at what she was saying and didn't realize it. She didn't like Elle at first and now she did. It had to be eating her up on the inside.

"I don't have a problem. I was smiling about the part where you said you think she's a great person. You have never really liked her before."

I waited for her to answer angrily, but she didn't. Instead, she sat back on the couch.

Cora just sat motionless. She didn't add anything to what Genevieve said. I guess she was still preoccupied with Riley.

"Well, I don't think there is any doubt about it. Bryce is the 4th," Riley said. "His bad dreams have been getting worse over the year, and he told one of the football boosters that he felt like someone else took over his body on the field when he was playing. That's classic Thusian. The only way for us to know for sure now is to find out when he started to gain his talents. It would have to be last year around the end of summer or right before he came to Winsor."

"How are we going to find that out?" Cora asked, now part of the conversation again.

Riley leaned toward Cora like he was going to reach out and touch her, but his hand never left his lap.

"We talked about that a while ago, right Riley?" Genevieve said, hoping that he would answer Cora's question.

"Yes, yes we did," he said. "The only way we can find out is for Nicholas to ask him straight out."

"What, are you kidding? Why me?" I protested. "A coach would have better luck asking him about gaining talents. You could pretend like it was football-related, you know for college or something."

"You need to ask him. He would think it was weird if I asked about last year's football season when football is over now," Riley said. "And we need more details than just football-related stuff."

"Are you kidding? It's going to sound so stupid coming

from me. 'So, Bryce, have you gone through any changes you want to talk about?' It sounds like I am some crazy person asking if he's gone through puberty yet."

"But you are crazy," Genevieve said sarcastically.

"No, Nicholas," said Riley. "He feels a real connection, a friendship with you. He's more likely to open up to you than any of us. When I was showing him around tonight, he kept talking about how much of a help you were when he first got to school. He thinks the world of you."

I couldn't really argue with that. I wanted to, but I couldn't. "Okay then, when should I ask?"

"You should wait a while," Cora said. "He had to answer a lot of questions tonight. I know time is not on our side, but we need to give him some space. We will be able to get what we need from him closer to spring." Her confidence made the rest of us nod our heads in agreement.

"Okay then. We need to start protecting Bryce and Elle at all times, even though Bryce is most likely the one. We can't take any chances. We are too close," Riley said. "It's important that both of them have someone watching over them at all times. Their safety is now as important as ours. I am guessing that the Council has to be on to us by now. They may play nice, but they're not stupid. And there is no doubt in my mind that there has to be at least one Seeker on the Council, so that means that Xavier knows, too."

My thoughts wandered to James Caldwell and how he treated me at the Council meeting. If there was someone helping Xavier on the Council, he was at the top of my list.

FAVOR

CHAPTER TWENTY-ONE

Our winter break started the week before Christmas. Elle and I spent every moment together, making it easier to guard her from any threat. Chase spent almost as much time with Cora that week as I did with Elle. She had turned down his marriage proposal, but in true Dr. Chase Letterby fashion, he told her that she was right to say no because he needed more time before he could make such a commitment to her. Cora couldn't exactly kick him out, because that would definitely make him wonder what was going on and possibly tip off Ester Theasing, if she didn't already know. We couldn't afford for the Council to find out any more than they already knew. Keeping Bryce and Elle safe was almost a 24-hour job. Cora was left at home with Chase. Genevieve and Riley took turns together watching Bryce, and I continued watching over Elle.

"Elle, could you please come up here," Elle's father yelled down to her halfway through a movie we were watching. A couple of minutes after Elle had gone up there, Mr. Canan raised his voice and Elle loudly answered back. She came stomping down the stairs.

"You have to go."

"Why?"

"My dad would like to watch TV. And yes, I already told him there are three other TVs in the house."

"No problem, Elle, I can see you tomorrow."

It was a problem, because I wanted to spend time with her in here, not sitting out in my truck watching her house. Over the last week my sickness had come back with a vengeance from the stress of protecting her. I was so worried about her. Once again, I was personally making the owners of Tic Tacs wealthy.

"Yes, you can see me tomorrow, but I am coming with you now," she said.

"What's your father going to say?" I asked.

"I don't care. I'll meet you at the truck."

I put my jacket on and walked out into the cold, brisk air, which stung my lungs. I started up the truck, leaving the lights off just in case I had to make a quick getaway. I stuck my hands under my legs, trying to keep them warm. The only bad thing about my dad's old truck was it was drafty, letting the cold air come right in. I could feel an icy breeze working through the truck. My breath was fogging the windows so I could only just see the blurry outline of her house. Then a figure started to get bigger and bigger. It walked to the passenger-side of the truck. Before I could get out, Elle hopped in.

"Sorry I didn't get the door for you."

"It's fine, Nicholas, just go."

I put the truck in reverse, turned on the defrost and pulled out. Elle had put her seat belt on, but put a lot of slack in it so she could lay her head on my shoulder.

"Is everything all right?" I asked.

"No, not really." She sat back up in her seat. "Nicholas, pull in that driveway up ahead."

The driveway belonged to Winsor Presbyterian, a local church close to her house. I drove around to the back of the church and put the truck in park. My truck was finally putting out some heat.

"Nicholas, don't you wish we could just run away?"

Elle was taking off her jacket. She left on her scarf and her bright, woven yellow hat. She looked adorable.

"What do you mean, run away?" I turned the truck off because it was getting too hot.

"You know, just you and me. We could be together forever, with no cares or worries."

"What's going on?" I asked.

"It's my dad. He wants us to break up. He wants me to start concentrating on colleges. He thinks you're a distraction."

I put my hand on her knee. She closed her eyes and sighed at the touch.

"You see, that's what he means, but I don't care. I want to be with you for the rest of my life. You're the best distraction ever."

I wanted to tell her how I felt, but I couldn't. I was afraid—afraid about what the future would hold for us. Her soft hand was under my chin, forcing me to look deep into her eyes.

"Nicholas, I know you have had to be careful over the years not to get deeply involved with anyone, but you and I are meant to be together no matter what you are thinking right now. I know you love me because you said so, and that is something I cherish more than anything. I know how difficult this is for you." She thought my past was holding me back.

She leaned forward and kissed me. Her warm breath was intoxicating. She pulled me close to her, taking both of her hands and putting them behind my head. I was lost, spinning out of control. In this moment of weakness, I wanted to confess all of my secrets, but our kiss, thankfully, was preventing me from talking.

The sound of knuckles tapping on my driver-side window pulled me out of my state of bliss. We both looked shocked that someone was outside the truck. All of the windows had fogged up completely. There was absolutely no way to see through the glass. Elle and I were both in the passenger seat now, which was shocking because I didn't remember moving over there.

The fire in me lit. I was fearful that it was a Seeker, or worse, Xavier. What was I thinking? I couldn't afford to make mistakes like this. I decided to get out of the passenger-side door, so if I needed to I could grab Elle. I opened the door quickly and got out, shutting it most of the way. Everything around me stopped. I had one hand on Elle's arm ready to go. Standing in front of me was a police officer. I sized him up and saw his squad car back farther. The flashing lights on the car were red and blue. With time stopped, the lights combined to create a glowing purple color in the middle. He was still looking down at the driver-side door. He could be trouble, but I felt a little better about him and the situation.

Time went back to normal.

"Yes, sir?" I said.

He looked shocked that I was standing outside the passenger-side door so quickly.

"What are you doing here?" he questioned.

"We . . . well, my girlfriend and I were just . . . talking." After it came out of my mouth, I knew he didn't believe me. It was laughable. The windows were glazed over. Sure, we were "talking."

"Listen here, Mr. Keller. You and Ms. Canan should get on home, and tell Coach Miller he owes me another one for letting you off."

"Okay, sir, we'll be on our way. But why does Coach Miller owe you in the first place?"

What was I doing? He could take us to the station if he wanted to.

"Mr. Keller, I think you should be more concerned with getting your date home, don't you?"

He was right. I nodded. I don't know why I asked him that. I walked around the truck and got into the driver-side door and started it up. I used my sleeve to clear the windshield and I backed out, avoiding the squad car and driving slowly through the parking lot.

"How did he know who we were?" Elle asked, putting her jacket back on.

"Elle, it seems like everyone knows who we are."

"What were you talking about with him?" she asked, trying to wipe some of the fog off the passenger-side window.

"He told me to tell Coach Miller that he owes him

another one for letting me off. Do you know what he's talking about?" I asked.

"Maybe, I think that police officer helped Oliver," she replied. I was shocked to hear her say his name. "Oliver was supposed to stay in jail after he got out of the hospital. I think he helped him so he didn't have to stay there long. I'm not sure, but that's what my dad said."

Why would Coach Miller do that, I thought? How could he help Oliver after everything he had done? Sure, it was Xavier's fault, but none of them knew that. The idea of Coach Miller helping him made me angry.

"But Nicholas, let's not think about that. Because we should really be laughing about how we just got caught in a church parking lot making out." She leaned over and kissed my cheek. I took her hand and raised it up, slowly rubbing my lips over her hand. She was right. I laughed.

"Nicholas, I can't wait for Christmas. Don't forget, I will be over at your house around 5:00 p.m. tomorrow for Christmas Eve."

"For what?"

"Didn't Cora and Genevieve tell you?"

"Of course," I played along.

"Well great, I'll see you at five."

I gave Elle one final kiss goodnight when we got to her house. She bounced down the sidewalk and in the front door of her darkened house. She flicked the light off and on. With two honks of my horn, I was on my way home.

Why couldn't I just have a night with Elle that wasn't consumed by thoughts of Thusians, Oliver, or her dad trying to break us up (which was a new one, but one I expected at some point)?

The next morning brought Christmas Eve. I was sitting at the kitchen table eating breakfast. Chase was snoring loudly on the couch in the family room. Riley and Genevieve hadn't been over to the house with Chase here. I was starting to miss them a little bit. Genevieve did pop in from time to time, just so we could talk about who got what shift for watching Elle and Bryce. But besides that, they were absent.

Cora was at the kitchen counter with hundreds of ingredients spread out everywhere. She was busy cooking.

"So how long is Sleeping Beauty going to be staying?" I whispered.

"He is leaving tonight after our dinner."

"When were you going to tell me about dinner? Elle told me she was coming over, but I had no idea what she was talking about."

"Actually, it was Genevieve's idea. I told her that we never do anything special for Christmas Eve, but she insisted that this year we would do a family Christmas Eve dinner. Before I could talk to you about it, she invited Chase and Elle."

"Why dinner?"

"She said she wanted everyone to have their loved ones close to them for Christmas this year. Because who knows what next year might bring?"

Chase started to stir. It was time for me to get out of the house. I slipped on my jacket and hurried out the front door.

I saw Riley pull into their long driveway. He must have just been getting back from the night shift watching Bryce.

With only three of us able to watch them it was beginning to wear on us. Riley had volunteered to take the shifts watching Bryce. Genevieve and I now divided up the duties watching Elle. We all agreed that in the morning, they would be the safest. So from 9:00 a.m. to noon we would all try to get some sleep. With Chase occupying Cora's time at the house, Riley guarded Bryce all by himself, running on just a couple hours of sleep a day. We were all hoping Chase would leave soon so we could then split up the responsibility four ways. We were really supposed to watch in pairs, but we had to do what we could right now.

I walked over to his car. He looked sick. His eyes had large dark rings around them and his face was a sick grey color with a little green mixed in.

"Riley, are you feeling okay?" I asked, opening his door.

"Of course. Just a little tired. Let's get out of the cold, then we can talk."

Once inside his house, he started to look better. He coughed a couple of times, then said, "I had a long night, but an interesting one."

He started to make himself some tea in the kitchen. I stood there waiting for him to finish his thought. Once he got his hot tea, he put both hands around the mug and sipped out of it. The color returned to his face, but the dark circles remained.

"Bryce is the one. I know it for sure." He took another sip.

"How do you know?" I asked.

"I was sitting in my car, parked in the large empty lot across from his apartment building. His dad came home around 1:00 a.m. He was carrying a suitcase. I assumed that he had come home to spend the holidays with Bryce. The lights in the apartment went on one at a time. Then Bryce's bedroom light came on. His dad was standing in the living room. Bryce entered the room. I could see everything because the curtains were open just enough. They got into some sort of heated argument, right away. His dad cocked back to hit Bryce. But then everything slowed down for me, because Bryce was in danger of getting hit by his dad. Bryce moved to the side, escaping his dad's blurred arms and fists. Then Bryce shoved him into the window, causing a crack that slowly spider webbed out from the impact. Time then went back to normal. I couldn't see what happened next, but his dad carried his suitcase out with him a few minutes later and left. Thirty minutes after he left, each one of the lights in their apartment went off slowly. The way Bryce moved to the side and avoided his dad's punch makes him, without any doubt, the 4th. He will complete The 7."

I sat there not knowing how I felt. I should be happy, relieved because the search was over, but instead I felt bad for Bryce. Who knows how long his dad had been hitting him? That must have been how he got that bruise around his eye. I was glad it was him so he could escape that life and start a new one with us, even though his new life would be filled with more horrible things. At least now he could fight back.

"So what's next?" I asked.

"We need to start protecting him around the clock, no more breaks until we tell him the truth. Also we can ease up on protecting Elle." I didn't like the sound of that, but before I could object, he continued. "Nicholas, don't worry. We still need to watch Elle because of Xavier trying to kill her last year. But I think she is safe at her home at night with her parents."

"Cora said we should wait until spring to tell him, because that will be the best time," I said, reminding him, because I was sure he wanted to go over there now.

"I know what she said, but I saw what he did with my own two eyes. He is it."

"Okay, but still we are not going to tell him anything until the time is right," I said, reinforcing that point. "We can't just tell him something like this and expect that he will be fine with it."

"He needs to know right now, so we can finally take on the Seekers, and Bryce can help me kill the Council members who were responsible for my parents' deaths." Riley's eyes widened.

"What did you just say, Riley?" I stared at him, not sure if I heard him correctly. "Kill the Council members?"

"Nicholas, I meant to say, 'Kill the Seekers.'"

"That's not what you said. You said, 'Kill the Council members who were responsible for your parents' deaths.' Is that why you were showing Bryce off to Ester? You were introducing her to her possible executioner? If I didn't know better, I would think you were working with—"

He interrupted me before I could say Xavier's name. "The 4th will be able to help us eliminate the Council."

"But you said Bryce will help you kill the Council members responsible for your parents' deaths. What did you mean?" I asked angrily.

"My parents were two of the last true Thusian historians," his Irish accent returned, "and the Council felt threatened by them, so they killed my da and ma." He was now gritting his teeth. The muscles in his jaw were twitching. He looked like he was going to explode.

"Do you even know what putting together The 7 means?" I asked, not sure of anything he told us.

"No, not exactly. No one does. But it's the only way to restore things to the way they should be."

"So this whole thing is about revenge for you? How could you not tell us this? I knew you had more secrets. You're trying to use us as your own personal weapon to get revenge on the Council, just like how the Council used the Seekers. Breaking them up is one thing, but killing them is another. You know that's not right. We can't be like the Seekers." He wasn't looking at me anymore.

"Look at me," I demanded.

He slowly looked at me.

"We are going to wait until spring to tell Bryce, like Cora said. This will give you enough time to tell Cora and Genevieve your secret agenda. And I suggest you do it soon so I don't have to. No one will approach Bryce, Riley. This is not about your revenge; this is about our survival."

SECOND CHANCE
CHAPTER TWENTY-TWO

Our Christmas Eve dinner was very nice. Everyone was there except for Riley, who was watching Bryce. I wanted to invite Bryce to dinner, so he could get away from his dad. But I didn't think it would be good to have Riley near him, so it was best not to ask. Riley wanted revenge and I didn't think he would stop at anything to get it. I wasn't sure if I could trust him yet, so I had to keep them apart.

Chase left around 1:00 a.m. to go home. He continued to hint about marriage, but Cora ignored every mention of it. I think he only left because he was tired of the rejection and, for him, that didn't happen very often, if at all. The whole Christmas vacation had turned out to be the best I could remember despite everything that had happened, because Elle, Genevieve and Riley spent most of their time with us. It was starting to feel like a family—a dysfunctional one, but still a family.

Genevieve and Elle acted like friends now. After the Christmas party, they didn't say anything bad about each other. Genevieve had been great, but still I didn't think Elle was completely sold on her.

Our Christmas break seemed like it was over in the blink of an eye. Cold weather blanketed Winsor. The low temperatures were in the negative numbers and the highs didn't get much above 10 degrees. The cold made it that much harder to return to school. Even my dad's truck struggled with it that first morning.

Eric and Livi were the first two I saw, which was normal with Eric and me sharing a locker. Livi was busy talking to a group of girls next to our locker.

"How's it going?" Eric said.

"Okay, what's up with you?" He was not his normal, cheerful self. He was quiet. After a long break to recharge, I would have expected him to be bouncing off the walls, ready to entertain.

"Have you heard the news?" he said. "Oliver's back."

I didn't quite grasp what he said. It sounded like he said Oliver was back in school. But that was impossible, because he had been expelled.

"Eric, I thought you just said that Oliver is back, but that can't be right."

"Yeah, he is. His parents and Coach Miller worked out a way for him to finish his senior year so he can graduate with the rest of his class. Does Elle know?"

"She didn't say anything on the ride here," I said.

"You need to tell Elle before she finds out, or worse, sees him. And get this: he is back to his old ways. It's as if nothing happened. His friends are back at his side and he's acting like he's king of the school again."

I grabbed my books and set off looking for Elle. I had to get to her. Down the long hall, I spotted Oliver and a couple of his friends. The closer I got to them, I could see that Elle and Amber were in the middle of his group. Chad was coming from the opposite direction. Both of us were heading right for them. We would get to them at the same time. I didn't really need Chad's help, but he was an intimidating figure. Hopefully, his presence would deter anything from becoming violent. The fire lit in my stomach.

We both entered into the circle, cutting Amber and Elle off from Oliver and his friends.

"Oliver, do we have a problem?" Chad asked.

Oliver had a thin, jagged scar that started above his right eye and went all the way down the side of his face to his neck.

"Chad, it's good to see you too, and look—you brought little Keller. Did you miss me, boy?" He blew me a kiss. I was consumed with fire. The acid in my stomach burned the back of my throat. Elle grabbed onto the back of my shirt to let me know she didn't want me to do anything.

"Oliver, I want to make myself clear. You stay away from Amber and Elle, or I'll have Keller kick your ass again," Chad said.

The scar on Oliver's face became distorted. I stepped forward.

"Oliver, do you understand?" I said firmly. He didn't back away.

"Alex or Nick or whatever you go by now, I don't care that you saved me. You are the reason why your girlfriend was in that car with me on the dock in the first place. If you were man enough to take me up on the rite of passage, then none of this would have happened. You may think this school is yours, but it's mine. It always will be. You and I will settle this before the end of the year, I promise. And this time, you will be the one licking your wounds."

He backed away and his friends followed, laughing as they went down the hall.

We turned to see if the girls were okay. They were, but I could tell that Elle was more upset than she was letting on.

"Don't worry about him," I said. "I will never let him hurt you again."

"It's you I'm worried about," Elle said, holding on to me tightly.

I walked her to class. All the while, I kept my arm around her for comfort. With all of the other stuff I was worrying about, now I had to add Oliver into the mix. I was close to overload. It was Coach Miller's fault he was here. He had helped Oliver with the police and now he helped him get back into school. My rage subsided but the fire was not going out, and for once, I was glad. It was a welcome friend.

After I dropped Elle off at her class, I didn't even attempt to go to my first period Spanish class. I went straight to the locker room in search of Coach Miller. At the door to the locker room I was stopped by Coach Hoff.

"Aren't you supposed to be in class right now?"

I tried to ignore him and walk by.

"Keller." He grabbed my arm. I wanted to jerk away, but I held back.

"What's the matter?" he asked. He looked concerned, not upset.

"I just need to talk to Coach Miller about something that only he can help me with."

He stood there for a moment processing what I had said.

"Okay, but next time, when I talk to you, you answer," he said in his best coach's voice.

"Yes, I will." I knocked on Coach Miller's door.

"Come in," he said.

He was sitting in a chair in the corner of the room reading a book. I couldn't hold back my anger any longer.

"How could you help Oliver?" I blurted out. "First you helped him with the police somehow and now you helped him get back into school. He doesn't deserve any of it, especially after everything he has done to Elle. He's nothing but a bully." I took a deep breath. He never flinched from my shouting. He simply put down the book he was holding and took off his reading glasses.

I grabbed the pack of Tic Tacs out of my pocket and nearly downed the whole box.

"So, Nicholas, it seems you have a problem with me. But before we talk, and I do mean talk, please shut the door." I shut it and turned to find him standing right behind me. He was a foot away, towering over me.

"Please sit down." He motioned for me to sit next to his desk. I sat and he did too, but this time at his desk.

"Nicholas, I am only going to discuss this with you once.

Not because you demanded it, but because I would like for you to learn something."

I immediately felt guilty for yelling. "Coach Miller, I'm so sorry for how I acted. It won't happen again."

He smiled and nodded. "Nicholas, you're right. I have helped Oliver several times and will continue to do so. First, I asked Officer Daniel Hill at the police station to allow Oliver's family to visit him in jail whenever they wanted to. District Attorney James Caldwell had his family barred from visiting him during those first few days out of the hospital when they took him into custody, which is against the law. So I had to intercede. Then I was also able to get Oliver released from jail to stay at home before the trial. Finally, he needed to get back into school so he could graduate and have a chance to go to college, so I worked out a way for that to happen."

"Coach, I understand why you helped his parents see him and get him released, because D.A. Caldwell is an idiot. But why help him get back in school this year? Why not next year? That would have been better because most of the people he hurt would have graduated."

"I did it because everyone needs a second chance."

"But he's a bully! Just this morning he trapped Elle and Amber. Chad and I had to get him and his friends to back off."

"Did you hear what he was saying to Elle? I imagine that when you and Chad saw him you didn't exactly welcome him back with open arms. When Oliver gets nervous, he falls into old habits and yes, one of those habits is being a pompous bully. When you get nervous, you become calm. These are just different ways you both react to stress. Let me be clear: there is no room for bullies at this school or anywhere else, but it will take him some time to readjust and I am going to help him each day to try to do that. Nicholas, I don't regret helping him, and I suggest you try to make the best of it. Who knows? Maybe one day you will decide to give him a second chance, too."

"I think I've given him all the chances he deserves. If he were a cat, he would already have used up his nine lives."

"Nicholas," he handed me a pass back to class, "there's nothing you can't do. Give him a chance." I took the pass and walked out of the office.

I couldn't concentrate on school or anything else. How was I going to deal with Oliver on top of everything else? My mind felt like mush. All I wanted to do was see Elle and be in her arms.

At lunch, I walked to our table, and Elle was sitting there with Bryce. Both of them were staring at a sheet of paper. They were smiling about something. I was glad to see her happy.

"Hey, what's going on, Nicholas?" Bryce said.

"Nothing, what's up with you?"

Elle pushed the paper they were looking at toward me. The flyer was for a local food pantry.

"We are going to have a Valentine's Day Dance to help the less fortunate in our community, and Bryce said he would help me with the planning." Thank goodness he did. It would make guarding them a lot easier if they were both together. I was sure she was putting all of this together to get her mind off Oliver returning. It didn't matter why; it was just good to see Elle being Elle.

"Bryce, be careful. You don't know what you're in for. She will work you to death." Elle hit me, giving me one of her crooked smiles. That instantly made my mind clear.

"Oh, I can't wait. It's going to be a lot of fun," she said.

"So how will the dance help the pantry?" I asked.

She began to explain how it would all work. People who came to the dance would have to bring five canned good items to get in the door. The table became full with our usual group. With the arrival of new people, Elle would restart the explanation of the dance and made it a little bit bigger and better each time. Eric was the last to join the table with no sarcastic comments or anything about the dance. He just ate his lunch, minding his own business. Oliver coming back was affecting him just as much as everyone else, maybe more. Eric was the quarterback of the team now, and I was sure Oliver had somehow found a way to make sure that Eric felt like he was a nobody.

VALENTINE'S DAY

CHAPTER TWENTY-THREE

I was right. Elle had Bryce over to her house a lot, helping with the different projects and plans for the dance, which made guarding them so much easier. I spent many evenings dozing off on her couch while she and Bryce worked on the different decorations.

"Nicholas, wake up."

"What? I'm not asleep," I said, opening my eyes.

"We need to go over to Genevieve and Coach Moore's house." Sitting up, I noticed they both had on their jackets. Why did they have to go there?

"Bryce is going to take me to their house. I will come over to your house as soon as we're finished," said Elle. I sat up quickly and slipped my shoes on.

"No, don't be ridiculous. I'll come."

"Nicholas, I can take Elle. You don't have to worry about it," said Bryce.

I didn't like Bryce insisting on driving Elle.

"Bryce, where's Erin?" He looked upset at the mention of her name.

"Nicholas, how dare you! Bryce and Erin broke up today." She took his arm and marched him up the stairs and out of the house. When did that happen? I got my jacket on and hurried after them.

I followed them over to Riley and Genevieve's. Elle still went with Bryce because she wanted to make sure that he was okay. Once in Riley's driveway, Elle and Bryce got out of the car and were let in by Genevieve. She looked like she was expecting them. I went home and sat down on the couch, waiting for Elle. Two hours later, there was a knock on the door. To my surprise, Bryce was with her.

"Nicholas, Bryce has never been over to your house so I invited him. Is that okay?" What, was I supposed to say no? I had to say yes.

"Of course, come on in." They walked into the family room.

Little did she know that soon Bryce would be here a lot more often.

"Bryce, I am sorry about before. I didn't know about Erin."

"No reason to apologize. I'm fine, Nicholas." He smiled. Elle looked sympathetically at him. I didn't like how close Bryce was standing to Elle. She was kind to everyone. I didn't want him to get the wrong idea. Friend or not, my relationship with Elle was far more important than anything else. It would make things awkward between us if he tried to make a move on her. I heard Cora in the kitchen. She must have heard the voices and was now cooking something up for us. This was my chance to get Bryce alone to set him straight.

"Elle, Cora wanted to talk to you about an idea for the dance." She looked excited and promptly walked toward the kitchen. I felt bad about lying to get her out of the room, but Cora was quick on her feet. We had been lying for a long time.

I turned to face Bryce, making sure he knew I meant business. "Bryce, do you like Elle?"

"Of course, she's great," he responded cheerfully.

"I mean, do you like her as a girlfriend."

"No way, she's just a friend. I would never try to steal your girl. You are my best friend." He smiled. Best friend, really? We were friends, but best friend? Did he really think of me that way?

"Oh, okay then. I was just making sure." I didn't know what else to say because I was shocked by the whole best friend comment.

"Can I use your bathroom?"

"Of course, it's back here." He followed me down the hall and I showed him where it was. I walked into the kitchen and, sure enough, Cora was cooking and talking to Elle about the dance, going along with my lie. Ten minutes had gone by and I hadn't heard Bryce. I left Elle and Cora still in a conversation about the dance. I walked into the hallway and saw Bryce walking down the last step of the staircase.

"Sorry, Nicholas, I washed my hands in the bathroom upstairs because I couldn't find any soap in the other one."

"No problem. You should get in there. They are talking about some more Valentine's Dance stuff."

**

A week before the dance, the National Weather Service had started predicting a winter storm that would paralyze the city, which was odd, because the weather had been so warm with temperatures in the upper 50s. With the weather as cold as it had been before, the warmth was welcome. It felt like a heat wave. Luckily, the day of the dance, February 13, fell a day before the storm was supposed to hit. But still, it was something that we had to keep an eye on because it might make guarding Elle and Bryce difficult.

The day of the dance brought even warmer weather. Bryce and Elle, along with a couple of underclassmen, were busy collecting canned food at the entrance. The lunchroom, which normally was decorated elaborately for Winsor dances, only had a couple of heart decorations here and there. The normal budget for a dance was all donated to the local food pantry to buy food. Elle made sure the dance committee didn't overspend so they could give the pantry as much as possible. She had a majority of the staff and their spouses there to help. Elle had managed to get Cora to come and help also. She was helping Riley and Genevieve with the auction, which would raise more money. Elle had asked specific teachers and their spouses to volunteer to be part of the Teachers' Dance Auction. Anyone there could place a bid to dance with a teacher or spouse for one slow song. Genevieve and Riley had agreed to be auctioned off. I felt bad for Riley because I knew that Joy Lemmins would be bidding for him.

I met up with Eric, who seemed to be in a much better mood, probably because Oliver wasn't around.

"Hey, Eric."

"This place looks like a dump. Where are the decorations?" He grinned.

"They are donating the money—"

"You would think that after two years, Keller, you would know my sense of humor by now. I'm joking."

"You sounded so serious this time." I smiled.

He reached into his pocket and pulled out a crisp 100-dollar bill. "I am going to bid 100 dollars for a dance with Mrs. Moore."

"I was thinking I would do the same," Chad said, walking up with Matt.

"Nicholas, is it true you know her?" Matt asked.

"Know her? She's a close family friend," Eric replied, holding up two fingers and crossing them.

"*Cora and I* are friends with them," I hissed.

"I'm kidding about bidding," Chad said. "Amber would kill me on the spot. You better watch out, Eric. Livi will do worse than kill you for sure if you win."

"No she won't. I make the rules in this relationship," Eric said. "And anyway, I am bidding because it's for a good cause, right?"

Matt laughed and said, "And the fact that she is hot has nothing to do with it." They laughed.

Sure, Genevieve was beautiful, but was she really that incredible? The guys were all collectively gawking at her.

CHAPTER TWENTY-THREE

Maybe she had the same effect on men that Chase had on women.

I walked over to the table with the guys and watched Eric and Matt drop their bids into the plastic box that had "Mrs. Genevieve Moore" written on it in bright pink letters with hearts. I left them to search for Elle. She was still stationed at the entrance, but Bryce was gone. I sat down next to her. She gave me a quick kiss on the cheek.

"How's it going in there?" Elle asked.

"It's going great, but Eric wants to know where all the decorations are."

"Tell Eric that he can take his wisecracks to a different school." She grinned, attending to the next person in line.

"So where's Bryce?" I asked.

"He's taking a quick break. I'm glad I asked him to help, especially after the breakup with Erin. He seems a lot better."

"Spending that much time with you would make anyone feel better."

She squeezed my leg.

"Could you check to see how the auction is going? I want to start reading off the winners in about 25 minutes," Elle said.

"Will do."

Walking toward the auction area, I saw Bryce. He was hovering around the tables, watching people put in their bids.

"Bryce?"

"Oh hey, Nicholas, how's it going?"

"Pretty good. You sure have done a great job."

"Thanks, but I think we both know it's your wonderful girlfriend who has done a great job. The rest of us are just along for the ride."

A half hour later, Elle and Bryce walked through the crowd up to the front of the dance floor with the auction boxes and put them up on the stage where the DJ was set up. Bryce handed the microphone to her and started going through each box, pulling the winners out to give to Elle.

"Hello, everyone, and thank you for coming to our first ever Valentine's Day Dance, to help our local food pantry. All of the food and money collected tonight will go to help people who are desperately in need."

There was a lot of applause. Then a voice cut through the crowd's applause.

"Come on, read the winners." It was Eric, of course.

Ignoring him, Elle continued, "I will read the winners and how much the winning bid was for. Once you have won, please make your way up to the side of the stage. After we have read the last winner we will have our auction dance. Good luck."

Bryce pulled the first couple of winners out. Some of the boxes had tons of bids and others only had a few. The ones who had a lot of bids slowed down the process because Bryce had to look through every bid to find the winner. They had finally announced almost all of the winners. The last two boxes belonged to Riley and Genevieve. There was excitement in the crowd as they waited for the remaining winners to be announced. Riley's box was full.

"And the winning bid for Coach Riley Moore is Cora Keller, with a bid of $350." Riley must have made sure that Joy Lemmins wouldn't get that dance. The next box belonged to Genevieve. It was busting at the seams. Bryce looked through each bid, then handed the winning one to Elle.

"We have saved the best for last." She looked down at the piece of paper. "This can't be right," Elle whispered, but it was still audible over the loud speakers. "The winning bid for Genevieve Moore is Nicholas Keller with a bid of $500."

What? I didn't bid that. When she said my name the audience *oohed* and then when she said the amount the *oohs* grew louder. Elle couldn't see me, but I could see her. Her face was pale. There had to be some sort of mistake.

"Thank you to everyone who put a bid in. We will start the dance in one minute."

She then disappeared from sight off the back of the stage. I went searching for her but she was gone. I saw Bryce and stopped him.

"Bryce, there has to be some sort of mistake. Let me see that bid."

He shook his head, "I went through them twice. There was a bid with your name on it and it had five 100-hundred dollar bills attached to it. I saw it myself and Elle did, too. I can go get it out of the trash if you want?"

"No. Where did Elle go?" I looked around frantically.

"Not sure, but she was in a hurry. She told me to make sure I closed everything up and to get all the money to the office after the dance."

Why did someone do this to me? I thought.

I pushed past him into the crowd of people. I had to find her. But where did she go?

Riley stopped me. "Nicholas, don't worry about Elle. Cora went after her. You need to give her some time to cool off."

"But I didn't make that bid. Someone else did it. I have to tell her."

"It doesn't matter. The damage is done. Give her some time."

The world began to spin out of control around me. Who made that bid? Two people came to mind. One was Genevieve herself and the other was Oliver.

The music began to play for the auction dance and the DJ said, "And now for a classic from the movie *Say Anything*, Peter Gabriel's 'In Your Eyes.'"

I turned and Genevieve was right there. She grabbed my hand and led me into the crowd of winners. I couldn't fight her; I was in shock. She put her arms around me and pulled me close to her. Everything became still.

"Did you put in that bid to mess things up with Elle?" I whispered angrily.

"You didn't put the bid in for me?" she asked. "I thought you were being kind and making sure I wouldn't have to dance with one of the perverse students who have been eyeing me like I'm a piece of meat," she responded.

"No, of course I didn't. I would never hurt Elle that way." I tried to push away, but I couldn't. My body wanted me to stay with her.

"Nicholas, even if you didn't bid on me, it's nice dancing with you." She pulled me closer so our bodies were pressed together. I felt uncomfortable with the contact, but at the same time, it was comforting in that moment.

"Genevieve, I'm glad I got to dance with you. I wouldn't want you to dance with any of those guys from the school."

For the rest of the song we stayed in the middle of the pack of winners, and she kept her body lightly pressed against mine. And all I could think of was Elle.

THE END
CHAPTER TWENTY-FOUR

When the song ended, I immediately went after Elle. I had to find her to explain. I didn't want to give her any more time, no matter what Riley said. I drove straight to her house. When I pulled up, Bryce was walking away from her front door. He must have left right after we talked. The fire inside me roared. He was trying to steal Elle. Some friend! I jumped out of my truck and ran up to Bryce. He flinched seeing me coming at him.

"Nicholas, wait, it's not what you think."

"What do I think, Bryce? Tell me," I shouted, grabbing him.

"I came here for you," he pleaded.

"I didn't ask you to do that, did I?"

"Listen, I lied and told Elle that I placed the bid for you. I told her I saw that some pretty sick guys were bidding on Genevieve, and you being like a little brother or something, I thought it would be okay. She didn't want to listen to me but I had to try. You and Elle are great together. I just wanted to be a good friend to you."

I was still angry at him for coming over to talk to her, but I guess the more people telling her it wasn't actually me, the better.

I let go of him and he walked away.

I had been to her house a thousand times, but this time it felt cold. I wasn't sure what was going to be waiting for me. Whatever it took, I had to make Elle understand, no matter what. I couldn't lose her.

I knocked on the door. The dark house didn't show any signs of life. I knocked again, but this time louder. A light turned on and the door opened. Elle stood in front of me. Her eyes were swollen and her face was soaked with tears. She didn't say anything. Her normally inviting eyes were hollow and distant.

"Elle, you have to let me explain." She turned and walked down the stairs, leaving the door wide open. I followed her, shutting the door behind me.

I didn't wait for her to sit on the couch.

"Elle, it wasn't me who put that bid in. You have to believe me. You are everything to me. I love you more than life itself."

"Did you dance with her?" she asked coldly.

"Yes." I became nauseated with my answer. Why did I dance with Genevieve? I should have chased after Elle.

"Then I guess you weren't too worried, were you?"

"Elle, I was. When I went to look for you, you were already gone. Riley told me that Cora went after you and that I needed to give you some time to cool off. I wanted to follow you, but I thought Riley was right."

"I didn't need time to cool off. I needed you. Cora was

kind enough to bring me home and Bryce wasn't far behind her. Did you tell him to come here?"

"No, I was angry that he did. He had no right to come here."

"You are lucky to have such a good friend. He told me that you didn't put the bid in—he did. But that doesn't matter to me because you danced with her."

My heart filled with grief and shame. Why did I dance with her? I reached out my hand. "Elle, I love you so much." Elle began to cry, pulling away. She put her hands over her face.

"I know you do, but why did you dance with her, Nicholas?" she said over and over, crying. I felt helpless. My world was shattering with each tear that fell. Everything was crashing down around me. Tears began to pour down my face. My head felt like it was going to explode.

After a couple of minutes, she calmed down. I tried my best to do the same, but it was difficult. I couldn't believe how much I had hurt her.

"Nicholas, I know you love me and I love you too, but we can't be together."

The words ripped through me like a white hot knife.

"Elle, please, I beg you, don't do this. You are everything to me. Please."

I said it several times, hoping she would change her mind, but she just kept shaking her head.

"No, Nicholas. We can't be together. It just seems that the more we try, the more things fall apart. And I can't live this way anymore."

In my panic to make her see, I started to tell her the secrets I had been keeping from her.

"Elle, let me explain everything to you," I rambled. "I have some things to tell you that will explain everything."

"Stop. I don't want to hear it. There is nothing that will make me change my mind. I want you to go, now."

Again, I felt the sting of her words as they pierced through my chest. I couldn't handle it. The world was spinning out of control.

"Please, Elle, please. I beg you."

She leaned forward and kissed me on my cheek.

"Nicholas, you must go."

She walked to the door and opened it. My body was moving toward her, but I didn't feel like it was me. I was hovering above myself as I walked, grief-stricken, up to the door. How could this be happening? After everything we went through.

I walked through the door. The warm weather was now mixed with a cold mist. I turned back to look at her. She was crying even harder now.

"I love you and I always will," she said, shutting the door before I could respond.

My world had just ended. I fell to the ground. My heart was pounding and I couldn't breathe. I pulled myself up and barely got myself to the truck where I put my head down on the hood, still sobbing uncontrollably. *Why? Why? Was this a bad dream?* For a fleeting moment, my grief mixed with anger. I pounded my fist on the cold steel hood and yelled as loudly as I could, "Why?" My voice echoed around me, but fell silent in the mist. I put my head down on the truck again. Elle was the only one who made me want to take on all of the challenges ahead of me, because I knew I would be with her until I made my Final Sacrifice. But now I had nothing.

The mist turned into a steady hard rain. My clothes quickly became soaked. I ripped my shirt off in anger and fell to my knees next to the truck. This was the end.

I stayed there kneeling next to my truck for what seemed like hours. Somewhere inside me, I was hoping that Elle would come out and make everything better. But the longer I waited, the more I realized that she wasn't coming.

Driving home was difficult. I couldn't concentrate on the road. I nearly hit a parked car that I didn't see until it was almost too late. When I got home, I sat in my driveway. I didn't want to go inside because I knew that the group would be there, waiting like always.

After a lot of yelling and pounding on the steering wheel, I managed to get myself to go inside. I was still drenched from the rain, which had stopped before I got out of the truck. Steam rose off my hot skin. Every light was on in our house. I went straight to my room. I pulled off my wet clothes and got into bed. The warmth from the heavy down comforter was the only soothing thing left. I wished my mom was there. She would help make everything better again. I missed my parents so much.

I began to float. This time the darkness was in the form of a person. This shadow person walked around me, sizing me up. I couldn't run or fight because I was helplessly floating, suspended like an ice cube in water. Then in one quick motion, the creature was on top of me, choking me, both hands firmly around my neck. As a reflex, I started to fight, but then I gave up, letting it do whatever it wanted to me. If it wanted me dead, then I would welcome it with open arms. Without Elle, there was no reason to fight back anymore. I opened my eyes and it was gone. It disappeared as soon as I stopped fighting. It vanished. It reminded me of the one other time when I let the darkness consume me last year. Maybe I wasn't supposed to fight this darkness. Then I felt warm spots moving around on my back. It was so comforting, like a warm washcloth being dragged across my skin, taking away some of the hurt I was feeling. I turned to see who it was and it was my mom. I began to cry again.

"Mom, I miss you so much."

"Nicholas, there is no reason to cry. I am always with you."

"But what am I supposed to do now?" I pleaded, hoping she would tell me.

"Shh, honey, that is not for me to decide. Your father and I will always be with you. You are never alone, no matter how dark the path becomes. Just remember to look ahead toward the light."

I awoke and began to cry again. Even with my mom's words to comfort me, it didn't make what happened with Elle any better. I needed her.

STORM
CHAPTER TWENTY-FIVE

I got out of bed around noon the next day. I didn't sleep much, making me feel like I couldn't do anything. All of my energy was gone. A large hole now replaced my heart. I was an empty shell. Cora hadn't come in yet to check on me, which was strange. No matter what was going on with me, she was always there to see if I needed anything, and most of the time, cooking followed.

I decided to take a shower, hoping it would make me feel better. I made the water as hot as I could possibly stand it and sat down in the tub. The steaming hot water was burning my back, but it felt good, like somehow it was getting rid of everything inside me that was responsible for what happened last night.

After a while, I got out of the shower and got dressed. I went downstairs reluctantly. All three of them were in the family room watching TV. None of them looked up at me. They were glued to whatever was on. Then it dawned on me that at least two of them should be guarding Elle and Bryce.

"Why aren't two of you watching Elle and Bryce?" It was

harder to say Elle's name than I thought it would be. It sent chills through my body. Like a reflex, my body remembered everything from last night and shuddered. I had to do everything in my power to fight back the flood of emotion that was sure to follow.

"Bryce's dad picked him up. I followed them to the Army base nearby. From the look of it, Bryce is staying there with him for the rest of the weekend. He will be safe there," Riley said without looking away from the TV.

"Elle hasn't come out of her house," Genevieve said, "and I don't expect her to for some time, at least not until Monday for school. I will go over there to make sure she's okay later," she added, never making eye contact with me either.

"We have other things to worry about right now. They will be safe for the time being," Cora said, pointing to the screen. The TV showed a graphic of a massive storm that would impact our area.

"This could be the snowstorm of the century," said the weatherman. "We are expecting at least two feet of snow. The Valentine's Day storm will arrive early tonight. It won't seem impressive at first, just steady rain, but it will intensify rapidly and turn to heavy snow. To complicate things further, we are expecting winds to be steady at 50 miles per hour with gusts up over 75 miles per hour, making it a dangerous, paralyzing storm. The temperature will plummet into the single digits, resulting in a fast freeze. A thick layer of ice will coat everything before the snow starts. Please do not be fooled by the warm, sunny weather that is out there now. This arctic low will draw moist air from the Gulf of Mexico, changing

252

the rain to snow quickly. It's important to prepare and take precautions now."

He continued to talk about the widespread power outages that would occur and warned people to make sure to stock up on food, water and any necessary medications. Cora and I had been through a couple of blizzards when we lived in Oklahoma, but I had never heard them say, "stock up on food and water," because that would normally cause a panic. It must be pretty serious for him to say that.

"We need to get ready at both houses," Riley said.

My mind cleared, pushing thoughts of Elle away so I could function.

"We need to get our house hooked up to your generator," I said. "Riley and I will take care of the power needs. Cora and Genevieve, you take care of the food and supplies." They nodded at me. "Once we are done, we need to do a final check on Elle and Bryce to make sure they are going to be okay through the storm."

They all just sat there, staring up at me.

"Okay, let's go," I said. I was back in control, but who knew how long it would last? Regardless, it felt good.

I followed Riley to his house where I helped him run the lines from the generator to our electrical box for backup power. It was amazing how much stuff Genevieve and Riley had in their house for emergencies. They were ready for anything that could be thrown their way. After several hours, we had finished most of our preparations. The warm, bright sun gave no indication of any storm coming. There was not a cloud in the bright blue sky. Genevieve and Cora had been to the store and were already back. They had filled both pantries full of food. Riley and I got enough fuel for the generator to last us a week, if needed. We also brought in enough firewood for our house to keep us warm if something happened to the generators during the storm.

I was left alone at our house for a while, sorting out some supplies. Riley left to check on Bryce without telling me, and Cora and Genevieve went to check on Elle. I began to feel empty again with nothing to occupy my mind. I began to replay everything from last night over in my head a thousand times. Why did I dance with Genevieve? The thoughts began to poison my mind and soul.

Luckily, all three of them returned quickly. Cora came in and laid our hand-crank weather radio, which we used often when we lived in Oklahoma, on the table in the family room. She then left to make us dinner.

"Riley, why didn't you take me to check on Bryce? Aren't we supposed to be together as much as possible?" I asked as he and Genevieve walked into the room.

"I just thought you needed some time alone," he replied. I definitely didn't need to be alone. "How are you feeling?"

"Fine, I guess."

"Nonsense, after a breakup like that, you should be crushed."

What did he want me to say? Genevieve hit him.

"What I mean is it's only natural to feel like there is nothing to live for," Riley said.

Again, Genevieve landed a blow on his shoulder, much harder than before.

"You will feel better after some time passes," he concluded.

I looked away from him, not wanting to talk about it. A loud beep and a red banner appeared on the TV screen that read "Emergency Weather Update: Valentine's Day Storm Upgraded."

"We bring you this special bulletin," the TV broadcaster said. "Our Winter Weather Warning has been upgraded to a Severe Blizzard Warning. The dangerous part of this storm will be the high winds and rapidly dropping temperature. Rain will quickly turn to ice, with the temperature falling 50 degrees in just under an hour. With the strong winds, it will make the wind chill below zero. Half an inch of ice is expected to accumulate before changing over to all snow. Please make sure you are indoors when this happens. We are expecting extensive power outages and crippling amounts of snow, with visibility close to zero."

We sat there. Not one of us moved or said anything. This update would normally send most people into a panic, but it seemed to be welcome news for us. We would finally have a break from our guarding duties. Even though nobody said it, I knew it was true.

ARRIVAL
CHAPTER TWENTY-SIX

After dinner at our house, Genevieve and Riley went back to their house to finish preparing for the storm. It was supposed to start in the next hour or so when the front pushed in. Cora and I would wait out the storm at their house. With all of the modifications that Riley had made to the design of their house, it would be an ideal place to ride out any storm. Cora and I went around our house to make sure all of the windows were locked and secured, closing all of the blinds.

Cora called me into the third bedroom, which we used for storage. She was having trouble locking one of the windows in there. The latch wouldn't budge. We both tried loosening it, but we weren't able to.

"We don't have time to deal with this right now," Cora said. "We'll take care of it later."

She gathered all the stuff we would need. I made sure our fireplace was ready to go in case we had to come back here. That was the only thing Riley didn't have built into their new house, because with a generator, they didn't need a fireplace.

A loud knock came from our front door. Cora was closest

to the door, balancing a pile of supplies in her arms. I was still attending to the fireplace, filling up the log rack next to it. Cora opened the door and I heard a familiar voice—it was Ester. What was she doing here?

"What a surprise, Ester. Is everything all right? Shouldn't you be home getting ready for the storm?" Cora asked, bringing her inside.

Ester walked into our hall. Cora took a couple of steps back to give her room.

"Everything is fine, Cora. I've come here to see Nicholas."

I walked into view.

"We have something to say to him." She said, "we," but she was the only one standing there. Our front door was cracked open just enough to see James Caldwell standing on the porch. The fire in me flared.

"James, if you would?" Ester said loudly.

He walked in and cleared his throat. He pulled out of his pocket a very old, worn, small, leather book. He opened it and began to read. "The Divine Council was formed to protect and manage the Thusian population, whose sole purpose is to protect mankind from unseen dangers. You have been called to serve on the Council by one of the members as his or her Death Rite. That member has just passed, fulfilling their honorable Final Sacrifice."

He closed the book and held it down by his side. I noticed a strange symbol on the spine that looked like a broken diamond surrounded by a jagged circle. The word "Thusian" was printed within it. The symbol looked familiar to me, like it was something from a different life.

"Nicholas, one of the members of the Council died last night, Mr. Reed Godfree. He was the one who explained The 7 to you at the Council meeting. He picked you as his first Death Rite recipient." She showed me a list of names—mine on top—on a piece of worn-out, yellowed paper. The same symbol that was on the book was stamped over my name.

"This is a great honor and we look forward to seeing you at our next Council meeting in two weeks. We will get you all settled in and discuss your new responsibilities. Nicholas, we are so excited for you," Ester said, giving me a big hug.

I didn't know what to say. Neither did Cora. I guess it could be good for us if I was part of the Council. At least I could keep an eye on them.

"Ester, James, I look forward to seeing you both at the next meeting," I said, my voice full of honesty and integrity, like I was talking to a judge. I hoped I was giving them what they wanted to hear.

Cora looked at me with concern. Ester looked pleased at my answer. She gave Cora a hug and they both left.

"Are you crazy? You should've turned it down, just like I did when I took you into hiding," she said after closing the door.

"Wait, you were on someone's list to serve on the Council?" I asked, shocked.

"Yes, but I had to take you into hiding, so I refused it."

"Who picked you for their Death Rite list?"

"Your mother did."

I was stunned. Why didn't she serve? I would think the Council could have better prepared us for this life, rather than being on the run for all of these years.

"Cora, we need to keep an eye on the Council and what better way than from the inside?"

"They are bad people," Cora said.

"Not all of them. This is a way for us to find out who is bad, right?"

"We need to talk to Riley about this, first."

I was so tired of her having to talk to Riley about everything. "No we don't, Cora. I am going to be on the Council no matter what anyone says. This is my decision. I don't need Riley's approval or anyone else's. And why do you need Riley's input on everything? It's annoying."

"Because I . . ." She paused, becoming very quiet. "I haven't been able to keep you safe lately. I don't trust myself. That's why I'm counting on Riley." She turned away from me.

I took her hand, making her look at me. "Cora, your decisions are the only ones I trust. You have kept me safe from all these dangers for a long time. That was you, no one else." She didn't say anything. She had her eyes shut. I wasn't sure what she was going to say or do.

After a moment, she opened her eyes and said, "Thank you. I needed to hear that."

We loaded up all of our supplies into her truck. We drove over to Genevieve and Riley's house and unpacked. We got there just in time. You could hear the powerful cold front starting to move into the area. The wind sounded like a stampede coming right at us through the trees. Then an intense rain began to pour. Outside their large window, it looked like it was raining sideways, with large water droplets chasing each other. The roar of the winds grew louder and louder, making a terrible, high-pitched howling sound that rattled the house. The large trees in the front yard were all swaying back and forth, twisting violently. We were busy putting away our stuff in the spare bedrooms when I heard the rain change over to ice pellets that pinged against the windows. We all settled into the family room, right when the snow began to fall. The change over from rain to snow only took thirty minutes, leaving behind a thick layer of ice coating everything. The trees creaked and groaned from the weight. Fifteen minutes after the complete changeover to snow, there was a bright flash out by the road. The lights flickered off, and then came back on. I heard the generator turn over and begin to power the house.

"The transformer must have exploded because of the ice. That weatherman was right. This storm is going to be a nasty one," Riley said, kicking his feet up and resting them on the coffee table.

From the couch, we all watched the storm rage outside. The snow and wind were impressive. We could barely see out the window.

"I have been chosen to replace Reed Godfree on the Thusian Council," I said.

Nobody said anything at first.

"Did you say Reed Godfree?" Riley asked.

"Yes, why?"

"He was a very good friend of my parents. He was on the Council for forty years. He joined when he was in his teens. His talents were in finance, just like Ester's. My parents considered him to be extremely trustworthy. It figures that they would kill him off also," Riley said.

"Nicholas, it's way too dangerous for you to sit on the Council," Genevieve said. "You can't put yourself in that type of danger." She sounded truly worried, like Cora had been earlier.

"I know, but it's the best way to find out who the Seekers are working with," I said. Riley nodded his head, agreeing with me.

"You may be right, but it's still too dangerous," Genevieve said, crossing her arms and frowning.

"You don't have to pout. I will be careful, I promise." I leaned forward and patted her knee. I didn't expect to feel anything when I touched her, but I did. It was a strange sensation. It felt like light was filling all of the dark places inside me. I pulled away, like I had received an electrical shock. I didn't want to feel anything like that. Dancing with Genevieve was what led to Elle and me breaking up, so any emotion triggered by touching her was unwelcome.

The storm continued to pound the house. My mind, too, was being bombarded by thoughts of Genevieve and Elle. I began to replay everything that had led to our breakup over and over again in my mind. This was all my fault. I danced with Genevieve. Nobody forced me to—I just did. But that still didn't answer the question of who actually put in that bid for me. My mind raced, going through all of the people it could have been, but the only name that stuck out to me now was Riley. Oliver wasn't there and Genevieve said that she didn't and I believed her, so that left him. He's the one who told me that Cora had gone after Elle and that I needed to let her calm down. Why would he interfere like that unless he placed the bid? But why would he want Elle and me to break up? Maybe he didn't want me to have any distractions when Bryce joined the group. Elle would be in the way. But if that was the reason, what about Cora? She wasn't really part of the group either. That answer was obvious: he had feelings for her.

"So does anyone know who placed the bid for me to dance with Genevieve?" I looked right at him.

"Good, Nicholas, you are trying to talk about it. That's a great start," he said.

I would let Riley think what he wanted if I could get the truth.

"So, does anyone?" I repeated.

Cora and Genevieve said, "No."

"Riley, do you know who would have done it?"

"No, I don't. It was probably someone who wanted you and Elle to break up," he said, continuing to look out the window.

"That's a great point. I thought the same thing. But each person I came up with either wasn't there or wouldn't do it. It left me with only one conclusion. It was one of you."

I had everyone's attention now. "You see, once Bryce is part of the group, we will need to concentrate completely on Xavier and the Seekers, right? So there should be no distractions for me. Cora would never do that to me because of her loss of Marcus. And Genevieve looked shocked when I asked her at the dance if it was her. So that leaves you, Riley."

He laughed. "You think it was me?"

"Well, you are the one out for revenge, aren't you? You don't want anyone to mess up your big plans."

He stopped laughing.

"Maybe you are working with Xavier somehow to get rid of the Council." I was filled with rage. Cora went to Riley and Genevieve to me, just in case there was going to be a fight.

"Yes, of course I think Elle would be a distraction," he said, "but I would never do that to you. I consider you a friend, a brother. Elle might be a distraction, but she's your inspiration. She is why you will be able to fight and win against any Seeker. The four Thusians will have to have a reason to fight, which will make us indestructible, unbeatable. This reason, and our bond, will add to our talents, making us the perfect weapon to fight Xavier."

I could see that he was sincere.

"I would never do anything to break our bond or take away our reasons to fight. And, yes it has been about vengeance for me, but now it's about protecting the people we love." He looked at Cora. "And I would never work with Xavier, even if he wanted to kill the Council."

I felt really stupid. My emotions were getting the best of me again. How could I accuse him of trying to break up Elle and me, and then accuse him of working with Xavier?

"Riley, I'm not thinking clearly."

"No problem, Nicholas. You are full of raw emotion. You've had a difficult couple of days." He smiled. "Besides, I haven't exactly been thinking too clearly myself."

The snow was really coming down now, covering

everything. The windows were starting to freeze over. The frost was climbing up the windows, branching out from the base and creating long, complex patterns. Their large window thermometer showed the temperature falling into the single digits. The wind chill had to be below zero now.

There was a loud cracking sound outside. I looked out the window to see if I could tell what it was. Maybe another transformer exploded. Then a split second later, a tree entered into my view as it fell toward the house. Everything around me slowed to a near stop. The large tree was falling toward the picture window with all of its branches spread out like it was getting ready to grab us. I turned the coffee table in front of me onto its side. Riley grabbed Cora and pulled her behind the table. Genevieve was already in front of me behind the table when the tree crashed through. I pulled Genevieve to my body and ducked down behind the table, wrapping her up so she wouldn't be hurt from any of the glass.

The sound of the tree hitting the window was like an explosion. A wave of snow and glass slammed up against the table. The cold air rushed into the room. The tree was halfway into the house. We scrambled quickly into the bedroom where our winter gear was waiting. It was still warm in there but soon it would be cold. The four of us put on our jackets, pants, gloves, hats and goggles. We grabbed our backpacks that we all had prepared earlier.

"We can't stay here, the house is compromised. We won't be able to protect ourselves and if we go to the basement, we will be sitting ducks. It will be too difficult to drive to your house in the snow. We'll need to walk. If we stick together, we'll be fine. But keep your eyes open; it could be a trap," Riley said loudly over the whistling sound of the cold air rushing through the house.

He was right. With all of the snow and ice, our trucks would already be buried. Riley had clips that he securely attached to our jackets, and he ran a rope through them, connecting us.

"This will make sure that none of us get separated in the snow. People have died just yards away from their houses in blizzards. I will follow my GPS unit to get us there safely." We ventured out into the family room. I was able to really see the extent of the damage. A tree that was at least four feet in diameter lay in the middle of the room. The family room was now covered by an inch of snow. Some places in the room already had small snow drifts. We walked through the house and left by the back door, linked together and carrying our backpacks. The wind outside was powerful, making it difficult to walk. On the side of the house there was more visibility because it shielded us from the full force of the wind and the snow. But I could still barely make out the shape of the trees that separated our two houses.

Riley checked the generator and then turned toward our house. If I hadn't walked back and forth a hundred times, I would never have known that it was right next door. When we got farther away from the house, the wind and snow intensified. The normally short walk was taking a lot longer. We had to cling to the trees so that the wind wouldn't knock us over. I could barely see Genevieve in front of me. Riley was leading us, I was in the back and Genevieve and Cora were in the middle. Genevieve was struggling. A couple of times, I had to help her regain her balance and get her to the next tree. The sounds of cracking and falling trees were the only things I could hear over the howling winds. The longer we were out here, the greater the possibility of being hit by a falling tree or limb.

Something moved off to my side. I turned to see what it was, but all I saw was snow. *There's something there,* I thought. I peered harder to see what it was, but still nothing. The snow was beginning to slow as the fire in me began to intensify. Then I felt the rope being tugged. I quickened my pace to catch up to Genevieve in case she was in trouble. She was face-down in the snow, not moving. I grabbed the back of her coat and backpack and pulled her up. She was struggling to stand. I put her arm around my neck and helped her the rest of the way, which turned out to be just a couple more yards. Both Riley and Cora were against the side of our house, pulling the rope to reel us in. We moved along the side of the house and in through the back door.

Once inside, I let go of Genevieve and she collapsed to the floor. I stripped out of my snow gear quickly. I began to unzip Genevieve's jacket as fast as I could. Cora joined in, taking off Genevieve's goggles, gloves and hat, even though she didn't know why I was doing it. Genevieve's cheeks were red and she was listless.

"Are you okay?" I pleaded, hoping she was. My pulse quickened, anticipating her answer.

"Yes, something hit me," she said. That got Riley's attention.

"What hit you? Nicholas, did you see anything?" he asked.

"I thought I saw something, but that's when you started to pull the rope. Then I found her face-down."

"I think it was a branch, because it felt like I was hit by something swinging."

Genevieve rolled over, regaining some of her strength. She grabbed her jacket, which was on the floor next to her, and flipped it over. There were several large rips running across it. She put her hand in one of the holes and retrieved a piece of a branch. Relieved, we all started cleaning up our stuff. Genevieve and Riley took their backpacks into the family room. Genevieve refused any help from us. Cora and I hung up the snow gear to dry. Cora then went around to each of the rooms, turning on the lights. Riley's generator was doing its job. I was glad we had run the cords on the ground earlier so there was no chance of falling trees or limbs knocking it offline.

Genevieve and Riley had already laid out sleeping bags on the floor when Cora and I came back in.

"We had the perfect house for anything but a falling tree. Why didn't I have those cut down?" Riley said. "The storm glass was supposed to stand up to anything." He shook his head in disgust.

Then the lights flickered and went out.

"What happened to the power?" Genevieve asked.

Riley turned on a lantern that he had in his backpack. "Not sure. I checked it before we came over here. It had enough fuel to last through the night."

While they discussed what could have happened, I started a fire. At first smoke poured into the room because of the paper I used to start it. The wind gusting over the chimney was not allowing the smoke to escape. But then the smoke diminished after the paper burned out and the logs caught fire. It cast a warm, orange glow over the room.

"I'm going to check the generator," Riley said.

"No, you're not." Cora entered the room with a couple of candles in hand.

"I'll be quick. I have the GPS to find my way back if I get lost."

"Not another word about it, Riley Moore," Cora said, sounding like a mother lecturing her son. It had been some time since I had heard that motherly tone and, luckily for me, it was directed at Riley.

"We have plenty of firewood to keep us warm for days and I have a lot of food here. You may check in the morning when the storm lets up."

"We will need to keep these doors to the family room shut at all times so we can keep the warmth in here. Nicholas, can you come and help me get some of the stuff that we'll need?" Cora asked.

I followed her upstairs. She pulled out a couple of brand new sleeping bags and pillows from the shelves in the closet. She also grabbed the comforters off our beds. I helped her down the stairs and back into the room. I could already feel the cold seeping into our house. It wouldn't be long until all of the heat in the house was gone.

Cora picked up the hand-crank weather radio and gave

it a couple of turns, bringing it to life. The recorded message this time didn't reveal anything different than the news had earlier. The room quickly became cold, even with the fire blazing.

Cora put my things on the couch. I climbed over Riley and Genevieve's stuff and sat on top of my down comforter, which was over my sleeping bag.

"Since we have all of this time with nothing to do, we should talk about how we are going to tell Bryce," Riley said.

Cora and Genevieve must have been thinking about the same thing because they both had their own ways of telling him. Cora's way was a gentle, motherly approach. First show him the Thusian Vault, just like she did for me. Genevieve had a more direct approach, hitting him over the head with it. Neither of those approaches seemed right to me.

"Are we sure he's the one?" I asked. No one spoke. I continued, "If we aren't 100-percent sure, we shouldn't tell him. We should put him through some sort of final test."

"Like what?" Genevieve asked.

"Riley, you said the 4th would display several different talents, kind of like us, right?"

"I did."

"If so, we should put him into a situation where he can demonstrate those talents for all of us to see. If he passes, then we tell him."

"What type of test?" Riley asked. "He has already shown several traits of a Thusian. What more do you need to see?"

"Something that is physical in nature, but it has to have a thinking component too," I said.

"You're right, Nicholas. You should challenge him to the rite of passage at the last quarry party of the year," Cora said. I was stunned at what she suggested. She went on.

"The physical part of the challenge is clear, going down the hill without getting hurt. Nicholas, if he doesn't show the physical talents he needs, you can help him like you did Chad. If he doesn't need your help, you can try to win this time. If he's the one we are looking for, he would have to use some of his mental talents to try to figure out how to beat you to the end of the hill."

"I guess that would work," Riley said with a stunned look on his face. I think he was shocked by what Cora was recommending I do. Then he added, "Cora you're right. He would have to show different physical talents during the challenge: balance, strength, and endurance. But he would also have to figure out how to beat Nicholas using his mental talents. That would definitely display all the things we need to see to prove once and for all that he's the one we've been searching for," he finished.

They were right. I knew deep down inside that this was the only way to know for sure. But if I had any chance of getting Elle back, I would have to make sure that she knew about it well in advance so it wouldn't be another shock. I didn't even know if that was a possibility. I wanted to call her just to hear her voice, but I couldn't. I was sure she would just screen my call so she wouldn't have to talk to me.

As time went on, it got colder inside the room. Even the lasagna that Cora made got cold before I could finish it. The fire helped, but only the ones closest to it could feel the direct effects of the heat. Sitting on the couch, I could start to see my breath. Small puffs of clouds formed as I breathed out. *Was Elle cold?* I thought. I started looking for anything to distract my mind from Elle, but it was no use. I was concerned about her. I knew that they had a fireplace in their basement if their power went out. They had plenty of firewood, because I had cut and stacked some up on the back of their house in the beginning of winter. Even though I was sure she'd be okay, I longed to be there taking care of her right now. Even if she didn't want me there, it would at least give me more time to try to explain myself and make things better, because the hole in my chest was still there.

After we were all finished with dinner, we settled into our sleeping bags. Cora was nearest to the fireplace with Riley next to her. I was on the couch and Genevieve was on the floor between me and Riley. I had offered the couch to both Cora and Genevieve, but neither wanted it. I watched the ominous shadows from the fireplace dance around on the wall. Outside was pitch black. I couldn't see the storm any longer, but I could hear it raging. I concentrated on the crackling of the wood in the fireplace, which helped me fall asleep rather quickly in the cold. I had a couple of Tic Tacs in my mouth just in case any nausea set in during the night. I was shivering so hard, I felt like I was going to come out of my skin, filling my dreams with being cold. No darkness, just the cold.

Halfway through one of my dreams, it became warm. I looked around and there was Elle. She was holding me, saying, "Shh, Nicholas, everything will be all right. You're safe." I knew it was a dream, but she felt so good. I held on to her tightly. Her warmth radiated through me.

I awoke to the sound of a tree falling outside and found I was not the only one on the couch. Genevieve was right next to me, fast asleep. She was warm, like a little heater. I pulled down the comforter and instantly felt that it had become freezing cold in the room. Riley had moved closer to Cora and the two of them were now sharing the large down comforter in front of the dwindling fire. Genevieve and I being just a few feet away from the fire made such a big difference in temperature. She must have climbed up with me to stay warm. Even though I didn't want her there, I didn't wake her. The guilt of being this close to her was nothing compared to the cold we were experiencing, so moving would be foolish. We had to stay warm, just to get through the night.

Genevieve's eyes fluttered and she groaned. She was having a bad dream. I held on to her and whispered, "Everything is going to be all right," just like Elle had whispered to me in my dream. Her body relaxed. I put my head down and drifted back to sleep.

The next morning, I found myself alone again. Genevieve, Riley and Cora were already up. I heard them out in the kitchen. I was relieved that Genevieve was gone, because it would have been awkward to wake up next to her. Maybe she was hoping that I wouldn't know she was there with me. It was impossible not to know because my sleeping bag and shirt smelled like her sweet perfume. The aroma was nice and comforting.

ASHLYN
CHAPTER TWENTY-SEVEN

The house was a lot warmer than the night before. Either the electricity or the generator must have kicked back on. I put my sweatshirt on and headed into the kitchen. Both Riley and Cora's cheeks and noses were bright red, like they had just been outside.

"I see the power came back on," I said.

"Riley got the generator working again. We went out to see what was wrong. A tree limb had somehow knocked the cord running to our house out of the socket. So Riley hooked it back up." Cora looked very pleased. I was too. The warmth was nice.

"So, what does it look like out there? The front window is entirely frosted over."

"It looks like a tornado went through, trees down everywhere," Riley said. "We're lucky none of them hit your house last night. There is at least a foot and a half of snow. The wind has died down, but the intense wind created drifts as tall as me. It may be calm now, but we're supposed to get another round of wind and snow later. It's supposed to get nastier than it was last night. At least, that's what they're saying this morning on the TV."

I grabbed a bagel and went back to the family room. The weather radio was sitting on the coffee table. I gave it a couple of cranks and it came to life. I sat down on the ledge in front of the window that looked out to the street. The radio whistled and began its emergency weather statement. "This is an all-weather radio alert broadcasting out of St. Louis. A blizzard warning remains in effect until 3:00 p.m. Monday for the following counties . . ." It listed dozens of counties including ours, and then continued with its message. "A second round of winds will gust up to 60 miles per hour, making visibility near zero. An additional six to eight inches of accumulation is possible by Monday morning." Then the automated message started over. I turned it down and peered out the window. I had wiped off most of the frost so I could see out. Every once in a while, I could see flashing yellow lights from snow plows that were trying to keep up with the snow. But from the look of it, they weren't having much luck.

Genevieve came out and sat across from me on the window ledge. She pulled the cover that I was using onto her. Her legs were intertwined with mine but we weren't touching. Our bodies were facing each other, but we were both looking out at the snow. I was uncomfortable with how she made me feel. I pulled my legs up to my chest and put my arms around them. I didn't want this path that Genevieve and I were on to go any further. As natural as it was being with her, I didn't feel that way about her, even though our connection was undoubtedly strong. Elle was still the love of my life, the one who owned my heart.

Some snow started to fall again and the flakes were as big as quarters. "Genevieve, what happened to you the day of the earthquake?" I figured as close as we were right now, this would be the best time for me to find out how she got to this point in her life. She took a deep breath and turned to look at me.

"First, let me show you something." She turned around and pulled her shirt up, exposing her naked back to me. I looked away.

"Nicholas, I know you are shielding your eyes, but I need you to look at my back. Don't worry, that's all you'll see."

I slowly looked toward her. On her back were three jagged circles from her left shoulder blade down to her shorts. Something compelled me to reach out and touch them. I felt each one of them, not sure what they were. I knew they were scars of some sort. Then, to my horror, I realized that they were bullet holes. I pulled away. She put her shirt back down and turned to face me. Her eyes were clouded with tears.

"When I was nine years old, my father died while trying to help a woman being mugged. He ran over to stop her attacker and was shot in the process. It was his Final Sacrifice, but neither he nor my mom knew anything about the Thusians and the sacrifice. All of our family and friends were devastated by his death. He was the glue that held our family together. We lived in a nice house just outside New York City. We had lots of friends to help us, but as time went on, my mom began to spiral out of control into a deep, dark depression.

"She started to drink a lot. It was understandable, because many nights she would cry herself to sleep, calling out for my dad. She said the alcohol helped numb the pain. But after a while, that wasn't enough. She started to take drugs. Slowly she began to spend all of the money that she and my dad had saved over the years. It was what we were supposed to live on for the rest of our lives, and she spent it all. So she sold our home and we moved into a really bad part of town. It was a slum. We managed to get by for years, but her drug use was now out in the open. Many nights she would come home stoned, not knowing where she was, or she wouldn't even come home at all. A couple of nights I had to call friends to help get her to the emergency room because she didn't look like she was going to make it. It got so bad that she began to buy the drugs right in front of us."

Us? Who else was in her family? Then she answered my question.

"One horrible night—the night I discovered my talents—my younger sister Ashlyn and I were sitting in the back seat of our car with my mom up in front. A man wearing a long, dark green jacket came to the passenger-side window and knocked. I always distracted my sister from what my mom was doing, so I could protect her from seeing all of the stuff that my mom was exposing us to. Ashlyn knew what she was doing, but she welcomed the distraction. My mom got out to talk to the man. She was only out there for a minute, then came back around, got in and started the car. The man yelled something and pointed a gun at our car. Then I heard the shots. That was the first time things slowed down for me. I turned my back to him, shielding my little sister. When I was sure she was protected, time resumed. I felt the three bullets hit me. It felt like I was punched in the back with fire, sending pain radiating into all parts of my body. My mother was killed by the man's gunfire, which was probably for the best, because it wasn't going to be long before she killed herself anyway. But Ashlyn saw Mom lying slumped over in the front seat covered in blood. She became catatonic, unable to speak from that day on. No matter how hard I tried to protect her, she still got hurt. She was taken with me to the hospital. The doctors were stunned to see how the bullets only went half an inch into my back and then stopped. They said it was a miracle and that the bullets must have gone through the car door and struck me after slowing down."

Genevieve sighed and continued. "I recovered in two weeks. Ashlyn was placed with my grandma, my dad's mom. Riley showed up right when I was supposed to be released to go live with my grandma. He told me why the bullets didn't kill me and how my main physical talent had to be shielding. He then explained everything to me, about who we are and about how we had to find you. I left the hospital with him that very night to start searching for you, leaving my sister behind. I figured that Ashlyn would be better off not being around me with the possibility of those Seekers coming to look for me. With my name being in the paper for miraculously surviving the shooting, they would definitely come looking." She began to cry. I had never seen her like this. She was so vulnerable and delicate, like a flower. She laid her head down on her knees, which she had pulled up to her chest.

"I miss Ashlyn," she said, crying. I leaned forward. I put my hands on her legs to comfort her and to let her know that I was there for her.

I sat in disbelief, because this callous, stubborn, arrogant woman was actually caring, loving and self-sacrificing. She was an incredible person who had been through a lot. I was so wrong about her. Her rough exterior was an act. This made me see her in an entirely different light.

"I left with Riley when I was 13, Nicholas. I know I shouldn't have left with a complete stranger, but I did."

"That makes you only 19," I said in shock. She looked like she was in her late twenties. The way she carried herself made her seem so much older.

"I'm actually 20. My birthday was in December. So I'm only three years older than you. You know how we all have a different reason to fight? Ashlyn is my reason. I want her to have a normal life and to never hear the word 'Thusian.' I don't want her to be hunted the way I am. I will do everything in my power to make sure that happens."

I was becoming overwhelmed with the amount of compassion I was feeling for her. The connection between us was real. I didn't feel uncomfortable any longer about us being close. I grabbed her and turned her around, pulling her back against my chest and I put my arms around her. Her body shook and she began to cry harder. I held her as tightly as I could to let her know that I was there for her.

After a half hour or so she leaned away from me and

turned around. "Nicholas, I am so sorry for what happened to you. I know how much you love Elle. I was jealous of that love because of my feelings for you."

She had feelings for me?

"I followed you to her house the night of the dance to make sure everything was okay. I saw what happened. As great as the dance was with you, I wish I could take it all back. I saw what you went through. It was agonizing. I was right by your truck experiencing all of your pain, as if I were the one going through it myself. I wanted to comfort you, but I couldn't. I had to leave because the pain was too overwhelming. You didn't deserve that. You are an amazing person. I am sorry I wasn't strong enough to stay with you and comfort you like you are doing for me now."

Tears welled up in my eyes. Her story was so emotional that it was easy to become upset again.

She turned around and pulled me into her arms, kissing me on the cheek, whispering, "Everything will be okay, I promise, everything will be okay."

We stared out the window for a long time, watching the light snow. That's when Riley and Cora came in.

"We need to go check on Bryce and Elle to make sure they are okay before the storm intensifies again. The road looks clear enough for our two trucks to make it. We should go in pairs," Riley said.

"Genevieve and I will go to Elle's," I said, without checking with her.

GOING BACK
CHAPTER TWENTY-EIGHT

The snow looked like it was going to stop, but I knew we were just halfway through this storm. I cleared the broken limbs out of both our driveways, and with everyone's help, we cleared the ice and snow off the trucks. Genevieve and I got in my truck, and it started with ease. Our trip was going to be faster than Riley and Cora's because they were going to have to check out Bryce's apartment and then the base. The roads were empty with no cars anywhere. The streets looked like they were part of a ghost town. I turned onto Elle's street, which had not been plowed in several hours. My truck easily maneuvered down the street with its large tires only losing traction once or twice. I was glad Dad loved having bigger tires on his truck.

"Nicholas, don't get too close to her house. You don't want her to see your truck," Genevieve said.

She was right. That would be devastating for Elle to see Genevieve sitting shotgun.

"Okay, stop here. I will run up and check the house."

"Why you?" I asked.

"I am lighter and I can move across the snow faster. Plus, I have more experience using my talents for this type of thing." What was she talking about?

"We searched for you for a long time, Nicholas. There were many nights when I needed to be in the snow. Riley taught me a way to help kick-start my talents when I need to use them. Like at the quarry party when I told you to imagine your friends in trouble, and that helped you to slow things down. Our bodies know we're not in danger, but we trick our minds to help us use a small part of our talents when needed. This will allow me to almost run over the snow without sinking completely in."

"You can use your physical talents on demand?" It was one thing to slow down my surroundings, but to be able to use my physical talents on demand would be very helpful.

"Nicholas, weren't you listening? I can only use just enough to allow me to be better suited than you right now because I've had a lot more practice. Now be a good little boy and stay here," she said smugly. That was the Genevieve I knew.

I really wanted to go, even if I sank into a five-foot drift and had to dig to her house.

"I know you want to see her. But trust me—this is not the time to try. I'm going to check the house and make sure she is safe, and then we are going straight back home. The storm will intensify soon and I don't want to get stuck out here just because you wanted to get a look at her." She got out of the truck. "Sorry, dear," she said and shut the door firmly.

She did move swiftly through the snow, barely sinking

in as if she were weightless. She was so graceful and agile. She looked like a deer running through the woods. She disappeared from sight. The snow had picked up just in the time I was waiting, reducing visibility. Elle's house and most of her neighbors' houses were barely visible from where I was parked.

Ten minutes had gone by. I was getting worried. If she wasn't back by the time I counted to twenty, I was going to look for her. *One, two, three, four, five, six, seven, eight* . . . The truck door swung open. A snow-covered Genevieve slid into the passenger's seat.

"Let's go, and turn up the heat—I'm freezing," she said, kicking off her boots onto the floor and shaking her snow-covered head.

I backed up the truck into a side street so that I wouldn't pass Elle's house.

"So?"

"So what?" she asked.

"You know what—is she okay?"

"Of course. No one has entered or left the house. Their fireplace is going. Elle, her dad and mom are down in the basement. There are big snow drifts covering the back of their house. The front door is no better. No one is getting in or out of there any time soon."

Relieved, I grabbed her hand. I don't know why I did it; it just happened. She gripped my hand tightly, as if she didn't want me to let go, just in case I had made a mistake. Her skin was so warm. She held my hand firmly in her lap.

We got home just as the storm's winds began to pick up.

The swirling, blowing snow stung my face as we ran to the house.

"Riley and Cora won't be home for another hour, I think," I said.

"We can call Riley's cell phone if you want," Genevieve suggested.

"Riley has a cell phone? We are supposed to avoid using them because they can be tracked. Cora told me all about it. That's why Thusians don't carry them."

"Nicholas, have you ever known Riley to follow the rules?" She was right, he didn't, but I still thought it was too big of a chance to take.

"No, they'll be fine. Let's make lunch for them before they get back," I said.

She agreed and we went to work preparing food.

SOMEONE
CHAPTER TWENTY-NINE

Riley and Cora arrived home earlier than I expected. Bryce was now with his dad at their apartment. They told us that the entrance to the apartment had a large snow drift in front of it, making it impossible to get in or out, just like Elle's. The four of us sat down to eat the lunch that Genevieve and I fixed—a family favorite to warm us up. We each had a bowl of Amish chicken and noodles over mashed potatoes with cornbread on the side. It wasn't as fancy as Cora's meals, but she looked happy to see it on the table. Cora stopped everyone from eating so she could bless the food. I guess she was hoping that a prayer would help us get through the night. I wasn't sure if it would, but I was glad she did. We needed all the help we could get.

None of us talked. I guess they were listening to the same thing I was—the storm had increased in its intensity again and the loud cracking of falling tree limbs was picking up. The sounds were agonizing. It seemed worse than last night. We cleared the table and ended up in the family room again, around the fireplace. Cora closed all of the doors into the family room just in case the power went out again. I stoked the dwindling fire and added a couple more logs to get it really going. Genevieve and I settled in front of the window again watching the snow fall. Cora and Riley were playing cards on the couch.

Genevieve had eased her way up against me with the cover over us. She had fallen asleep. I was so hot with her body against mine. I didn't mind, but why? I loved Elle more than anything, but the connection with Genevieve had become so strong. I felt like I needed it, too. The connection we had was because we were part of the 4, and also because we had no secrets. It was nice to be able to share everything with someone. Elle and I were soul mates; she was and always would be the love of my life, but maybe Genevieve was part of my soul too, or at least right now she was helping to repair it.

Riley and Cora continued to play cards while we sat there. They were laughing and giggling so hard at one point that it woke up Genevieve. They were like two kids who had crushes on each other. The white blur of falling snow was slowly turning to grey. The sun was trapped behind the thick wall of clouds and was now setting. Cora and Riley both got up and went into the kitchen, hopefully to make dinner.

The fire in me began to burn, taking me by surprise. The snow slowed to a stop in mid-air. I could see through all of the snow. Someone was standing out by the street. Something round and grey caught my eye. It was suspended in the snow just a couple of feet away. It was coming right toward the top of the window. It slowly worked its way closer to us. Where it touched the window, it looked like it was being pushed in, like a bulge was forming in the glass. I examined it more closely. Behind the glass on the outside was a large, polished grey rock. It was pushing into the glass and was about to break through. I fell off the ledge, pulling a sleeping Genevieve onto the floor with me. Then time resumed. The rock broke through the window and slammed into the wall across the room. Both Riley and Cora were next to us as soon as the window shattered. I didn't wait for anyone. I jumped out of the broken window and chased after whoever was running down the road away from me. I was moving so fast that snow was slowly falling around me. My muscles flexed violently, propelling me forward even faster. The snow began to fall at such a slow rate that time was almost standing still. The person running left a tunnel clear of any snow. Whoever it was, was running almost as fast as me. Riley was behind me. He was pretty far back, but I knew he was there, following us. I didn't have on my jacket, but I didn't feel the cold at all. I was gaining ground rapidly. I was almost within striking distance.

The person turned sharply down a street and I followed. When I made the turn, a snow truck was barreling right toward me. I moved out of the way of the blade that was closing in on me. I swung my head and body clear of it, but it still managed to graze my shoulder. I could feel the warm blood running down my arm and back. The figure I was following disappeared. I stopped. What if this was a trick to get us away from the house? Instead of trying to pursue the vanished figure any farther, I stopped and turned back. Riley grabbed me as I went by, but I pulled away from him. There was no time to talk. He chased after me toward the house. I couldn't let anything happen to Genevieve and Cora.

Back at the house, I saw the figure enter the side yard and begin climbing up our wood pile, trying to get on top of the roof. From there it would be easy to get in through the unlatched window. I ran as fast as I could. I lowered my shoulder and tried to hit the person just like I was playing football. I didn't hit squarely, but I did manage to make some contact, knocking both of us back into a tree. I jumped back up, looking for another chance, but the person fled into the woods. I didn't dare chase whoever it was. I had to check on the girls.

I ran past the broken window to the front door, which was locked. I banged on it. Riley was next to me now, banging too. "Let us in," we yelled.

The door flew open. Genevieve and Cora both stood in a defensive position. We pushed them back into the house and I slammed the door, locking it. Genevieve and Riley went through the house quickly to make sure it was secure. Cora and I went to the garage and grabbed a sheet of plywood that the previous owners had left. We put it up over the broken window, securing it tightly with nails where the window used to be. Then we took another piece and put it over the window that wouldn't latch in the spare bedroom. Cora saw the gash on my shoulder. She ripped open my blood-soaked shirt and began to treat it. The fire in me had died down. I could barely feel it, but I knew it was there for me, ready at any time.

"Nicholas, don't leave without backup next time," Riley said, still trying to catch his breath, sitting down on the couch next to Cora.

"You were behind me, weren't you?"

He rolled his eyes at me. "We need to go somewhere safe," Riley said, "and we need to check on Bryce and Elle, because I am sure that whoever that was could easily get to them if they wanted to."

I pulled on my jacket when Cora finished up my bandage.

"No, I didn't mean that we have to check on Elle and Bryce right now, Nicholas. It's too dangerous to go out. It could be a trap. They want us out in the open to separate us," Riley said.

"We need to take care of ourselves right now. They will be fine," Cora said.

"You may be right about that, but we have to be sure," I said.

Genevieve hadn't said a thing. She was holding something in her hand. She opened her hand to reveal the grey rock that smashed through the window.

She held it up and said, "The rock has words on it. 'We know what you are looking for,'" she said, and then she dropped it like it was a poisonous apple. It tumbled away from her, ending up near the fireplace.

"I'm going," I said. No one stopped me. They all put on their jackets and followed me out into the raging blizzard.

My truck slipped and slid all the way to Elle's house. Genevieve held on tightly to the handle above her head next to the window. When we got to Elle's house, I didn't give

Genevieve the option of checking on Elle like she did last time. I was going to do it. I got out and sank into the snow. I began to run; I didn't run with as much grace as Genevieve. Each one of my steps sank deep into the snow. I must have looked like a mini snow tornado moving around the house because of the amount of snow I was kicking up. Elle's house was surrounded by towering snow drifts that would make it impossible to get in and out. They were safe.

Riley and Cora got home right after we did.

"So what did you find?" I asked.

"Both Bryce and his dad are still in the apartment. The front door had been dug out, but it's now covered by more snow. And you?"

"Elle's house was exactly as we left it," I said. Genevieve nodded.

"God help us if Bryce isn't the 4th," Cora said, taking Riley's hand. After that there wasn't anything else to say. We were all on pins and needles, flinching every time we heard something outside, just waiting for the next attack. I was unusually tired, feeling as though all of my energy was gone, just barely alive. The night was long and none of us slept. We just listened. We decided that our house was still the safest place to be. Even though we couldn't see outside any longer, we knew that they couldn't see us either.

We all huddled near the fire, because the electricity went out again around 2:00 a.m. It wasn't because of any foul play or stray branch; it was because the generator needed more fuel. It was too dangerous to go out there, so each of us wrapped ourselves in extra blankets. It was colder than the night before. All of the heat from the room was being sucked out much faster through the plywood.

"I am going to put fuel in the generator. We might freeze to death if we wait until morning," Riley said, standing.

"No way, Riley, it's way too dangerous to go out there. We will be fine in here," Cora said, standing up, grabbing him, and sitting him back down.

"Don't be ridiculous. I am just going to be gone for ten minutes."

I had a bad feeling about this too.

"No, you aren't going out there," I said. "We agreed this would be the safest spot and now it is the warmest spot, too. We can't split up again. We need to stick together so everyone is safe. We are the strongest together. It has taken me far too long to realize that, but I do now."

The rest of the night the four of us huddled together next to the fireplace, trying to stay warm. I kept the fire burning as hot as I could all night. We just had to make it until morning.

UNSURE
CHAPTER THIRTY

The next day brought relief from the storm. Both the snow and the wind had stopped early the next morning right around daybreak. The sun was even trying to come out from behind the thick morning clouds. To my surprise, the road had been somewhat cleared already. There was still a good four inches of snow on the streets, but the driving conditions were much better than yesterday. School had already been canceled for Monday, giving us enough time to get both of our houses back in order. We boarded up the large window at Riley and Genevieve's and got rid of the large tree in their house.

As bad as the snowstorm had been, we still had school on Tuesday. It was surreal driving to school between the large piles of snow on both sides of the road. Normally, I would be talking with Elle about all of this, but my passenger seat was empty. So much had happened in the last couple of days. I had lost the love of my life, gained a relationship with someone I couldn't stand before, got attacked, survived a blizzard, and now I was going back to school. It made what was about to come that much more difficult to face. I knew everyone at school must have known about the breakup, because word always traveled fast in our school, but I was hoping that the blizzard would be the major topic of conversation. To my disgust, Elle and I were what people were talking about. I had so many people come up to me and say that they were sorry. Most of them were girls, some asking if I needed some company, which I thought was odd. I hadn't seen any of our mutual friends yet, and luckily I hadn't seen Oliver either. Eric and Livi were absent from the row of lockers when I got to school, but I knew that I would see them later.

Before lunchtime, I was so nervous that I ate a whole pack of Tic Tacs. Was she going to be there? What would she say or do? I felt like going and sitting under the stairs like last year to hide, to get away from this. I ate some more Tic Tacs and went to lunch to face my fear. Every eye was on me, or at least it seemed that way. Our table was empty when I got there. I was glad to be the first one there because I didn't want to experience that awkward "where do I sit" part of a breakup. I sat down and started eating. Bryce was the first to join me and he sat right next to me.

"I'm sorry about you and Elle. I was hoping I could have saved you guys from breaking up."

"It's okay, Bryce."

"Don't worry, you two are meant for each other. It will only be a matter of time before she realizes that she made a mistake."

I smiled.

Both Elle and Erin arrived at the table at the same time. Erin looked at Elle and sat down quickly next to me. Bryce gave Erin a dirty look. I couldn't tell if Bryce's look was because he was mad about their breakup or if he was upset because she was sitting next to me. Elle sat down next to Bryce. Luckily, before anyone had a chance to speak, Eric and Livi, followed by Amber and Chad, sat down. No one spoke. They had to feel as uncomfortable as I did.

"So, what about that blizzard?" Eric asked, breaking the silence.

That was what we needed. Everyone chimed in. I didn't talk at all. I just ate. I glanced up one time toward Elle to see if she was looking at me. She was staring right at me, but immediately looked down to avoid eye contact. Erin kept trying to start a conversation with me, asking me what I was doing this weekend. I just shrugged my shoulders hoping she would shut up. The last thing I wanted was for Elle to think I would give Erin the time of day. She was still everything to me.

Bryce and Elle were talking. I couldn't tell what it was about, but she was laughing at whatever he was saying. Again, jealousy in me rose toward Bryce. I wanted to knock the sandwich out of his hand and push him off his seat. Was this how I would be without Elle? Looking at them would probably be a bad idea because I didn't want to show myself as being jealous over an innocent conversation.

This was torture, sitting there and listening to them. My anger toward him was growing every second. I shouldn't be feeling this way. He was probably the 4th and I needed to maintain some sort of friendship. But every time she laughed or sounded happy, it sent anger pulsing through me. I wanted her to be as miserable as I was. *Bryce is my friend*, I reminded myself. It wasn't working. *Remember, Nicholas, Bryce is the one we are looking for,* Riley's voice echoed. That didn't help me either.

Actually, the thought of him being the 4th raised more questions rather than helping me calm down. Was he really the 4th? I knew my jealousies were raising these doubts, but I continued down that path of questioning in my head. I couldn't help it. What if he wasn't the one? What if Elle was really the one? Or maybe I made a mistake and it was Eric's brother Seth? Then a twisted image came to me. What if it was Oliver? My jealousy was driving me to insanity. There was no way that Oliver was the 4th, but the questions were valid to me right then. How could we be sure who was the one we were searching for? There was only one way to know and I knew what it was.

**

"No way, Nicholas. It's not smart to go check out the records at the Thusian Vault by yourself," Riley said, pacing back and forth in our kitchen. "I know Bryce is a Thusian. We can all see that. And from what I can tell, he is more the 4th than anyone else we have seen so far. His talents have been growing over the year."

How could he be so sure? I thought. My doubts had grown into an impassable obstacle.

"I definitely agree he's a Thusian. But is he the 4th? I

can't be sure. We need to know 100-percent, not 99-percent, because if we are wrong, the consequences could be devastating. You know I'm right, Riley."

"But how are you going to know what to look for? Only a Keeper would know what to look for in those records. Keepers are the key to all of those books in the vault. That's why the Council needs someone to track the Thusians' lineage—because they can't figure out the books," Genevieve said.

"A Keeper wouldn't have to look in there. They would already know who the 4th was. And since we don't have a Keeper, this is the next best thing," I said.

"Ester told Cora and me last year that all of the records are kept in that room, and hopefully the lineage book of Thusians that Michelle Lightfoot keeps will be there. I even know what the book looks like. That book will give me a chance to check out Bryce's lineage and then let me see if there are any other Thusians we have missed."

"You expect to find that in just your first day of going through there? Even if you knew where to look, it would take you a couple of days to get through it. It's going to take you months if not longer to find anything starting from scratch. And we don't have that kind of time," Riley said impatiently.

He was right, but I had to try.

"Okay, but at least give me a couple of tries to find the information we need. I will look before my first Council meeting and then I will go back two more times. If I don't find anything, then we can move forward with me challenging Bryce and testing him at the quarry party."

Cora was not taking part in the conversation, but then she spoke. "Nicholas is right. We need to exhaust all avenues before we jump to any conclusions. Bryce is the best candidate, but we must give Nicholas a chance to make sure he is the right choice."

Riley didn't need any more convincing. He still thought it was a waste of time, but he really didn't have a choice. Disagreeing with Cora was pointless, and we had over two months until the next quarry party anyway.

**

I was busy getting ready to leave for the Council meeting when Genevieve knocked on my bedroom door. I hadn't seen her since we discussed me going to the vault.

"Before you leave, I would like to talk to you for a minute, if that's okay."

"Of course, come on in." I sat down on my bed and she walked over and sat next to me.

"Do you still have that coin I gave you?" she asked.

I reached into my pocket and retrieved it.

"Have you discovered its meaning?"

I looked down at the blank coin, still seeing nothing, and shook my head.

"Don't worry, because I didn't know what it meant either when it was given to me." She reached out for the coin and I placed it in her hand.

She took the coin and showed me the edge. It never occurred to me to look on the side. It read "0.999% pure silver" in very tiny print, almost undistinguishable if you weren't looking for it.

"The reason why the coin is blank on both sides is because it doesn't matter what's on the outside, it only matters what's on the inside. The face of the coin is where you expect to find the decorations. But that is just for show. What it's made of is what counts the most. I couldn't think of anyone that represented what this coin means better than you. You are as pure as anyone could be on the inside: 0.999% pure."

I just sat there. That was one of the nicest things anyone had ever said to me.

"Genevieve, thank you so much, but I can't keep it. It was given to you."

She took my hand and put the coin back into it, covering my hands with hers.

"When my father gave it to me, I really didn't understand what it meant. And up until I met you, I still didn't know. You can obviously tell that from the way I treat people. But the way you are and how you treat others is inspiring. You are definitely the kind of person my dad was talking about when he told me the meaning of the coin. And I am happy knowing that I was carrying it all this time, just waiting to give it to you, a person who is truly deserving of it."

Hearing that her dad gave it to her made me want to give it back even more.

"I can't take this. Your dad gave this to you. Please, Genevieve, take it back. If my dad had given me something like this, it would have meant the world to me. I would never give it—"

"Nicholas," she interrupted, "I think you know this by now, but you and your happiness mean everything to me. That's the reason why you must keep it."

I knew she had feelings for me, but all of this caught me off-guard. She got up and left my room. I was left sitting there, speechless. I knew how I felt about Elle, because that would never change, but the feelings I was having for Genevieve were unlike anything I had ever known before.

I wandered into Cora's room with the silver coin still in my hand.

"Nicholas, I'm glad you came in. I need to tell you how to get into the Thusian Vault."

I nodded my head, still speechless after my time with Genevieve.

"Once you are at the entrance, it takes 144 steps until you get to the door that leads down the stairs. When you get to about step 130, close your eyes and walk carefully. Open the door and then slowly open your eyes so you aren't blinded." She looked at me to make sure I was listening, and then she continued. "After you walk down the stairs, you go inside the copper room with all of the wheels on the right side. Remember each wheel has a series of letters going around the outside of it. It's important to line up the knobs on each wheel exactly with the right letter to complete the combination. Did Beth or Joseph sing you a lullaby when you were little?" What a weird question.

"Yes, I think they did, but I can't remember it."

"Did it go like this? *Go to sleep, my little one. Go to sleep, my little one. Close your eyes and rest your head. Dream sweet things while safe in bed,"* Cora sang.

"They did sing that to me, almost every night."

"That is the lullaby that most Thusians sing to their children. Start with the first wheel closest to the large metal door and work your way back to the entrance. The first letter of each of the words from the beginning of the lullaby is the combination to get in. Once you are finished, make sure you hold onto the last wheel until the door starts to click. After the clicking stops, a handle will appear. If you let go too soon, the room will flood, trapping you inside. The second part of the lullaby is used to get you out of the records room if you shut the door."

MR. WEATHERS
CHAPTER THIRTY-ONE

I planned to arrive two hours before anyone else. This would give me enough time to begin my search of the records room. I had no idea what I was really looking for, but I had to try. I would start with the lineage book and any other one that had that diamond looking symbol on it.

The long drive there was filled with the singing of my parents' lullaby in my head so I could get into the vault. I pulled up to the gate and was greeted by Mr. Weathers, the caretaker. He was wearing a pair of denim overalls and a red flannel shirt. He looked like he was ready to go out on a hunt.

"Nicholas, what a pleasant surprise. It's so good to see you."

"I know I'm early, but I wanted to look around the records room before my first Council meeting."

He just stood there giving me the most peculiar gaze. I started to feel uneasy. Maybe he was a spy for the Council or Xavier. Maybe he would report me right away.

"Interesting," he said.

I didn't like the way he said that. Just then James Caldwell popped into my mind. Nothing would make him happier than catching me coming to the vault early to snoop around. I had to think fast.

"Oh, if that's a problem I can come back. I just wanted to learn more about my heritage." I put my truck in reverse.

"You can go in. It's your past. Nothing wrong with a curious mind."

"Then what was so interesting?" I asked.

"I thought it was interesting that somebody like you was now part of the Council. That's all. Feel free to look around. I love to look around when I have time to kill, and I always have that. I don't get too many visitors or guests, and what a shame, because I have so much to talk about."

He opened the gate with a big smile. I drove up the mountain drive toward the empty lot. What did he mean when he said that it was interesting that I would be part of the Council? I parked my truck and walked back down to the little house next to the gate to get some answers. His comment was bothering me. I knocked on the back door. The door opened before I could get a second knock on the door.

"Come in."

The small guard shack was a lot bigger than it looked from the outside. It was very nice and well-decorated. It was not what I was expecting. It had several oversized orange couches and some of the most beautiful paintings I had ever seen. Along two of the far walls were some ornate bookshelves that spanned the whole wall, filled with all types of books.

This home looked like a miniature combination of a library and an art museum.

"Please, Nicholas, sit."

Why was I in here? I was wasting time. But I had a feeling that he knew something, so I would have to be careful talking to him.

"So how long have you been here?" I asked smiling.

"Guarding the vault has been a forty year mission for me. You know, being a Thusian, this is my sacrifice; at least I think it is." He never took his eyes off me.

"I have a question for you," I said.

"I know you do," he responded with a smile, taking a sip of something from a tea cup. "Oh, how rude of me! Would you like some tea? It's from the Himalayas."

"No, I'm fine. Why did you think it was interesting that I was on the Council?"

He paused. "I just assumed you had better things to do with your time now." He sipped his tea again.

What did that mean? Maybe being alone out here for this long had made him mad. While I was here, I might as well see how much he knew about the people who came and went from the vault. Maybe I could skip the vault altogether if he truly knew everyone that visited here. He might know if any of Bryce's parents or grandparents had come here before. Even though the majority of Thusians had no idea about the Council or what they were, I figured it was worth a shot. But I would have to ask about other people first, just in case this was some sort of trap.

"I think it's amazing how you remember everyone who comes here. Do you remember Riley Moore's mom and dad?"

"Oh yes, they were such a delight." He gestured for me to have to some tea, but I shook my head. "I considered them to be trusted friends. We used to have long conversations discussing history and other things like that. It was wonderful." He looked off into the sky out a nearby window, reflecting on his friends. "I also enjoyed their Irish accent. It was delicious."

Delicious? Okay, he was starting to sound like Joy Lemmins. Maybe I had found her a match. Who knew her match would be a hermit living in the hills by himself for forty years?

"So do you remember my mom and dad?"

"Remember them? I loved them both dearly. Two of the kindest, most gentle souls I have ever encountered. I can truly say they made me a better person just by knowing them."

I swallowed hard and pushed on. "I have some other questions, if you don't mind," my voice cracked. I cleared my throat and continued, "About some other people that may have come here over the years." I had to test him further.

He nodded, welcoming more questions.

"Do you know Genevieve? You know, the girl that came here with Riley Moore."

"Oh, yes, Genevieve Marlee-Anne Pereira. Axel Pereira and Angela Patel-Pereira, her parents, were great people."

I don't think I ever knew Genevieve's full name, but I was sure her parents hadn't been here to meet Mr. Weathers.

Genevieve told me that her parents didn't know about their Thusian side. Riley had told her everything about her past. His memory had to be slipping. I sank back in the chair, defeated. I was pretty sure this wasn't a trap now, but it was a dead end. I wasn't looking forward to the task that I faced. Looking through thousands of books was not going to be easy.

"Thanks for talking to me, Mr. Weathers," I said. I got up and walked back toward the door. Then another question came to me about something he had said when the four of us were summoned here.

"Mr. Weathers, the last time we were here, you said that you were happy to see such a unique group of people here. What did you mean by that? You've seen all of the Council members hundreds of times. The only others who were different that day were Cora, Genevieve, Riley and myself." Crazy or not, maybe his mind could give a single rational explanation.

"Finally, the question I was hoping you would ask," he said. "Nicholas, I think you know the answer to this, the most important of questions."

I had no idea what he was talking about. "I do?" Great, he was speaking about more craziness and nonsense.

"Let me rephrase it for you. I thought it was interesting that you *four* unique people were together."

This had to be a trap; it had James Caldwell written all over it. He was on to me. I had fallen right into it. I grabbed the door handle to escape.

"When did you have your Realization, Nicholas?" he

called to me. "Are you sure you know when it was?" he asked. I stopped in the doorway. I cautiously walked back in, not sure if he was friend or foe, but since I was the only one here with him, it couldn't hurt to see where this was going.

"My Realization happened the day of the earthquake. But you already know that. Everyone knows that."

"Do I? Self-Realization starts when the individual knows they have some sort of talent or talents. Did you know then that you had any talents?"

"I had to know something. It's not every day a fifth grader pulls two classmates and a teacher out of an earthquake-ravaged school."

"You're right, but did you know about the talents you used to save them? Think hard, Nicholas. It's important."

I had to have known something helped me, but I always got angry when people called me a hero. I never thought I was anything special, just ordinary. I thought it was blind, dumb luck that I saved them. If I didn't go through my Realization then, that would make Riley and Genevieve's search for the 4th all wrong, because they picked the wrong person to help them look. I wasn't part of the group of four.

"But if I didn't go through it then—" I stopped midsentence.

"Nicholas, think about who else may have had their Realization that day. This will help answer all of your questions."

Well, I knew Riley and Genevieve had theirs, but I didn't want to say that aloud just in case it was still a trap. "How am I supposed to know that? I've been hiding most of the time."

CHAPTER THIRTY-ONE

"Nicholas, I can't tell you. You have to discover this on your own."

Discover what? My mind was spinning. The only other person I could think of was Cora.

"Cora?" I said.

He smiled, nodding yes.

But how could Cora be part of the group and not me? She didn't know what she had to do until later that week after the earthquake. Her Realization of her talents came when she made her Final Sacrifice.

"Now, it's time to think about your Realization. When was it?"

Who cares? I thought. *I'm not even part of the group anymore.*

"Nicholas, stop feeling sorry for yourself and focus. When was your Realization?"

The first time I remembered having something odd happen to me that would clue me in on having a talent was right before I moved to Winsor, when I saved Andy from being hit by Marshall's Mustang.

"I guess it was about a year and a half ago," I said.

"All right then. You have all of the pieces of the puzzle now."

What? I was even more confused.

"Listen here," I said to Mr. Weathers, becoming frustrated by his riddles. "I don't know what you're trying to get out of me. If you're working with Xavier or the Council, you can tell them it's not going to work." I was becoming upset because I felt like this mad old man was setting me up and wasting my time.

"You just discovered that Cora had her Realization the day of the earthquake. Think what that means," he said, not paying any attention to what I had just said.

"But she didn't. It was days later, when she performed her Final Sacrifice and took me into hiding."

"We are not talking about her sacrifice, are we? We're talking about her Realization of talents. Her Self-Realization was that day when the earthquake happened."

"How do you know that?" I demanded.

"I know because the Council members trust me. Cora told Ester she had a feeling that she would have to do something right away when she heard that the earthquake struck your hometown. She had already made preparations to take you into hiding before Ester and Chase visited her. She was already planning on breaking up with Marcus. Ester and Chase never wanted her to flee with you. It was Cora's decision. Ester told me that Cora felt like she couldn't make a wrong decision when it came to your safety and protecting you."

Now I knew he wasn't crazy, because he knew about Marcus. His story didn't match Cora's story, but he had to be right because no one told Cora to do anything unless she already was willing to do it.

"Genevieve, Riley and Cora all had their Realizations the same day. No other Thusians had their Realization that day and are still living now. So that brings us back to you," he said. "You said you went through yours a year and a half ago. When did you first meet up with Riley and Genevieve?

"They caught up to us in Winsor."

"Are you sure that's when they were first around you and Cora? Think."

I knew that they had just missed us right before we left for Winsor. The look on my face must have tipped him off that I knew what he was getting at.

"Then you must know what this means, don't you?" he asked.

I backed away, stumbling out of the door, falling to the ground. I was the 4th. We had been looking for me all this time. I was the one, and Bryce wasn't. We assumed I had my Realization the day of the earthquake like Genevieve and Riley did. Cora was never considered because of my publicity during the 10-10 Earthquake.

"But why should I trust you? You said that you knew Genevieve's parents. But that's impossible because Riley told her about the Thusian stuff, not her parents."

"Nicholas, did your parents tell you? Some choose not to tell their children until they get older, if at all. But the fact remains—"

I finished his thought. "That's why it was unique for all of us to be together, right?"

He nodded his head yes. How did he know so much?

"You couldn't know all of this just by sitting here as a guard, even if people did talk to you about all of this stuff." Then it hit me. He was a Keeper. His secret was bigger than mine. That's the only way he could know all of this.

"Mr. Weathers, you're a Keeper."

He smiled, never confirming or denying.

"I thought the Keepers were all dead."

Again smiling, "Some things can't be eliminated, Nicholas, no matter how hard they try."

"Then you must know why The 7 was formed in the first place. Because it doesn't seem like anyone knows for sure."

A car's headlights lit up the window.

"You'd better go. I don't think it's best for you to be seen in here with me. And Nicholas, you have to discover on your own why The 7 was formed. No one can help you. Once you do that, you will know your purpose." He walked out the side door to greet the car pulling up to the gate.

Great, something else I had to figure out. I ran up along the driveway to the entrance of the vault, keeping close to the woods so no one would see me.

One thing I know for sure is I'm the 4th, I thought, running along the driveway in shock.

I waited in my truck until the car parked. Right after that car, more people arrived, some people in cars or trucks and a few in helicopters. I decided there were enough people for me to go on down. I didn't want to be there. I had to go tell the others. But leaving would cause unwanted attention for us.

I was greeted by some of the members as I walked through the vault. Even James Caldwell acknowledged me, which came as a shock. The large stone seat that was mine was right next to James Caldwell, and it was extremely hard. I looked around and everyone else had pillows and blankets that made their chairs look much more comfortable.

"Well, good evening. I would like to welcome our newest member, Alexander Nicholas Taylor Keller."

I hated when people used my full name. The group clapped in a very controlled, subdued manner. Walter Reed gave a high-pitched whistle with a big smile.

Ester continued. She called on the same woman, Sydney Reese, for an update of their financial holdings. She said pretty much the same thing that she did before. Ester then called on Michelle Lightfoot to discuss the Thusian lineage. She, too, said pretty much the same thing. Not much had changed since the last meeting.

"Now let's talk about Riley and Genevieve. I believe that is the next order of business," James Caldwell said. "I am still convinced they are searching for the Thusians to form The 7." He looked at me out of the corner of his eye.

"They are convinced that either Bryce Adams or Elle Canan is part of the group, even though they would deny it. They think that one of them will complete The 7, even though there is no way to confirm they are even Thusians, since neither of them is in our lineage book."

He paused, and then continued. "Obviously, everyone knows the problem with them continuing to try. Without the guidance of a Keeper, they will not be able to succeed, thus bringing on another catastrophic loss of life. The Seekers will gain power again over the Council and our brothers and sisters will die, never fulfilling their sacrifices. I make a motion for the Council to stop their attempts to assemble The 7 by any means necessary," he said, pounding his fist on his seat.

"All right, James. We can call for a vote, but first, do we

have any discussion on this topic?" Ester asked. Everyone looked around at each other. Nobody made a sound.

"Then if there is no discussion, let's have a show of hands from those who are in favor of stopping Riley and Genevieve and anyone else who tries to form The 7 from this day forward."

My first day on the Council and they are voting to prevent anyone from trying to form The 7. They had to know I was part of it. Did they think that if I was now on the Council that I would all of a sudden do what they wanted? Riley warned me about not trusting them. I began to boil. This was definitely a trap. My anger was not going to be contained any longer. They couldn't stop what had already taken place. The fire in me exploded, filling my entire body. About half of the Council had their hands raised when I jumped to my feet.

"Yes, Mr. Keller, do you have something you would like to add to this subject?" Ester asked, almost like she expected this reaction.

"What if we could figure out how to use the Thusian lineage book to aid in completing The 7?" I asked. I was hoping to buy myself some time. "Xavier and the Seekers are growing stronger and bolder each day. Cora and I were attacked at my house during the blizzard." Some of the Council looked shocked, even scared, looking over their shoulders, while others didn't show any emotion at all. I was hoping to delay this vote and get home.

Walter Reed stood. "Before we take this vote, we need to protect our newest Council member and the other Thusians under attack. If Xavier has become this bold, we need to immediately send some of our most skilled and trusted Thusians to Winsor and kill him. This is our chance to end all of this and I will lead this charge."

"That sounds excellent, Walter, but we first need to carry out the vote on the motion on the floor," Ester said.

I still was standing.

"The lineage book won't help us. I have already stated that. Mr. Keller, do you need more time to think about it?" James Caldwell asked in his district attorney voice.

"I don't need more time. I have had enough of this joke," I snapped.

"You are all correct. Riley, Genevieve, Cora and I have been looking for the 4th to complete The 7 for some time. But what you didn't realize is that we have already formed it and found the last part we were looking for. It's me. I am the final piece."

Ester started to laugh along with some of the other Council members who were following her lead.

"Very well, Nicholas, but there is no way to be sure, so you need to support the Council on this. A Keeper is the only one who can verify it, officially. We can get protection like Walter has suggested for all of you. We will forgive you four for lying to us. You are now part of the Council and you have to take it seriously. You shouldn't proclaim to be something that you're not or can't prove, because there are consequences, Alexander, dire consequences."

"I know what you're trying to do and I will not go along with it. We have completed The 7 because I had help from a Keeper. You think just because Keeper Wren was killed off that the Keeper tradition died with him? Thusians are bigger than any Council, divine or not." The Council had stopped laughing.

"And for the last time, my name is Nicholas," I said, while walking out of the vault.

The drive home from West Virginia went quickly. I didn't dare stop to call, just in case they were coming after me. If they wanted to beat me home, they could easily. I just had to get home before the Council showed up. I couldn't believe it. The whole time I was the 4th. How come we didn't figure it out? Our assumptions about my Realization were part of the reason, but now what? First I had to tell everyone what happened. I was sure they weren't going to be too thrilled about me proclaiming I was the 4th to the Council.

HOME
CHAPTER THIRTY-TWO

Cora was the only one at our house when I arrived, which was a relief. I rushed into the house. She was busy in the kitchen, cleaning the dishes from what looked like a big dinner.

"So how did it go?" she asked.

I took a deep breath. I had been anxious to get home to tell her about everything, but now for some reason it was difficult to say something that I had no problem yelling to the Council earlier.

"When I got to the vault, Mr. Weathers—you know, the guy at the gate—said to me that it was interesting that I would join the Council—instead of going down to the record room to look around, I went back to talk to him—I found out he's a Keeper." My words were running together. I wasn't sure if she understood what I was saying. I didn't know if I was making any sense.

"Slow down, Nicholas. How did you find all of this out?" She stopped washing the dishes and turned to me.

"I asked him if he remembered different people who had

314

been to the vault over the years. I wanted to see if he could be of use to me in trying to find out if Bryce was the 4th. I asked him a couple of test questions. I tried to trick him by asking him about Genevieve's parents to see if he knew them. He did. At first, I thought he was crazy because they had never been there. But then I concluded that he was a Keeper after a couple more questions, and he didn't disagree with me when I told him what I thought."

Cora was now listening intently to my story. I was wringing my hands because I had to get to the part I had been avoiding.

"But that's not what I discovered first, Cora. Mr. Weathers guided me into discovering who we have been looking for to complete The 7."

Cora stopped breathing in anticipation of what I was about to say.

"We have been looking for me."

"That's impossible," she said, like I was playing a joke on her. "You know that Riley said that the three of you went through your Realizations the same day as the 10-10 Earthquake," she said.

"Right, Cora, that's what he said. But the real question is: when did you go through yours?" Great, I was sounding like Mr. Weathers.

"Well, I guess around the time of the earthquake. I knew I had to do something right when the earthquake hit, but I didn't do my Sacrifice until a couple of days later when we went into hiding."

"Your Sacrifice has nothing to do with your Realization. I

said the same thing to Mr. Weathers, and he told me to focus on the Realization. You see, Riley assumed I went through my Realization the day of the earthquake too. But I didn't start noticing something was different about me until the night before we moved here."

She sat down at the kitchen table. She was concentrating, trying to take everything in. She nodded her head after a minute. It looked like she understood and agreed with my conclusion.

"If that's true, then what about Bryce?"

"I have been thinking about that most of the way home. I'm not really sure. I think he is just a Thusian. This town has its fair share of them. I never got around to asking Mr. Weathers about Bryce. But I have something else to tell you." I cringed, thinking about what she was going to say next. "I told the Council we had already formed The 7."

"You did what?"

I pulled back. "They were trying to get me to vote with them to stop anyone from forming The 7, no matter what. It was a trap. They just wanted me on the Council to stop us. I couldn't sit back and let them."

"Nicholas, I know you thought it was the right thing to do, or maybe it was your anger getting the best of you, but it doesn't exactly keep us under the radar anymore. It puts us right out in front."

"I don't think we would have been able to hide much longer, especially when we start to go after Xavier and the Seekers," I said.

"But what about our home? We were finally settled," she

said. She looked frightened, which was a look I had never seen in her before.

"Wherever we are will be our home, Cora. At least now we have a family. Where are Riley and Genevieve? I have to tell them what happened."

"I think they already left for Bryce and Elle's houses to watch them for the night," she said with a concerned look. "Nicholas, you know they are both going to have to come with us when we leave."

"What?"

"Riley didn't want to tell you this, but Elle and Bryce will have to leave their homes even if they aren't the ones, because the Seekers know we have been watching them. They will target them for sure after we leave to try and draw us back in."

How could I have not seen this? The secret life I had been hiding from Elle was going to be a part of her life no matter what. I felt sick. A pit in my stomach grew. We drove over to Elle's house and Bryce's house to see if we could find either of them, but they were nowhere to be found. So we went home. I would have to wait until morning to talk to them. We both went up to bed. I was engrossed with the thought of Elle being with me, even if she didn't want to be. How was I going to make her understand all of this and then convince her that she had to leave everything behind? That would be hard enough to accept by itself, but adding in the fact that Genevieve was going to be with us—that seemed impossible. I checked outside again through my window. There were still no signs of any of the Council. Maybe they wouldn't come.

My night was just like the million before it. It was full of nightmares, but Bryce and Elle were in them. The darkness surged toward Bryce, but he moved in tandem with it and was able to get away. Elle needed my protection, but I struggled to help her.

The next morning I got dressed for school and left early, hoping to catch Riley and Genevieve at their house, but they weren't home. Cora said she took a chance and called Riley's cell phone last night when we got home and told him I had something important to talk to them about, but didn't go into details. I told Cora to tell Genevieve everything when she got back and I would tell Riley at school. Then we would meet back at our house after school to prepare for whatever would happen next. The fact that the Council didn't follow me home was unsettling. It should have made me feel better, but it didn't.

HELP
CHAPTER THIRTY-THREE

When I got to school, I went straight down to the locker room to look for Riley, but no one was in the coach's office, not even Coach Miller. I saw Coach Hoff hurrying to his first period class in front of me, but he was too far ahead for me to yell to him to see where Riley was. I would have to wait until a little later in the day to track down Riley, because he had a free period in the beginning of school.

When my Spanish class ended, I walked down the hall toward Riley's classroom. I saw an unusual glow coming from the lunchroom. It looked like someone was turning on the lights to the stage in the theater. When I got closer, I could see there was smoke too. It was a fire! I ran to the edge of the lunchroom and it was all ablaze. The entire room below me was engulfed in fire and heavy black smoke billowed up. I could hear someone yelling for help somewhere below. My body reacted; I hopped off the balcony into the fire and ran through it with ease. The dancing fire slowed down around me, allowing me to move by without it having a chance to touch my skin. But the smoke burned my lungs, making my chest hurt. I covered my mouth with my shirt, trying to filter out some of the smoke.

Oliver was yelling for help. He was trying to get into the kitchen, but was unable to get through the flame-covered door. Was he the one who started this fire?

"Oliver," I yelled, "what are you doing?"

"Nicholas, there are people trapped in the kitchen. I can't get in there to help." He looked frightened. The look on his face told me that he wasn't responsible for the fire.

"I'll help them; you get everyone else out."

"Okay," Oliver said and went running off.

I heard some screams from behind the door that led into the kitchen. I kicked it open to find three of the lunch workers trapped back behind a stove that was engulfed in flames. Everything slowed. I grabbed a metal tray and put it underneath me as I jumped into the air and over the fire so the slow moving flames wouldn't burn me. The three of them were gasping for air; I had to get them out. The back door that they were trying to use to escape wasn't opening. With one swift thrust from my shoulder, the door swung open. The door had been locked from the outside by a thick chain, which now lay on the ground next to the door. The three lunch workers staggered out into the fresh air. The smoke was still burning my lungs, and my eyes were beginning to sting, but I knew I had to go back in. Something wasn't right. It had to be Xavier and his Seekers. My thoughts raced to Elle. I had to find her.

I ran back into the kitchen and into the lunchroom, jumping and moving through the flames to get out to the hallway. My strength had increased. I could feel the blood and adrenaline pumping through my veins. I had to get to Elle. At every exit on my way to find her, crowds of people were trying to escape, but the doors were chained shut like in the kitchen. I had to keep pushing to the front of the crowds to break down the doors, helping everyone get outside to safety. At one of the exits Oliver was breaking a window with a chair for more people to escape, and at another exit I saw Riley. He, too, was moving as fast as he could, breaking open door after door to free the people trapped inside. He saw me, nodded, and continued to the next door. I knew he and Oliver would take care of the remaining doors so I continued on, looking for Elle.

The school was now totally consumed by flames. I ran back toward Elle's classroom, avoiding falling pieces of the burning ceiling. Everyone was out of the room already, which gave me hope that Elle was safe outside with the others. I ran past the counselor's office and searched in there. It was empty too, just like every other classroom I checked. My last stop was the coach's office to make sure no one was in there. The sprinklers finally went off. Water was falling onto the fire, having little effect on the flames. It doubled the amount of smoke, making it harder to see. At the bottom of the stairs to the locker room and coach's office, I saw someone lying motionless. I took all of the stairs in a single bound and rolled the person over. It was Oliver. He had blood running down his neck. It appeared he had been hit. I got him sitting up. He was delirious. He stood quickly, trying to get somewhere but he didn't seem to know where.

"Nicholas, thank God you're here." He grabbed my

shoulders. "After I finished helping get people out of the school, I came down here to check on Coach Miller. But then something hit me."

Oliver staggered down the hall, pulling me along with him toward the locker room. As we got closer, I could see a body lying right inside the door.

"No!" Oliver screamed, running over to him. Coach Miller was on the floor, covered in blood.

We rolled him over. He didn't move at all. Oliver started to pull him up and I helped. We had to get him out of the burning building. We carried him to the hall when I heard a scream from behind us.

"Oliver, can you get him out? I'll go back to help whoever is left."

"I can," he said, pulling Coach Miller down the hall toward the outside door. I ran back into the locker room to see who was still in there.

"Is there someone here?" I yelled. The fire hadn't reached in there yet, but the sprinklers were going. I moved quickly to the back of the locker room to search. The water was slowing down, making each droplet look like it was suspended in mid-air.

There in front of me was Bryce standing over Elle. The drops of water slowly hit him. Elle was groaning; she looked like she was in agony. I couldn't move. I was paralyzed at the sight. I couldn't tell what was going on. Seeing her there made me flash back to the night when I pulled her out of the water. Bryce stood over her like a lion guarding his kill. His grin was sinister.

"Bryce what are you doing?" I screamed.

"Come on, Nicholas, you're not that stupid, are you?" he responded calmly. "We have been watching you for over a year now, and it's your turn to accept your fate and join the Seekers. Xavier will be happy to clear a spot for you."

Elle groaned.

"What? Are you kidding? I'll never join Xavier."

His eyes lit up with joy. "I was hoping you'd say that."

I moved toward Elle, but he moved just as fast as I did. He turned and kicked her back into the showers behind him. She landed with a groan, her head hitting the tile violently. I lunged and hit him, flipping him over me. I turned to see him moving slowly through the air just like the water was. I drove my fist into his stomach with all the fire in me, catching him mid-air, driving him to the ground with a loud, thunderous crash. He didn't move.

I got to Elle who looked more dazed than hurt, which was a relief. I looked back at where Bryce had been lying. He was now standing up, looking like nothing had happened.

"Not bad, Nicholas, not many get the best of me. But I have bad news for you—there's no way you will be able to get both of you out of here. No one gets the best of me twice."

"Bryce, it's not too late to—"

"Nicholas, give me a break. Do you think we're in a movie? I don't see any cameras, and I hate to break it to you, but the bad guy is not going to have a change of heart in the end." He took a bow and grinned.

"I've been waiting for this day for such a long time," he said. "I knew you wouldn't join us. If it were up to me, I would have killed all of you before the start of school, but Xavier had his plan, so I had to wait," he sneered. "First, we fixed up this stupid school of yours. He knew it would upset you. It was just something to throw you off your game and it worked. Also, it made it a whole lot easier to start this fire with all of those new flammable decorations. Then school began and I had to act all pathetic, like you, so you would feel sorry for me."

Bryce was pacing back and forth. He looked so happy, like he had been waiting for this moment for a long time. He was loving every minute of it. I had to keep him talking to buy me some more time to get Elle out of here.

"So it was you who loosened the video screen at the quarry party, wasn't it?"

"Very good, Nicholas. I have to admit that it was pretty clever of you to get everyone away from the stage by challenging Chad to a rite of passage. Simply brilliant. But what wasn't brilliant was me having to date that twit Erin," he said with a disgusted look on his face, and then he laughed. "I hope she doesn't make it out of the fire today. That would be a perfect ending. If you want to know the truth, I would have much preferred to cuddle up with Genevieve. That's one hot piece of—"

"You're a coward," I yelled, interrupting his thought and hoping that he would keep talking. I could hear the fire raging outside the locker room. I also thought I could hear sirens coming from outside the school. I got down on my knees and got Elle into a sitting position.

"Coward, ha! This was all part of the plan. Like when I placed that bid for you to dance with Genevieve. You should have seen Elle's face. It was priceless. She looked like you had just chosen Genevieve over her. That was a thing of beauty and I did that one on my own." He took another small bow and then continued walking back and forth even quicker than before. "Elle was playing right into our plan to isolate you from the rest of the group; it was perfect. Xavier was right. All of these distractions have hindered you from finding the 4th," he scoffed.

"Oh yeah," Bryce continued, "it was so nice of you guys to check on me and my dad, or should I say, Xavier and me, during the storm."

Xavier has been right under our noses this whole time! I thought.

"The attack during the storm was to determine who was the strongest out of the three of you. We had to make sure you were Seeker material. You were faster, stronger and smarter than all of the others. Instead of pursuing me farther into the snow after the plow hit you, you turned back to the house, clearly showing that you were the best. Most would have just fallen further into the trap. You only took the bait in the beginning."

"You broke the latch in our spare room, didn't you?" I said, remembering when I saw him walking down the stairs at our house.

"Of course I did. I was going to kill the girls, but you got there just in time."

There was a loud bang that sounded like it was above us.

Caught up in his storytelling, Bryce had drifted past the exit. I saw our path to escape.

"And after you proclaimed last night at the Council meeting that you had formed The 7, we couldn't take any more chances. So we lit this fire to trap and kill you if you wouldn't join us, hopefully killing other Thusians in the process, like Coach Miller. We can't let those weak Thusians have hope. But I do have some good news. You're at least going to die trying to save your beloved Elle. And I do emphasize the word *try*. You will either die in the fire or from the water in the pool above us. I don't think the supports can hold the weight much longer after all of the damage they've taken."

He kicked a column close to him and it cracked. Looking around, I saw that most of columns were already cracked or damaged to the point of collapsing.

"And knowing you, this is how you would like things to end anyway. The fire should be at the point where it has spread all the way down the hall. I will have just enough time to escape, but you and Elle won't be so lucky."

He was just far enough away; it was my chance. I got to my feet and scooped up Elle. The water coming out of the sprinklers overhead stopped again in midair. I got past him with ease because he was still marveling at what he had done. Bryce scrambled after us, realizing we were trying to escape. I was carrying a weightless Elle in my arms. I was halfway to the exit when the double doors exploded into flames. Pieces of the doors splintered out everywhere, knocking us backward and making time return to normal. I fell to the ground, making sure to cradle Elle from the blast and fall. The blast had knocked Bryce back, also. He was lying just feet from us. He looked up, scared. He had a large gash on his forehead. This was not part of his plan. I got to my feet, picking up Elle. Then there was another loud explosion, but this one came from the ceiling above us.

"So, Bryce, was this part of your plan, to die with us? You are nothing to Xavier, just an expendable pawn."

"I don't care, Nicholas. All I know is that you will die, too." He ran past me, blocking the burning exit. "Nicholas, you can't win. Don't you know that no matter what you do, you can't escape your fate, your Final Sacrifice?" he screamed.

I set down Elle to confront Bryce because I couldn't take him on with Elle in my arms. Even if I were able to defeat him, there was no clear way to escape. "If you don't fight, you will die," I said.

"What are you talking about?" Bryce said, confused.

I closed my eyes and a complete calmness took over. The fire in me was gone, but I knew exactly what I had to do. I opened my eyes and ran toward the lockers, tearing off a locker door like it was a piece of paper. Bryce went after me. He swung wildly at me but missed. He was moving slower than me. His movement was slightly blurred. I swung the locker door as I passed him, hitting the column in the middle of the room and lodging the door halfway into it, taking a large piece of the concrete out of the back. Time returned to normal.

"How pathetic, you missed," Bryce laughed. "You're faster than me and you had a chance to kill me and you missed."

"Who says I missed?"

I got back to Elle, just as a large chunk of the ceiling started to cave in on top of us. Time slowed enough for me to get us out of its way. When time returned to normal, Bryce was lunging at the place where Elle and I were before we moved. The largest part of the falling ceiling hit him.

I put Elle down and rushed over to Bryce. He was covered with part of the ceiling. I removed the pieces off the top of him. He had been crushed by the weight. Blood was everywhere, and he was barely breathing.

"What were you trying to do?" I said, not sure why I cared.

In a broken voice, he replied, "I saw that you were about to get crushed and I tried to knock you out of the way, but you had moved already." He wheezed and blood trickled down the side of his mouth. "Seekers can't deny our Thusian side, either. I guess my Final Sacrifice was to save you guys," he laughed. "Or maybe it was to share some information with you." He coughed up blood onto his chest. He was dying and there was nothing I could do for him. "Nicholas, you are destined for great things. Xavier is not really interested in you at all. He is searching for the book."

His eyes fluttered and then rolled back into his head. He was gone. He had died from the same curse that haunted me, the Final Sacrifice.

There was a roaring sound from above me. I picked up Elle and moved her back into the showers away from the fire and the falling ceiling. The column that the locker door went into was giving way like I had hoped. The ceiling couldn't hold the pressure of the water anymore. It caved in, sending water from the pool above flooding into the locker area. I held Elle up as high as I could lift her. The water rushed out of the locker room into the hallway, quenching all of the fire that was in its path. The water filled the shower too and swept us out toward the hall. The water revived Elle enough to hold on to my neck. We rode the wave of water toward the exit, allowing us to escape without getting burned. The water knocked down the outside door, washing us onto the ground. We were safe.

GONE
CHAPTER THIRTY-FOUR

Once outside, I was able to see that Elle looked okay. She only had a bump on her head and a few scratches.

"Elle, does anything hurt?" I asked.

She didn't answer. She pointed behind me. I turned to see Oliver there, leaning over Coach Miller. I ran to him and bent down. Coach Miller wasn't breathing. I started to do CPR. Oliver sat frozen, just staring down at him.

"Nicholas, you can stop. He's gone. I have been doing CPR for the last ten minutes," Oliver said.

Elle grabbed the back of my shirt and I stood up, backing away. We just stared at this great man lying there on the ground, dead. The school was engulfed in flames behind us, with emergency vehicles and personnel swarming around, but none of that mattered. Coach Aaron Miller was dead.

Riley, Genevieve, and Cora found us. Genevieve put her arms around Elle for support and led her away. Riley and Cora pulled me away from Oliver and Coach Miller because a group of paramedics had arrived.

"We have to go, it's not safe for us," Riley said, leading

me to Cora's truck where Genevieve and Elle were already waiting. We all climbed in. I wanted to hold Elle, but she was being taken care of in the back seat by Genevieve. I didn't know what to make of anything. Almost everything I thought I knew was a lie, one that Xavier had planned from the beginning—and I had believed it all.

Back at my house, Cora and Genevieve took Elle into Cora's room. I sat down on the couch, still wet. My lungs and eyes burned from the smoke. It was the only thing that made me believe this wasn't one of my nightmares. The image of Coach Miller's body lying there, not moving, was etched into my head.

"What happened to you in there?" asked Riley. "One minute I saw you and then you disappeared."

"I went to make sure Elle had gotten out and then went to check on Coach Miller."

"And?"

I then explained to him about Bryce. I told him all about how he pretended to be the 4th, but was actually working with Xavier. I had just started telling him about the book, when I saw the girls walking into the room. I stopped.

"Go on," Riley said.

"Don't worry about Elle. She knows some of the Thusian stuff. Genevieve told her last night," Cora said.

Elle didn't look at me.

"Genevieve, how dare you tell her! You had no right to do that. Now there is no way to keep her from getting involved. Do you know what you have done?" I screamed. Genevieve didn't look at me.

Elle walked over to me, leaving Genevieve's side, and took my hand. The anger inside me was gone. I took a deep breath, regaining some composure. She put her hand to my face and looked into my eyes. Her hypnotizing eyes calmed my soul, which felt like it had been burning.

"Nicholas, please tell everyone what else you discovered at the Thusian Vault," Cora said calmly.

I turned to them and explained how Mr. Weathers was a Keeper and how he helped me discover that I was the 4th, the one we had been looking for. Then I ended by telling them that I told the Council.

Riley jumped up. "What? We have to get out of here right now. We don't have much time left. I'm surprised they haven't been here already." He went to the window to look out of the blinds.

Just then the front door opened and before we could move we were surrounded by a dozen people including James Caldwell, Walter Reed and Ester. They walked right into the middle of the room. Walter was closest to Elle and me. He put his large hand on my shoulder.

"Nicholas Keller," James Caldwell said, "your declaration to the Council is something we are taking very seriously. Everyone on the Council has voted to keep what you said quiet, to protect you and the others. But if any Thusian or Seeker finds out what you said at the meeting, there will be dire consequences for all of you." James stepped back and Ester spoke.

"You are all forbidden to talk to anyone about this, and that goes for you too, Ms. Canan. Do not disobey this order and please, Nicholas and Cora, be careful, because there is very little I can do for you now," Ester said.

She gave both of us a sympathetic look and walked out the door, with the group following behind her.

"Nicholas, a group of us are going to help protect you now. I will do everything I can to keep you all safe," Walter said, following the group out the door, leaving the five of us alone.

Riley, Genevieve and Cora walked out of the room into the kitchen, leaving Elle and me alone.

"Nicholas, I don't care where I have to go or what I have to do now. I will do whatever it takes for me to be with you." How could she say that? She was willing to give up everything for me.

"I can't put you in danger. You have already gone through too much. These secrets have ruined my life. I don't want them to ruin yours." I fumbled with the pack of Tic Tacs that was on the coffee table. Elle slowed my shaking hand and got the Tic Tacs out for me.

"Shh, relax," she said, holding my hand and pulling me close to her. Her breath was calming. I had missed her effect on me.

"I know that you didn't place that bid at the dance— Genevieve told me," Elle said. "She also explained how she forced you to dance with her, Nicholas. I thought about you a lot during the snowstorm. Genevieve explained that you were always watching over me, protecting me, even after I broke up with you. I don't completely understand what is going on, but I want you to know that I love you and Genevieve cares about you too. She wants you to be happy, even if that means you being with me. She loves you, Nicholas, and I can't be upset with her because of that."

Elle was more concerned about Genevieve than any of the Thusian stuff. I closed my eyes and put my head on her shoulder, wondering how much she really knew. I finally had Elle back, but at what cost?

GOODBYE
CHAPTER THIRTY-FIVE

"**N**icholas, I know this is going to be difficult for you." Genevieve was standing in my bedroom dressed in a long black satin dress. She walked over to me and straightened my tie.

"Yes, it is," I said, "but I guess this is something we will have to get used to—death."

The fact that Coach Miller was gone still hadn't really sunk in yet. He died by Bryce's cold Seeker hands, which were trained to kill the weak, but Coach Miller wasn't weak. He was stronger than anyone I knew. We went downstairs where both Cora and Riley were waiting for us. We walked out the front door and were followed to our truck by our new bodyguards. The Council had sent four Thusians to protect us. They weren't allowed to talk to us, but they went everywhere we did. Elle had a bodyguard too, but he stayed out of sight at all times.

All four of us got into Cora's truck. Riley drove and Cora rode next to him. It had been a week since the fire, and yet it seemed like it all happened just an hour ago, still fresh in my mind. It didn't seem like we should be going to Coach Miller's memorial service yet. Genevieve was looking out the window, but made sure she held my hand for support. I didn't fight it. I needed it. Elle and I were back together, but that didn't seem to influence Genevieve's behavior. She was there to support me no matter what.

We sat near the middle of the sanctuary. So many people wanted to attend—thousands is what I heard on the news—that they made the actual funeral by invitation only. There would be a public visitation later. The seating was in a circle around the central pulpit. Over the pulpit, the ceiling was tall. It looked like it went up into the heavens, with a stained glass dome covering it.

The pastor came to the center shortly after we sat down. "We are here to pay tribute to Aaron Michael Miller, a truly remarkable man who has touched so many lives," he said. His voice echoed through the sanctuary.

Then from the entrance came ten firefighters dressed in their full firefighting equipment, axes in hand. They lined each side of the casket. What were they doing?

I remembered the small service we had for my father and mother two days after the earthquake. Only a few people were there, including two men from my dad's unit. I never cried that day. I didn't fully understand what had happened, or maybe I just didn't want to deal with it. Thinking about it now made my eyes tear up.

The ten firefighters raised their axes above the casket, and with one uniformed motion they all sent the heads of their axes into the casket. The sound was deafening. His casket had a thick piece of wood down the middle where the axe heads hit. All ten of the firefighters dropped their arms, leaving the axes in place. One by one, each of them took the handle out of their axe head and returned back down the hall where they had come from, leaving the blades where they were embedded.

When the last fireman left, the pastor spoke again. "When Aaron was a fireman, his axe was one of the most important tools he had. A man was only as good as his axe and his unit. So leaving the axe head behind is symbolic of how when one person from the firehouse dies, a piece of everyone goes with them. The tradition of the axe head being left behind in the casket is the highest honor for any firefighter. This is a tradition that the Winsor Fire Company started when the company lost their first brother."

He then invited people to come up if they wanted to say something. At least fifty people got up and said different things about Coach Miller. Some read passages of scripture from the Bible, and some told stories about Coach Miller. I looked around for Elle, but never saw her. I knew she was there, but from where I was sitting I couldn't see her.

The last person that went up to speak was Oliver. He looked out over the silent crowd. His face was pale. He tried to speak several times, but his voice wouldn't come. Tears began streaming down his face. The pastor came over to help him. With some words of encouragement, Oliver began to speak.

"Coach Miller, I will miss you. Thank you for giving me

a second chance when nobody else would. I will never forget you."

He stepped away from the microphone and rushed out of the sanctuary.

"Coach Miller, if you can hear me, I promise to give Oliver a second chance," I said in a whisper, hoping he could hear my prayer.

Elle and I were watching TV in my family room right after the funeral. She was lying against me. I don't know how she escaped her parents, but she did. I knew we had to eventually talk about what happened, but I didn't know where to start, still not sure what Genevieve had told her. Now that I could tell her everything, I didn't want to. At this point, I felt like the more she didn't know, the better we could keep her safe.

"Nicholas, are you okay?"

That was a loaded question.

"Not really. Are you okay?" I asked back.

"Yes."

How could she be okay after everything?

"Elle, you have to be kidding. How can you be fine?"

She sat up. "For the last year, I knew that you were hiding something. You were always so guarded, never really opening up. I couldn't figure it out, but I knew there had to be a good reason for you not telling me. Once Genevieve told me, things started to make sense. I didn't tell you, but when you saved me from the car last year in the water, I thought I saw you punch through the windshield and break my seatbelt, sending us up to the surface. But I was in and out of consciousness, so

I thought it was just a hallucination or a dream. Then when Bryce grabbed me in the hall, I wasn't scared because I knew you would find me. I had faith in you, Nicholas. That's why everything is fine."

"Elle, how can you be okay when you just found out about all of this? I have a hard time with it still and I've known a lot longer than you."

"It's easy. I believe in you."

"But I didn't save Coach Miller and I got lucky saving you again."

"Coach Miller died protecting Oliver and me. He saw Bryce dragging me down the hall toward the locker room. Oliver was already in the locker room, and Bryce hit him as we went by. Coach Miller pulled Oliver out of the locker room to safety and then went back in to get me." She paused, taking a deep breath. "He died protecting us."

She stopped, taking my hands. "I don't understand what you are about to face, but I believe in you and so do Cora, Genevieve, and Riley. And no matter what, you don't have to feel alone anymore. Your fears are no longer just yours to bear because I will be with you every step of the way no matter what." She snuggled up to me and laid her head on my chest.

She was right. She would be with me the rest of the way. But I wasn't sure if I had the strength to protect her and everyone else I loved.

END OF BOOK TWO

Are you a fan of
THE HERO CHRONICLES?

Be the first to get fan exclusives and insider Thusie information by engaging with *The Hero Chronicles'* author online.

Visit the links below to talk directly to Tim Mettey, stay up-to-date on his writing process, get insight into the world of *The Hero Chronicles,* and even catch some sneak peeks of future books.

Join other Thusies around the world on:

Facebook.com/tim.mettey

Twitter.com/TimMettey

Pinterest.com/timmettey

#Thusies #TheHeroChronicles